# BRAVO

## HUNT BROTHERS SEARCH & RESCUE

## JESSICA ASHLEY

B.A.D. PUBLISHING CO

# BRAVO

**Their love is a risk neither can afford—but it might be the only thing worth fighting for.**

Former Special Forces Operative Bradyn Hunt may have left battlefields behind for his family's Texas ranch, but he's still fighting—now as the head of Hunt Brothers Search & Rescue. He and his team tackle the toughest missing persons cases, reuniting families and seeking answers.

Kennedy Smith has been on the run for years, living under different names and never getting attached. Her latest hiding place is as a ranch hand at the Hunt family's property, figuring there's no safer place than among a group of Army veterans. But she didn't count on falling for Bradyn, the quiet, determined leader who just rolled back into town.

Just as she considers staying, her past catches up. The danger she fled is at her doorstep, and now Bradyn is in the line of fire. Kennedy must decide—keep running or fight for the only man she's ever trusted. But the secrets she's kept could destroy them both.

**A pulse-pounding romantic suspense about trust, redemption, and the kind of love that refuses to let go— even when the past threatens to destroy it. Will they survive the firestorm, or will her secrets bring every- thing crashing down?**

B.A.D. PUBLISHING CO
believing in the power of reading

By Jessica Ashley
Copyright © 2024. All rights reserved.

*Edited by HEA Author Services*
*Proofread by Love Kissed Books, LLC*
*Proofread by Dawn Y.*
*Cover Design by Covers by Christian*
*Photographer: Wander*
*Model: Brandon*

# NOTE FROM THE AUTHOR

*"If you keep quiet at a time like this, deliverance and relief for the Jews will arise from some other place, but you and your relatives will die. Who knows if perhaps you were made queen for just such a time as this?" Esther 4:14*

There are days where the weight of the world crushes down on us. Where the darkness seems to smother everything around, doing whatever it can to snuff out the light.

Don't let it.

In those moments, where I question my purpose in a world riddled with pain, fear, and anxiety, I am reminded of that verse. *"Who knows if perhaps you were made queen for such a time as this."*

Who knows if perhaps WE were made for such a time as this.

God's plan is a mystery to us all, but we know that He doesn't make mistakes. Every person has a path set out in front of them, and each of us have our own part to play in this world. And at times, it might seem impossible to keep praising Him when the storm is raging all around you and you're struggling to keep your head above water. DO IT ANYWAY. Fight back in the best way you can.

PRAY. PRAISE. LOVE.

Brandon Lake said it best in his song, Hard Fought Hallelujah...

> "There's times when my hands go up freely
> and times that it costs. There's days
> when the praise comes out easy, and
> days when it takes all the strength I've
> got. I'll bring my hard-fought, heartfelt,
> been-through-hell Hallelujah." (I love
> that song so much!)

So when the darkness tries to smother you...when those intrusive thoughts attack...remind yourself that you were born for a time like this. That you were created by a loving God who will never leave you.

You are not alone...EVER.

In this series, Bradyn and his brothers will travel all over the world, helping pull victims from the darkest moments of their lives.

There will be trials. Pain. Grief.

But there will also be hope. Love. Salvation.

We were never promised peace during our lifetimes. In fact, the deeper into our faith we get the more dangerous the battle becomes. As Christians, we are at war with an unseen enemy. And that enemy doesn't pull punches.

But we are more powerful than him because we have God on our side.

Because our Savior already defeated death.

Every time the enemy's fiery arrows come for me, I remind myself that I am strong because God makes me strong.

I am saved because of the sacrifice Jesus Christ made on that cross.

And there is nothing the enemy can do to rob me of that.

Just as there is nothing he can do to rob you of the promises God has made.

**You are loved.**

**You are cherished.**

**You are a warrior.**

**KEEP FIGHTING.**

-Jessica

*If you are in need of prayers, reach out to me at jessicaashley@authorjessicaashley.com. I will add you to my prayer list and send more warriors your way!*

*To those who feel lost.*
*Psalm 46*

# CHAPTER 1
# BRADYN

Sweat beads along my brow, but I don't dare wipe it away. Weapon trained straight ahead, I move near soundlessly through the jungle with my German shepherd, Bravo, at my side. He doesn't make a sound either, both pointed ears poised as he listens for any sounds that might mean someone is onto us.

So far, so good, though. I pray our luck stays strong.

"We're closing in on the north side," Alpha team whispers through my earpiece. They aren't my men, but over the last couple of months, we've worked so closely together that they feel like an extension of my family.

"Zulu is closing in on the south." Another callout whispered in my earpiece.

"Foxtrot is nearly on the east side."

I glance over at the only other man currently on my team. Silas Williamson, my cousin on my mother's side, is a former Navy SEAL turned private security operative. Since my brothers were all otherwise occupied, with one finishing up another job and the others working our family ranch in Texas, I called him in to help me wrap this thing up.

And even though he currently resides on the East Coast with his pregnant wife and the niece he's raising since his sister's passing, he didn't hesitate to step up and help.

He offers me a nod, so I whisper, "Bravo is closing in on the west."

It's been three months of me living off of MREs and sleeping only four hours a night. Three months of solo work, tracking men across the ocean and through jungles on the other side of the world. And, hopefully, all of this is about to come to a happy ending.

Well, as happy as it can be.

I can only pray we're not too late.

What started as a missing person's case turned into a full-on human trafficking bust. Thirty-seven girls aged fourteen to twenty-two were traced back to the same place our girl went missing. A gas station out of San Antonio.

And now, with God on our side, we're about to take thirty-seven names off the missing person's roster.

Ahead, a branch creaks, and I shift my weapon, peering into the jungle as I prepare for someone to come out of the brush—but no one does. A bird takes off into the sky, a screeching *caw* filling the air as it goes, so I keep moving forward, my gaze trained ahead except for the moments I shift it to check Bravo's body language.

Aside from my brothers and Silas, the German shepherd is the only one I trust to always have my back. He's sharp, fast, and lethal when necessary.

That is unless we're home and my mom is sneaking steak into his dog bowl. Then, he's a hundred-pound ball of goofy fluff.

*Home.*

How I cannot wait for mom's home-cooked meals, sleeping in my own bed, and watching the sun rise over the ranch. *Soon,* I remind myself. Soon, I'll be home, and what will make it even better is that these girls will be with their families, too.

Finally, the building comes into view.

According to our inside source, the structure is comprised entirely of cinderblocks they flew in so they could keep the construction of this place off any record. We're in the middle of a jungle in South America where the nearest coastline is a three-day walk. If we hadn't found an inside source, we likely never would've found the place.

But we did. And here we are.

*Thank God.*

Shots ring out, booming through my earpiece and echoing through the jungle. Birds scatter, and Silas and I both hold our position—the shots aren't being fired at us.

"Shots fired, shots fired! Zulu team pinned!"

Silas and I pick up speed with Bravo maintaining right beside me. We sprint through the plants and trees, still doing our best to keep our steps as quiet as possible. My back presses against hot concrete as we take positions on either side of the door. With the teams engaged in gunfire, our hope is that we can get in and get the girls out so they aren't caught in the line of fire.

Silas bows his head for a moment, and I do the same.

*God, protect us. Guide us so we can rescue these girls. Please, Lord. Be with us. In the name of Jesus. Amen.*

I open my eyes and wait for Silas to do the same.

He does. I offer him a nod then plant charges on the hinges of the heavy metal door. We turn our faces and step to the side as I set them off.

*Pop. Pop. Pop.* The hinges break. Silas lets his weapon dangle from its sling as he pulls the door free then steps aside so Bravo and I can take the lead.

"*Zook,* Bravo," I order. *Search.* He doesn't hesitate before plunging into the darkness. I follow, Silas coming in right behind me.

Adrenaline surges through my veins as we make our way down a narrow hall, all while the other teams battle on the opposite side of the compound.

Bravo stops and begins pawing at a closed door. I glance back at Silas, who offers me an understanding nod, before I grip the handle and shove the door open, raising my weapon as I go.

"No! Please!"

I lower my weapon slightly and take in the scene before me. The room is smaller than the average living room, but it contains girls and young women plastered up against the walls and each other. Their eyes are wide and terrified, their faces and clothing streaked with dirt.

"Please don't hurt us," a woman pleads. I turn to my right, and my gut twists. *Something isn't right.* I can't explain it, but something feels—*off.*

"We're not here to hurt you," I tell them. "Everyone, on your feet. We're here to get you out."

The woman who spoke is the first to stand, and she rushes toward me, wearing a gleeful smile on her face. And then I catch the shimmering sight of a dagger as she draws it out and poises to jam it into me.

Bravo lets out a warning before he leaps onto her arm, teeth sinking into her flesh.

She screams, and the knife clatters to the ground.

"*Aus!*" I order him. *Let go.*

Immediately, he releases her, taking his place at my side, and the woman stumbles back. Silas pushes her into the far wall and zip-ties her arms behind her back.

"You can't have them!" she roars.

"Bravo team here, we got the girls. Headed out to the rendezvous," I say to the other teams. The gunshots have ceased now, and the comms have been full of chatter about arrests being made. "Woman attacked us;

she's zip-tied in the back room and ready for transport."

"Copy," I hear. "We'll handle her. Good work, Bravo. See you on the other side."

I take a look at the terrified faces before me as I count each and every one. *Forty-one.* Even more than we'd planned on. *Thank* You, *God.* "Rebecca Fisher?" I call out, hoping that the girl we're here to find is among the rescued.

"Here." A seventeen-year-old high school senior pushes to her feet and walks forward. She's still wearing the same clothes she'd last been seen in, and aside from being terrified and dirty, she doesn't appear to have been hurt. At least, not physically. Mentally is another story. I know all too well what these girls are going to have to go through to get their lives back.

"I'm Bradyn. That's my partner Silas, and this is Bravo." I point to the dog who is sitting at my side. "Your parents hired us to find you."

"My parents?" She lets loose a sob. "They were looking for me?"

I know from the report that they'd had a big fight when Rebecca wanted to go off and meet an older boy. Even as they'd forbidden her from going, she'd gone and was abducted. Their last words were exchanged in anger, and I'm so glad I get to be the one to bring her back so things won't end there.

"They never stopped," I tell her with a smile. I turn to

address everyone in the room. "All right, ladies. How about we go home?"

---

"You do good work, Hunt."

"I can't take any of the credit, Frank. It's all God."

Frank Loyotta chuckles and takes a seat behind his desk while I remain standing and staring into the conference room where all of the women are waiting to be collected by their family members. They've showered and been fed and tended to medically. We were beyond grateful to know that, aside from some bumps and bruises, nothing else happened to them.

They were lucky.

So many aren't.

My thoughts take a dark turn, but I shove them down. Today is a victory. I will not have that stolen by ghosts of the past.

"Your cousin head home?"

I nod. "Silas was out on the first flight today. His wife went into labor this morning, so he took off."

"That's wonderful. You'll pass on my congratulations and my many thanks?"

"Will do," I reply. "What happened to the men we arrested?" I take a seat beside him, grateful to be back in the States. It was a long nine hours on the flight back from South

America, but the Dallas skyline was a welcome sight, if not brief, as we shuttled to the building that serves as the main headquarters for Find Me, a nonprofit made up of other veterans who are working to put an end to human trafficking.

As soon as I'd realized just what I was dealing with, they were my first call. While not actual police, Frank has far more contacts than I do.

"They'll never take another breath as free men," he says. "We turned them into local authorities in South America and are keeping tabs on what's happening with them. But my contact out there says they'll never walk free again."

"Good." I know vengeance belongs to God, but there are moments like this where I wouldn't mind taking it into my own hands. If not for the ones we rescued, then for the ones we didn't.

"You know, we have some openings—" he starts.

"I appreciate it, Frank, but you know I've got my team."

He smiles. "I know, but you just say the word. I'll open up spots for all five of you and your canine partners." Frank offers Bravo a smile.

"I appreciate the offer."

The door opens, and I hear a woman yell, "Rebecca?"

*Her parents are here.* "That's my cue. Thanks again, Frank."

"Anytime." He shakes my hand. "Call us up if you want to work together again."

"You do the same." I release his hand and head out into the main room at the same time Rebecca opens the conference room door and rushes into the open arms of her sobbing mother. Both parents surround their daughter, holding her as the three of them cry.

My own eyes burn with emotion as I take in the view. I don't have kids yet, and I can't imagine the pain they must have suffered while she's been missing. The horror of not knowing what happened, and whether or not their child was still alive.

I remain where I am until her father, William Fisher, turns toward me and wipes his eyes. "Bradyn. I can't— I don't—" He breaks down and wraps his arms around me. Shoulders shaking, I return the embrace, my heart full that I was able to return their daughter to them.

"You don't have to say anything."

"You saved her. You saved our girl," he sobs as he pulls back.

"God saved her," I tell him. "He put me where I needed to be."

"And I will thank Him every day of the rest of my life." He wipes his cheeks. "I don't know what we would have done if—"

"You don't have to worry about that," I tell him as I

clasp a hand on his shoulder. "Because everything worked out."

"I'm so sorry," Rebecca sobs. "I should've listened. I should've—"

"Baby, it's okay. Please, it's okay," her mother cries. "You're home now. That's what matters."

"You helped me bring these girls home," I tell Rebecca. "Stand on that when the darkness closes in."

She looks up at me with red-streaked blue eyes and nods. Then she rushes forward and wraps her arms around me again. "Thank you, Bradyn."

I return the hug. "You're welcome."

As she pulls away and gets settled back with her parents, I offer them a smile. "If you head to the front desk, they'll get you cleared to take her home. They have resources, as well, to help with the transition period. It can be hard, going from a high-stress situation back to normal day-to-day. PTSD isn't just something soldiers face."

"We'll make sure she's okay," her mother says as she sniffles then reaches forward and takes my hand. "Thank you, Bradyn. For everything."

"No need to thank me," I tell her. "I'm just glad we had a happy ending."

Rebecca and her mother head toward the front desk while her father reaches into his pocket and offers me a check.

"I wish I could give more."

"You don't need to pay me at all," I tell him. We work on a pay-as-you-can system, wanting to make sure no one feels like our help is out of reach.

"I want to. I know you said it wasn't necessary, but I want you to keep doing this. I want you to keep bringing little girls home to their parents." His eyes fill again, and he shoves the check into my hands. "Please. It's not much. But it can help."

Because I sense he won't take no for an answer, I accept the offering. "Thank you, William."

"Thank you," he replies. "You gave us our entire world back. And for that, we'll never be able to repay you."

# CHAPTER 2
## BRADYN

Exhausted and more than ready for a hot shower and a good night's sleep, I guide my truck up the long drive to the place I've spent most of my life. Given the early January climate, the large magnolia trees lining the drive are bare, but I can picture them as they were when I left in late October—lush and green, and caging over the road like a protective archway guiding me in.

Man, it's good to be home.

"You ready, boy?" I ask Bravo, who's currently sitting in the passenger seat, peering out the window, clearly ready to get out and run. He glances over at me, big brown eyes excited, tongue hanging out the side of his mouth. His tail starts wagging, thumping happily against the seat. I laugh. "Me, too, boy." We missed Thanksgiving, Christmas, and the New Year celebration, but missing those is such a small price to pay for getting those girls and young women home where they belong.

Three months well spent, though I am more than ready for a meal that didn't come premade in a sealed pack. My cell rings, so I hit the button on my steering wheel to answer it hands-free. "Hunt."

"You make it home?" Silas sounds as exhausted as I feel.

"Just pulling in now. How's Bianca?"

"She's a rock as always. Still no baby, but we're thinking it could be anytime now."

"Then why are you wasting time on me?"

He chuckles. "Just wanted to make sure you made it home okay."

"I did, thanks for checking. And thanks for stepping in on the assist. I really appreciate it."

"No problem. You did most of the work. I just showed up."

"You showed up," I tell him. "So thanks."

"Well, anytime. It's not like you haven't ever shown up for me before."

"Fair enough." I laugh. "Tell Bianca I said good luck."

"Will do. I'll let you know when the baby arrives."

"I'm counting on it. Talk to you soon."

"Talk soon."

The call ends right as I'm pulling into the drive of my two-story farmhouse. I put the truck into Park and stare out the windshield at the wraparound porch with the swing I hung last spring, the white brick siding, and the large picture window I enjoy standing in front of when the weather isn't quite good enough to be out on the porch first thing in the morning.

"Home sweet home," I mutter to myself then grab my duffel and call Bravo out of the truck. He jumps out of the driver's side then takes off toward the back of the house before racing back toward me. Laughing, I unlock the door and step inside.

I'm greeted with the heady scents of cinnamon and clove, thanks to the oil diffuser currently spitting out steam on my counter. The plants on my shelves all look perfectly healthy, thanks to my mom coming to water for me while I was away. She's clearly been cleaning, too, since the coffee mug I'd rinsed out and set upside down on the drying rack next to the sink is nowhere to be seen.

"Oh, Mom."

The porch creaks behind me. "Do I hear my name?"

I turn as Ruth Hunt rushes into the house wearing a white dress with lavender flowers printed all over it and a heavy black jacket. "Only in appreciation," I reply then drop my bag and wrap my arms around her. We get our height from our father, so my mom's head barely reaches my chest, but I drop my head and breathe in her familiar floral perfume.

*Home.* It doesn't matter that I'm four years away from forty; my mother will always feel like home to me.

"I've missed you, kid. Let me take a look at you." She releases me and steps back, her brow arching as she takes in my unkempt appearance. "You need a trim."

"I've been living in the jungle for three months," I reply with a laugh. "I didn't even sleep in a bed until last night."

She shakes her head. "You still need a trim. Come early for dinner, and I can do it for you."

I laugh, knowing she would too. "I'm headed into town later and was planning to stop by Floyd's." At the mention of our local barber, she nods.

"Good. How was the trip home?"

"Not too bad. No traffic coming out of Dallas, so that's nice."

"Glad to hear it. We missed you around here."

Before I can respond, Bravo bounds into the house, and she drops down to pet him. "There's my good boy! Keeping my son safe, that's what you do, isn't it? You work so hard." Bravo flops down and exposes his belly so my mom will pet it.

You'd never know that, forty-eight hours ago, he had his powerful jaws locked onto the arm of a woman prepared to take my life.

Now, he's a puppy. A goofy, fluffy, German Shepherd puppy.

"What time is dinner?" I ask, mouth already watering.

"Seven," she replies.

"Anything I can bring?"

"Yourself and an appetite."

"I've had an appetite for three months."

She laughs. "Well, good. We'll do something about that tonight." Mom stands. "You doing okay?" Her expression is serious now, and I know it's her fishing for how this latest mission might have affected me.

Truth be told, they all weigh on me like stones around my ankles. The things I've seen, the places I've pulled people out of—they haunt me. But I wouldn't change this mission for anything else. I bring the lost back to their families. And if I must, I'll cut myself to the bone to do it.

"I'm good, Mom."

"Honey—"

"I even managed to hand out those Bibles Dad gave me."

"Really?" Her expression lights up.

"Really. Some of the veterans I worked with and each of the girls I rescued."

Her eyes fill with tears. "The Word of God will help them."

"Yes," I reply. "It will."

"Good." She wipes her tears. "Did Silas make it home okay?"

"He did. Bianca is still in labor, but he made it home okay."

"Home birth. That is one brave woman," she says, her tone laced with admiration.

"Bianca is as tough as they come," I reply honestly. The woman walked through hell and back, managing to come out with more faith than some of the people who warm pews every Sunday.

"Very true. She's a perfect match for our Silas." Mom beams. "Well, I'm going to head up to the house. I'll see you at seven?"

"See you at seven." I step forward and kiss her cheek then give Bravo the command to sit and stay. Otherwise, he'd follow her out happily and not get the bath he so desperately needs.

"I love you, Bradyn, and I'm so glad you're home."

"I love you, too, Mom. And me too."

She smiles, then closes the door behind her. I take a moment, standing in the silence of my living room as the weight of what I dealt with settles over my shoulders. I can still see their faces. Dirty and bruised. The pain in their eyes only eclipsed by the fear as we burst into that room.

My heart is heavy.

My soul worn.

But they're at home with their families.

As I do every time I return home, I bow my head. "Lord, thank You for bringing me back safely. Thank You, God, for guiding me to those girls and giving me what I needed to bring them back safely. I ask that You watch over them, wrapping the victims in Your light and Your love. In the name of Jesus, I pray, amen." I take a deep breath then open my eyes and look down at Bravo, who is watching me curiously, his tail wagging.

"All right. It's bath time, bud. I didn't want to say it earlier, but you smell horrible."

FRESHLY SHOWERED and dressed in jeans, a sweatshirt, and the boots I missed almost as much as my bed, I make my way into the small town of Pine Springs. With only a single stoplight—installed last year to most of the town's disdain —we're not known for our lavish nightlife. Which, in my opinion, is a gift from God above.

Small towns are a dying breed these days, and I'm grateful mine has stayed relatively untouched. Stoplight not included.

I pull into a spot right in front of the barbershop and put my truck into Park then take a second to just sit in the peaceful silence. Bravo is back at my parent's house, undoubtedly being spoiled rotten by my mother, so this is the first time in three months that I've been completely and utterly alone.

Honestly, I'm not sure I care for it. The silence is deafening.

I climb out and make my way up to Floyd's shop, a

man who has been cutting my hair since my first haircut over thirty years ago. Before I can even reach for the handle, though, I hear my name.

Turning, I face the street as an elderly woman wearing black slacks and a puffy black jacket crosses quickly. Her cheeks are red from exertion, her expression wide-eyed and excited.

"While I live and breathe! It is you!" she cries out as she reaches me, the lines at the corner of her brown eyes crinkling in delight.

"Hi, Mrs. Shannon." The woman had been best friends with my grandmother from childhood up until my gran passed away two years ago. She's an honorary grandmother to me and helped my mom tremendously as she grieved the loss of her mother.

"It is so good to see you!" She envelopes me in a floral-scented embrace, squeezing gently.

"You, too."

"When did you get back?" she asks, pulling away.

"Just a few hours ago," I reply.

Her brow arches. "Boy, you look too handsome to have just come in on a plane."

I laugh. "It's amazing what a hot shower and a nap will do."

Her smile spreads. "Fair enough. So, how are you?" It's a question I get whenever I return home from a mission. While the intimate details of what we do are confidential, the town has a decent enough idea. And given that my mom puts us on the prayer list at church whenever we're out, I can bet on being asked this same question over and over again until I've personally seen every person who lives here.

"I did good work, and I'm glad to be home."

"You did amazing work, my boy. I may not know details, but I know that you are doing what needs to be done."

I smile softly even though the weight of her words settles onto my shoulders like a boulder. I do the best I can, but there are plenty of things I've done that I'm not proud of. Not that I'd ever be able to get her to see it that way. "Thanks. How are you?"

"God woke me up this morning; therefore I have no complaints." She smiles. "Well, I better get back to the diner. Francis will be wondering where I ran off to when he gets back from the restroom."

I chuckle, knowing that her husband would assume that she was doing just this—chasing someone down to ask them about their day. It's just who she is. I offer another hug. "It's good to see you."

"You, too, honey. I'll see you around. Don't be a stranger."

"Wouldn't dream of it," I reply with a smile. After offering me a wave, she rushes back across the street and toward the diner. I watch for just a moment, doing my best to stifle the darkness of what I've seen as it tries to creep back into my mind.

Then I turn to head back toward the barber shop and smack into a soft frame.

"Oh, sorry!" Instinctively reaching out, I settle my hands on top of slender shoulders then find myself losing the ability to breathe as I stare down into the most gorgeous blue eyes I've ever seen. They're impossibly blue, really. Like the sky on a cloudless day.

"I'm sorry," the woman says, pulling back.

I withdraw my hands from her shoulders, and because I'm not sure what to do with them, I shove them into my pockets. "My fault. Sorry."

Wearing jeans, boots, and a Carhartt jacket, she's dressed like a rancher, though I've never seen her. Honey-colored hair is braided over her shoulder, and a baseball cap is tucked on her head. It takes me a few seconds to realize that it's my family's brand on the front of it. An HF with cattle horns coming off each letter.

"Oh, Hunt Ranch?" I point to the hat.

"Yeah." Color paints her cheeks. "I am sorry, I didn't mean to run into you like that—"

"Bradyn Hunt," I reply, holding out my hand.

Those impossibly gorgeous blue eyes widen as she reaches out and takes my hand. "The eldest brother returns home, then?" she asks with a hesitant smile.

*Why is she affecting me this way? Like I've been struck by lightning and can't remember how to function?*

I clear my throat. "It would seem so."

"I started work at your ranch about a month ago and have heard nothing but stories about how you were off on an adventure, saving the world and all that."

After withdrawing my hand, I rub it over the back of my neck in an attempt to ease the heat enveloping me as she stares up at me with wide eyes I would happily drown in. "Yeah, well, I wouldn't go that far."

"Everyone else would."

Because I have literally no idea what else to say, I just stare at her—because that's what a hardened soldier does, right? Stares at a beautiful woman because he has no idea what else to say?

"Well, I need to get to the post office. It was good meeting you, Mr. Hunt."

"Bradyn, please. And your name is—"

"Sammy," she replies. "I'll see you around, Bradyn." Without another word, she turns and heads down the street toward the post office, all while I continue staring after her like an awestruck teenager.

Somewhere close by, a bell dings.

"Bradyn?"

"Huh? What?" I finally turn away from the direction Sammy walked in, only to find Floyd standing in the doorway of his shop, grinning like he just caught my hand in the cookie jar.

Which actually happened once at a Hunt family barbeque when I'd been trying to get my hands on dessert before dinner.

"I thought that was you. Are you planning on coming in?"

"Yeah, sorry. I just—"

"Oh, I saw." He chuckles. "She's a looker, for sure. Come in so we can make you at least mildly presentable for the next time your paths cross."

# CHAPTER 3
## KENNEDY

"Just this today?" the aged man behind the postal counter asks as he sticks a stamp onto the postcard I just handed him. "I bet your grandfather misses you something fierce."

The words make my stomach churn. "I miss him, too. And yeah, just that, Shep, thanks."

"Anytime, Sammy. That'll be fifty-six cents." As I reach into my pocket for the change, he sets the postcard aside. "How are you liking it here in Pine Creek?"

"I love it," I reply, grateful that it's one of the few truthful things I get to answer these days. "It's a great town, and the Hunt family has been very welcoming."

"Yeah, they treat their ranch hands like family. Most never leave."

"Well, I'm glad at least one did," I reply with a smile, handing him the coins.

His cheeks turn pink, and he smiles back. "This is true." He offers me a receipt. "Have a good day, okay?"

"You, too. See you next week," I reply with a wave then head back out onto the street. My gaze drifts to the place where I had a face-to-face encounter with Bradyn Hunt. Part of me wants to linger just to see if I can catch another sight of him.

Ever since I arrived, I've been hearing stories about the Hunt brothers. They might as well be local celebrities around here for all the work they do for the community and the military service they all carry with them. Local heroes with small-town charm.

Now that I've met Bradyn, though, I can honestly say that the stories didn't do him justice. Don't get me wrong, the other four are just as great to look at, but there's something about Bradyn. Something that had me dang near swooning like some woman in an old black-and-white movie, even though he hadn't said anything even mildly close to swoon-worthy.

I laugh to myself. *Swoon-worthy.* What an under-statement.

His hazel eyes were so bright they might have pierced my soul if I'd stared too long. His dark, shaggy hair was a lot longer than his brothers' and somehow perfectly tailored to his dangerous look. And the man is tall. I thought his brothers were, but Bradyn stands even taller than them. Not by much, but he's definitely far taller than any one man should be.

And those broad shoulders. He'd been wearing a thick jacket, but when I'd reached out to steady myself, I'd gripped those arms. Strong, muscled arms.

I shake my head. *Get it together, Kennedy.*

Seriously, though, could he be any more handsome?

Since I have the afternoon off, I head down the street and toward the market to grab a few things before going back to my cabin on the ranch. Even though it's January and freezing, the sky is blue, the sun shining brightly. It's a truly beautiful day, but there's a cloud hovering over me.

Likely due to the nightmare that had me up before dawn, even though it was the first morning in two weeks that I got to sleep in. My smile fades slightly as I step into the market, my thoughts on everything I need to grab.

"Afternoon, Sammy!" Jim, a teenager who restocks on the weekends, greets as I make my way inside.

"Afternoon, how's it going today?"

"Not too shabby," he replies with a flirtatious grin. I'm far too old for him, something I'm sure he realizes, but that doesn't stop him from chatting me up whenever we cross paths. "You look rested today. Day off?"

"That's right." I head toward the back of the store, a small basket in hand. After piling some bananas, apples, and a jar of crunchy peanut butter inside, I head back toward the front.

"Breakfast of champions?" the cashier asks as she rings me up.

"You know it," I reply.

"I thought they fed you better at that ranch."

I laugh. "They do. But I'm not big on hearty breakfasts," I reply. It's a lie, of course. Who doesn't love hearty breakfasts of pancakes, eggs, bacon, and hash browns? The truth is that I can't stomach taking any more from the Hunts than I already have.

Not when I'm lying to them with every breath I take.

"Ahh, well, I hear those breakfasts are amazing. Maybe give one a try. You could do with a little meat on your bones, Sammy," she replies with a wink.

I smile. "Maybe."

That's the one thing about small towns that I had always thought was a rumor but turned out to be true. Everyone knows everyone. Secrets can't hide here, which makes it incredibly interesting that I've been able to. This is the longest I've stayed anywhere. Even though it's only been a couple of months since I first crossed into the small town of Pine Creek, Texas, and a month since I started work at the ranch, everyone in town remembers me. And they all take time to say hi whenever our paths cross.

This place is the closest I've come to home in a long time.

But I know better than to get too comfortable. Because that could all change tomorrow.

"Thanks, Brenda," I say to her as I pocket my receipt and change, taking my paper bag with me.

"You're welcome, honey. Have a great day."

Stepping outside, I slip sunglasses over my eyes and head toward the beat-up old truck I bought in a used, cash-only lot six months ago. It's parked right between the market and the post office, so the walk is quick. Even as I know it's likely an impossibility, my gaze scans my surroundings for anything that doesn't quite fit.

Like a person in a place they shouldn't be.

After setting my bag on the passenger seat, I climb behind the wheel and take off. Music drowns out the silence around me during the fifteen-minute drive back to Hunt Ranch. It's hardly the only ranch in this area, but it is by far the largest and has been in the Hunt family for generations—1906 from what my research told me.

The Hunts are known around this town as kind people who love God and cherish their neighbors. Something they prove whenever someone is in need of anything. Take me, for example. They had no openings since they weren't planning on hiring a replacement for the last ranch hand who left, but the second I showed up at their door, asking for a job, they found a place for me.

Ten minutes after Mrs. Hunt pulled the door open, I was walking into the house and being welcomed with a tall glass of sweet tea and fresh homemade banana bread.

They're a perfect example of money not changing a person.

Despite the fact that they have a ranch that has to be worth millions of dollars, they're a small family at their core, doing what they can to help others on their way through this life.

It makes me yearn for something I'll never have again. Family. My throat constricts as a wave of emotion hits me. *No. Shove it down, Kennedy.*

Instead of letting the past consume me, I focus on what's ahead.

Unlike a lot of ranches in the area, the Hunt ranch hands have a row of cabins rather than a bunkhouse. We each get our own space—a bed, bathroom, small kitchen—that we can call our own as long as we're working here.

While we do share a parking lot, the cabins are all our own, separated by a magnolia tree planted strategically between each of them for privacy.

It'll be gorgeous, especially when the trees are in full bloom. All that dark wood contrasting with the waxy green leaves and white blossoms. I've only seen it in pictures so far, but I'm hoping that I'll get to remain here long enough to witness it for myself.

Unlikely, of course, but maybe.

I'm just putting my truck in Park when I notice a shadow creeping around the left side of my cabin. The blood in my veins begins to pound, and adrenaline surges through my system.

Instinctively, I reach for the small firearm I always keep on me, my hand closing over the grip as I abandon my groceries and slip out of the truck. All while I'm kicking myself for not bringing my go bag with me when I left this morning. I *always* have it on me. But today, I'd left it behind. Why didn't I bring it with me?

If I'm lucky, they haven't gotten into the house yet and I can slip in through the side and grab my bag. If I'm not lucky—well—I won't be walking out of here at all.

A man is peering through my back window, but when I get close enough to get a better look at him, I breathe a sigh of relief and hold the firearm behind my back. It's Texas, so legally, I can carry it, but I don't want anyone here noticing it. The questions that may come from it are ones I don't want to answer. "What are you doing here?"

Arthur Kidress turns, his cheeks flushing with color. "Sammy, there you are. I was looking for you."

"You were peering into the back of my house," I say. "Did you not knock?"

"Of course I knocked." Arthur arrived about a month before me and has made it no secret that he's attracted to me.

Unfortunately for him, even if I were drawn to him, I have a strict 'no dating' policy.

He comes down the back steps with a friendly smile on his face. "You didn't answer."

Since he was already on the ranch when I arrived here, it's unlikely he's a threat to me, but I can never be too careful. Not when I have enemies lurking everywhere I turn. "Which makes peering into my back door less creepy?" I question.

"Sorry." He runs a hand over the back of his head and then shoves both hands into his pockets. "I wanted to see if you were doing okay."

"It's my day off."

His embarrassment is written all over his face. "I'm making a mess of this, aren't I?"

"I don't know what you're doing, but I would say stalking my house isn't a great start to whatever it is."

He laughs. "I wanted to ask if you'd be up for dinner."

"When?"

"Tonight."

"A date?" I question.

"Yeah," he replies. "With me. I think it could be fun." He shrugs, and I almost feel bad for the impending *no* that's hanging in the air.

"I appreciate the invite, but—"

"But?"

"I'm not big into dating." Another not-lie for me today; it must be a record. Dating means getting attached. I can't afford attachments because they inevitably lead to pain and death. Two things I'm trying to avoid for myself and everyone around me.

"Oh." His face falls.

"I'm sorry, Arthur."

"Nah, it's good. I get it. Might make things awkward if the date sucks. You know, given that we have to work together."

I force a smile. "Very true."

"Well." He pulls his hands out of his pockets. "I guess I'll see you tomorrow?"

"See you tomorrow," I reply, moving to the side and keeping my back away from him so he doesn't see the gun I'm still holding.

Arthur walks around the side of my cabin, headed back toward the parking lot, so I shove the firearm back into the waistband of my pants before withdrawing my keys and heading back out to my truck. Heart still pumping, I grab my stuff from the truck and slip into the house.

As I do every time I come home, I clear the rooms one at a time, ensuring no one snuck in while I was away. After securing the small cabin and making sure all the windows and doors are locked, I finally take a seat on the couch and let out a sigh.

I miss having someone to talk to. Someone to share my day with. Now, I'm living so much of a lie I can't risk idle conversation just in case something slips out. Solitude cuts deep, but there's no way around it. Not yet anyway. Maybe not ever.

For some reason, Bradyn Hunt's handsome face swims into my mind. I can see him standing there, bathed in sunlight as he'd stared down at me. My stomach twists into nervous knots. He's exactly the kind of man I could have fallen for once upon a time.

*Once upon a time when my life wasn't one nightmare after another.*

Those pesky feelings rear their ugly head again, so I push to my feet and head into the bathroom to wash the day off of me. Pajamas and a book. That's what the evening has in store for me.

Anything else can just wait outside until morning.

# CHAPTER 4
# BRADYN

The scents of Dad's smoked brisket and Mom's fresh-baked apple pie hit me as soon as I step through the front door. Taking a minute to savor it, I remain in the brightly lit foyer, taking in the hearty scents and the sounds of my brothers laughing in the kitchen. Photographs of my siblings and me in various stages of our lives line the foyer walls, along with crosses my dad has handmade for my mom over the years.

*Home.* It hits me again, and I smile. Man, I missed this place.

My brother, Tucker, younger than me by four years, sticks his head around the corner. "You planning on coming all the way in, or are you no longer accustomed to being indoors?" He heads down the hall and envelops me in a tight hug.

"Something like that," I reply with a laugh then follow him down the hallway into the kitchen.

Tucker and his twin Dylan are the youngest of us, having turned thirty-two last month. I'd been gone for that, too, and unable to even make a call, given the sensitive nature of the mission.

"Happy birthday, by the way."

Tucker grins at me. "Nice of you to remember, big brother." He winks, letting me know he understands and in no way, shape, or form cares that I didn't call. Not that I expected him to. He's a part of our company too and knows that sometimes communication just isn't possible.

Dylan is the next to peek around the corner, his grin matching the one still on Tucker's face. He steps out and wraps his arms around me. The quietest of the twins, he's had a haunted look in his eyes ever since returning from his final deployment five years ago.

Though he won't talk about what he saw, I can imagine, and it breaks my heart that the little boy who wanted so badly to be a superhero ended up a man haunted by war.

"Good to see you, brother," he says.

"You, too, Dylan. Where are the dogs?" Since I haven't seen Bravo —or Dylan and Tucker's dogs, Delta and Tango —I'm assuming they're outside.

"In the backyard with Dad," Tucker replies. "They're playing fetch."

I smile, happy that my boy can finally unwind and relax.

We head into the kitchen where my mom is standing in front of the stove, a wooden spoon in her hand. She glances over her shoulder. "Your hair looks nice."

I cross the tile flooring and wrap her in a one-armed hug, pressing a kiss to her temple. "Thanks, Mom. I told Floyd you said hi."

"Good." She returns her attention to the stove. "Now go and convince your father to see Floyd because he's refusing to let me cut his hair, and he's starting to look shaggy."

"Who's starting to look shaggy?" My father's deep baritone fills the room, and I turn as he steps into the kitchen with a smile. His beard has gotten a bit longer since the last time I saw him, now down to his sternum, and his gray hair has grown out so it's curling over his ears.

The same hazel eyes I share with Dylan and Elliot stare back at me, full of joy. "It's good to see you, son." He embraces me then pulls back to look at me. "You look good. Not at all shaggy. I think your mother's eyesight must be getting bad."

My mother rolls her eyes, but a smile toys at the corner of her lips. "*He* went to see Floyd today. Which is more than I can say of you, Tommy Hunt," Mom replies as my father releases me and wraps his arms around his wife's waist.

What used to gross me out when I was a teenager now

has me yearning for a marriage of my own. A partner to share this life with. Maybe someday, God willing.

"Where's Elliot and Riley?" I question.

"There was a fence down in pasture two, so they're fixing it."

"A fence down? From what?"

Dylan leans back against the counter. "A tree fell on it during the storm a few days ago. There's another storm gearing to hit later this week, so they wanted to make sure it was up just in case we need to rotate due to more damage."

I nod and make a mental note to ride through the pastures tomorrow and make sure there's nothing else that needs repairing before storm number two hits.

This time of year, we get more sleeting ice than anything, which can cause downed trees and impassable roads.

"Hey, we already did it."

"Did what?" I ask, my gaze fixing on Tucker.

"We rode through the pastures and checked all the fencing. That was the only one down."

It shouldn't surprise me that he knows exactly what I was thinking. When you not only grow up with someone but also spend every waking moment working alongside them, it's difficult to keep even your thoughts a secret.

"I don't know why you're telling him that," Dylan adds, plucking a grape from the fruit tray my mom set out on the counter. "You know he's still going to take that ride. I'm surprised he's not out there now, double-checking our work and whatnot." He grins.

I laugh. "I've been gone for three months, and yet you can still read my mind." I don't even try to pretend like he's wrong. I'm a micromanager when it comes to this ranch, even though I don't have to be because they love this place as much as I do.

"Always, brother." He grins. "Can't get anything past us."

My phone buzzes, so I withdraw it from my pocket, and my own smile breaks out when I see Silas' incoming video call. "Hey there, cousin," I greet as soon as I answer.

"Hey, I want you to meet someone." He shifts the camera, showing me the most adorable tiny pink baby I've ever seen. "This is our son, little Asher Matthew Wiliamson."

"Let me see!" My mother practically shoves through my brothers to get to the phone. "Honey, he is perfect!"

"Thanks, Aunt Ruth," he replies. I can hear the smile in his voice, and knowing everything my cousin has suffered in his life, I cannot thank God enough for this happy blessing He bestowed on both Silas and Bianca.

"You are so welcome. How is Bianca?"

"I'm good!" we hear her call out from the background. The camera shifts, showing us the dark-haired beauty who captured Silas' guarded heart. She smiles happily, looking exhausted but thrilled. "He's perfect."

"He most certainly is," Mom replies.

The camera shifts back to Silas, and my dad peeks around Mom and into the phone, his eyes misting with happy tears. "How is our sweet little Eloise liking being a big sister?" he asks.

"She's so excited. Eliza and Lance took her out for ice cream just before I called."

"Good. I'm so glad. She'll have a best friend for life now," my mom says.

"Yes, she will." He is absolutely beaming with joy, and even as happy as I am, I can't help but feel a tad jealous too. I want children as badly as I want to take my next breath. *All in good time. All in God's time.* "Well, I better get going. I need to hand this little guy off to his momma then grab us both something to eat."

"Let us know if you need anything," Dad offers.

"Will do, thanks."

"We love you, honey," Mom says with a wave.

"Love you, too," he replies.

Mom heads back to the kitchen while Dylan and Tucker remain standing beside me.

"Congrats, Cuz," Dylan says. "He's handsome."

"Thanks, guys. I'm—" He smiles. "I'm so happy. I thank God every day for this. For all of this. I don't deserve any of it."

"None of us do," I reply. "We love you. Hopefully, we can get out soon to meet the little guy."

"I hope so too. Talk soon." The call ends, and I shove my phone back into my pocket.

"I'm so happy for them both," my mom says from in front of the stove.

"Same."

The front door thuds closed. I step out of the kitchen and grin when I see my sister Lani strolling toward me, wearing slacks and a button-down shirt. She looks exhausted, but when she sees me, her face lights up.

"Bradyn!"

I catch her in a big hug. "Hey, little sister."

She pulls away, and we finish the walk into the kitchen. "I'm so glad you're back. How was the trip?" She reaches in and plucks a grape from the fruit tray.

"I accomplished what needed to be accomplished."

"You always do." She smiles softly then grabs another grape.

Her black hair is shorter than it was before I left and is pulled back into a ponytail. She looks happy. Tired but happy. I guess running one's own medical practice will do that to a person.

Silence descends into the kitchen as my father steps up toward the oven and opens it, withdrawing a foil-covered pan that I know will be full of the most delicious brisket in the Lone Star State, something that over a decade of BBQ competition wins has proven.

My mouth waters.

"So what's new here at the ranch?" I question, hoping the conversation will not only distract me from the hunger pangs but also swing in the direction of a certain gorgeous woman I haven't been able to stop thinking about.

Even the news of Silas' new addition couldn't completely get her off my mind. She's lingering. And it's been a long time since a woman captivated me the way she did. Especially in the span of only a minute or so.

The way I asked the question must have raised a few flags for Tucker because he arches a brow. "You been out wandering?"

"No." I clear my throat. *Fess up, Hunt.* "But I did meet our new hand in town, and it had me wondering if there was anything else I needed to know."

"Ahh, you met Sammy," he replies with a knowing smile toward Dylan. The two of them grin at me.

"I did."

"Oh, she's adorable," my mother interjects. "Beautiful inside and out. And great with the horses. Even your night-marish one." She points at me.

Tucker barks out a laugh. "That's right, you'll have to fight her to get Rev back," he tells me.

"Rev likes her?" I ask, honestly surprised. Since we rescued him from an incredibly abusive owner, it took me nearly two years to earn Rev's trust. The Appaloosa didn't give it easily, but he's become my favorite horse on the ranch. Loyal, gentle, and bombproof. For me, at least. No one else can get close to him…usually.

"He does. Probably prefers her," Dylan replies. "I bet she smells better."

"Sammy is great," Lani agrees.

Tucker opens his mouth to respond, but the front door opens, and I hear the bootsteps of Elliot and Riley. *Thank you, God, for the distraction.*

The last of my brothers come around the corner, looking absolutely exhausted, but the moment they see me, their expressions turn joyful. Relaxed.

Elliot's baseball cap is on backward, his jeans dirty, his white shirt stained with dirt from the fence repair. He steps forward and offers me a handshake in lieu of a hug. "I'll hug you later," he replies, gesturing to his clothes.

"Appreciate that." I laugh.

"Glad you lived," Riley says with a lopsided grin, his own clothes smeared with grime.

"Bianca and Silas had their baby," Mom announces.

"Seriously?" Riley asks. "Awesome."

"That's great," Elliot adds.

"Bianca sent me pictures," Lani says. "He's so precious."

"He really is," Mom agrees. "Dinner will be ready in five."

"I'll go wash my hands then," Elliot says before heading down the hall.

"Same." Riley follows, disappearing down the hall toward the bathroom all six of us shared growing up. Even as quaint as the three-bedroom farmhouse is, it never felt crowded. Not once in the entire time I was growing up.

Jesus is the cornerstone of my life. Without Him, I could not stand. But God also blessed me with a foundation of family that is simply unmatched. And, as I help my mother carry food to our table and take my seat in the same chair I once occupied as a child, I am beyond grateful that He has brought me through the hellish things I've faced so that I may sit here and share another meal with the most important people in my life.

As they so often do these days, my thoughts turn dark —haunted by the things I witnessed when I'd been deployed as well as the experiences I've had since I first started Hunt Brothers Search & Rescue.

The people we rescued.

And above all, the ones we couldn't.

It's so easy to get dragged down into the darkness when it's constantly shackled around your ankles though, so I do what I can to force my thoughts elsewhere, opting instead to think back to that moment I'd shared with Sammy on the sidewalk outside the barber.

Gorgeous blue eyes. Sun-kissed honey hair. Stunning smile. And yet, there was something else about her too...

something that might as well be a beacon for the tattered remnants of a soul worn down by the darkness of the world.

---

"YOU DID GOOD, SON," my father says as he gets up to refill his glass of water.

It's silly that, even now, at creeping up on forty years old, hearing my father say those words still has the same effect as it did back when I was a child seeking his approval. Thankfully, unlike so many other kids, I never had to search far.

"I can't get the image of them hunkered down in the dark out of my head," I admit. "It's burned into my soul." The debrief went well with me filling in on the mission details, what happened, who was apprehended, and how many were saved. Even though our father isn't an active part of the rescue portion of our business, he typically sits in during every meeting and mission assignment, offering insight and support where needed.

My brothers, who are all sitting around the dining room table, nod in agreement. The dishes are done, the kitchen dark, and Mom has turned in for the night since she's helping organize the church bake sale first thing tomorrow morning.

"Pray for them," my father says as he sits back down.

"It's all you can do now. You've already given them back the lives stolen from them."

"It doesn't feel like it's enough." Crossing my arms, I lean back in the chair. "Every day, there's a new alert. A new missing person. These kids are innocent. Why them? Why do they have to suffer?"

"The devil is rampant these days." My father sighs. "But we already know who wins in the end, and until then, you're standing right where you need to be. Between the innocent and the evil." He drains his glass. "Any ideas when the next job will be?" he asks.

"No," I reply. "Next up is Elliot, though. We'll keep our ears to the ground, and as soon as something comes up, we'll handle it. Just like we always do." I let out a sigh and stand. "I'm exhausted, though. Think I'm going to turn in for the night. Come on, boy," I call to Bravo, who jumps up from where he's lying near my brother's dogs. Riley's dog, Romeo, lifts his head but places it back down when he realizes Riley isn't going anywhere just yet.

"Sleep well, son. See you bright and early."

"See you bright and early," I reply with a smile then head for the door.

After slipping into my jacket, I step onto the porch. The moon is bright tonight, casting a soft glow over the rolling hills just outside my parent's home. I breathe in the crisp, cold air and take just a moment to absorb the silence of the ranch.

This place is my heaven on earth. My refuge from the chaos I face every time I head down that driveway.

The moon is bright tonight, casting a soft glow over the barn straight ahead. Turning, I scan the landscape, pausing when I see the dim cabin lights where our employees live while they work here.

I can't help but wonder if one of those lights belongs to Sammy.

Is she down there awake right now? Or sound asleep? What brought her here in the first place? Most of the time, our help comes from either those not wanting to settle down or those who are running from something. Which is she? I'm betting on the latter. There was heaviness in her eyes. A darkness one only gets when they've lived through trauma.

Even though I really should be getting home, I pass by the side-by-side I drove over earlier and head for the barn. Since my parents' house is the heart of the ranch, the barn is only a short distance from their place.

I remember being a kid and sprinting as fast as I could across the distance, hoping to get there so I had at least a small chance of winning the hide-and-seek game my brothers and I played every chance we got. There are so many times I miss those days. When things were simple. When I hadn't seen the corruption of the world and everything felt right.

The walk is something I know by heart and could do

even with my eyes closed, though, thanks to the moon, I don't have to. Gripping the large iron handle, I pull the sliding door aside enough that I can slip in. Trained well, Bravo walks just inside the door then sits down at the entrance, keeping his distance from the horses.

Most of the animals here won't care either way, but since we have rescues come in occasionally, it made sense to train the dogs to know their place regardless of the horse. Then we never have to worry.

As if he can sense me, Rev sticks his large head over the gate and snorts in my direction.

"Hey, boy." I smile then offer him my flattened hand so he can smell me. He leans into my touch, so I move in closer and run a hand over his massive head. "I missed you, too, buddy. How are you?" In response, he lifts his head and nuzzles my shoulder with his nose. "I'm glad. I'll be by first thing in the morning. We'll head out before the sun comes up, okay? Just like before." After petting him on the head one final time, I secure the barn, climb into the side-by-side, and Bravo and I make our way back home where I will undoubtedly struggle to find rest, thanks to the memories still haunting me.

# CHAPTER 5
# KENNEDY

Morning comes far quicker than I would've liked, but as soon as my alarm goes off at four forty-five, I'm up and prepping a cup of hot coffee to drink out on the porch. As I step out, fully dressed and ready for the day, mug in hand, I breathe in the cold morning air and scan the horizon.

There are no lights on in the other cabins, though that's not unusual given I'm always the first one out of bed. A strategic move since I've always needed at least thirty minutes of alone time in the morning in order to be fully awake.

Heaviness weighs on my thoughts as I recall the person I shared that particular need with is no longer breathing. I swallow hard. *No time for those thoughts*, I remind myself. One day, maybe. But not now. Not today.

A light flicks on in the barn, and I jump, trying to peer into the darkness.

A horse whinnies.

No one should be in the barn. Even the Hunts aren't up and moving around the ranch for at least another hour. My heart begins to pound. Is it possible someone's trying to steal the horses? Do people still do that?

I rush into the cabin and set my coffee down on the counter; then I grab my keys, lock up, and head up toward the barn. It's more than likely someone is just getting an early start, right? Surely, no one would be foolish enough to try to steal anything belonging to the Hunt family...

But if I see something off and don't go check it out, I won't be able to forgive myself. So, still not quite awake, I try to quietly approach the barn, stepping carefully so I don't alert whoever is inside to my presence.

If someone is just getting an early start, I'll slip away and finish my coffee. And if it's not—the gun at my back is cool against my skin, and while I hope to never use it, if someone is hurting these horses—

A dog barks. A single alarm that has me stepping back in response.

A low growl emits, and a German shepherd walks out of the barn door, his gaze trained on me.

*A Hunt brother.* It has to be a Hunt brother. They all have working dogs. And given that I've never seen this particular dog, that must mean—before I can fully register it, Bradyn Hunt steps from the barn, a flashlight in his hand. He aims it at me, and the expression on his face relaxes. "*Halt,*" he orders.

The dog immediately quiets.

"You're up early," I blurt. "No one else is ever up this early."

A shadow of a smile graces his handsome face. "I've always gotten up before everyone else. It's when the world is at its quietest. Come on in; it's warmer in here." Without waiting for me to follow, he turns and heads inside. "*Hier,*" he orders his dog.

Just like his other brothers, he uses German commands when speaking to his dog. I'd asked Elliot about it after I first arrived, and he'd told me that it's easier to keep the dog focused when very few people know the same commands.

I stand where I am, lingering just outside the barn, unsure whether I should go in or not. It's none of my business that he's up early, and the more time passes, the more foolish I feel that I came up here in the first place.

This ranch is locked down tight at night and run by brothers who served in the Army as Special Forces. The likelihood of anyone getting onto the property without them knowing is basically zero.

It's one of the reasons I've felt safe settling here for a time.

*I shouldn't go in.*

So why do I *want* to go in?

Because I need this job, and the last thing I should be is rude to the guy that basically runs the place. While their father is still a part of the ranch, I was told that Bradyn is the lead for it. Maybe I would have thought twice about working here if I'd known that my boss would be an absolutely gorgeous, strong, seemingly kind man with eyes that make me want to spill all of my secrets.

*Buck up, Kennedy. You've faced down worse than a handsome cowboy.*

With that in mind, I walk into the illuminated barn. His dog looks up briefly from where he lies beside the door but stays put and drops his head back down.

Bradyn Hunt stands with his back to me as he runs a brush over Rev's massive back. I'm monetarily stunned to see Rev standing so still for him; then I remember Elliot telling me that Rev is Bradyn's horse, and the only one—besides me apparently—who can handle him is the eldest brother.

And with that knowledge, I pause a moment so I can fully take in the sight of Bradyn Hunt in all his glory. I'd been too stunned on the street to do so yesterday, and it's not until this very moment that I realize how much I was missing.

Standing at least six foot four, he's the kind of strong built by a life of physical labor and hard training. He turns his head to mutter something to Rev, granting me the sight of a strong jaw coated in stubble even though he'd been clean-shaven just yesterday.

His brows are sharp, his dark hair a bit longer than his other brothers' but shorter than it was yesterday when we ran into each other on the street.

Dark jeans hug broad hips, and since his Carhartt jacket is hanging on a hook by the door, the black thermal shirt he's wearing hugs his torso like a second skin.

He's gorgeous.

Stunning.

Too beautiful to be real.

Something nuzzles me, nearly making me jump. I reach up and run my hand over Midnight's forelock, a black Appaloosa mare with a white blanket over her back. "Morning, girl," I greet, smiling a bit to myself in embarrassment. I'm only glad it was the horse who caught me and not Bradyn.

At least, she can't tell everyone I was gawking at him.

"So, are you an early riser too?"

"Huh?" I shift my gaze to Bradyn as the question registers in my un-caffeinated mind. "Yeah. Sorry, didn't finish my coffee."

"Why not?"

"I thought someone was stealing the horses."

He stops brushing Rev and turns to fully face me. "You

thought someone was in here stealing horses, and you ran up here, unarmed, ready to stop them?" He doesn't ask in a mocking tone as some men would have, but rather one of genuine curiosity.

"I'm tougher than I look." Besides, he doesn't have to know that there's a firearm tucked at my back and I'd been more than prepared to use it. Not that I think he'd care—especially given the firearm currently holstered at his waist.

But that will lead to questions about where I learned to shoot and why I started carrying, and both of those questions will only have me spouting off more lies. I really don't want to lie to Bradyn.

I can't exactly tell him I learned the weight behind pulling a trigger in a moment when my life was on the line. That I'd never held a gun before it was me or him walking away.

And I certainly can't tell him how an elderly war veteran—who pulled me out of an alley, bloody, battered, and nearly dead—took me to a range every weekend for a year.

"I definitely get that feeling," he replies with a smile my way then returns to brushing Rev, the gorgeous gelding I'd grown rather fond of over the past few months.

Warning bells ring in my mind, the urge for me to turn and run getting stronger. What is it about this man that calls to me? Never, in my entire life, have I felt so drawn to someone I just met. Even though I know I should turn and walk away, I don't want to.

And that equals danger in my world. I clear my throat. "Elliot warned me you'd be wanting your horse back." *Way to go, Kennedy. You're bringing him back into another conversation instead of just leaving.*

Bradyn turns toward me and smiles. My stomach twists into knots in response. *I'm in big trouble here.* "Yeah, I'd say Rev and I are old friends."

"He's a great horse," I reply.

"I'm actually surprised he took to you," he says as he sets the brush aside and heads into the tack room, appearing a moment later with a saddle already fit with a pad. "He barely tolerates anyone else."

"We hit it off," I say. "Bonded over pasts we'd both rather forget, I suppose." Even as the words leave my mouth, I regret saying them. The last thing I need is this man—or any of the Hunts—looking too deeply into my past.

The secrets I've built around me like walls will collapse beneath the weight of even the slightest pressure.

He sets the saddle onto the gelding's back, and although I know he heard me, he doesn't comment. *So he's not one to pry. That's good.*

"What do you usually do when you're up this early? Work around here doesn't typically start until right at sunrise," he asks.

"I usually get started on chores. Cleaning stalls and prepping feed buckets. Helps the day go by smoother."

"Leave anything for anyone else?" he asks with an arched brow. When I don't immediately answer, he adds, "If you're up this early, I imagine there's not much left for the rest of us."

I shrug. "I like to be busy."

He tightens the cinch. "Something I relate to all too well. It's Sammy, right?"

"That's right," I reply, even as I wish I could hear my actual name leave his lips. *What is wrong with me? Get it together, Kennedy.* "Why are you up this early? And why are you saddling Rev? It won't be light for another half hour or so." *Woo-hoo, brain is finally working.* Except then I realize I just questioned the boss.

It's his ranch. His horse. He can do whatever he wants.

If the inquisition bothers him, he doesn't show it. "I don't mind the dark. I like to catch the sunrise at the top of the hill; then head out to do a quick ride through the pastures closest before coming back here and officially getting the day started."

"Sounds peaceful."

"It is," he replies then steps around Rev so we're both on the same side of the horse. "Why don't you join me this morning?"

"What? Why? It doesn't sound like a two-person job."

He grins. An adorable crooked grin that sends my heart

racing. "No, but the company might be nice. And the view is breathtaking."

*I'll say.* This man should come with a warning label.

*WARNING: His smile can lead to heart palpitations.*

I start to accept, but something in his expression has me pumping the brakes on this runaway train of attraction. There's pain hidden in there. And I know myself well enough to know that, even though I carry my own demons, as soon as we started getting close, I'd start longing to slay his.

But the connection I feel is only going to put both of us at risk. Either we'll hit it off, things will be beautiful, then I'll have to break both our hearts when I inevitably have to leave, or things go sour and Bradyn decides to do a deeper dive into my past, forcing me out anyway.

It's a lose-lose all the way around.

As he waits for my response, he slips the bridle onto Rev and removes his halter then turns to face me. "Interested?"

*Now that's a weighted question.*

I clear my throat. "No thanks. Maybe some other time. I need to go finish my coffee and grab some breakfast before the sun comes up."

His grin falls just slightly, and my stomach sinks right along with it. Even as I tell myself it's for the best, the disappointment on his face drags my mood right down to the ground.

"Sounds good, Sammy. I'll see you around." With a smile lacking the brightness it had earlier, he leads Rev out into the dark, Bravo trailing right beside him.

---

EVER SINCE MY first day here at the ranch, I've felt mildly intimidated by the Hunt brothers. They've always been kind, sure, but there's no mistaking the lethality lurking just beneath the surface.

These men are built and trained for war.

Soldiers masquerading as cowboys.

Like they're one breath away from marching into battle. I know that they'd defend this ranch to the very last breath in their chests, and that's something I can appreciate.

Bradyn is leaning back against the wall of the barn as Elliot gives us our task list for the day.

Tree limbs need to be trimmed.

Stalls cleaned out and filled with extra bedding.

Cattle moved to the pastures closest to the house.

Honestly, it's a relatively lean day compared to the last few.

We just had a particularly nasty storm two days ago and had quite a few downed trees.

I'm glad it's over, but now the news is predicting the one hitting us at the end of the week will be worse. Lots of sleeting rain. Which, thanks to the cold January weather, will then lead to ice and impassable roads. Hence the need to move the cattle even closer.

Riley, Tucker, and Dylan are all relatively quiet this morning. While that's normal for Dylan, Riley and Tucker are typically a lot chattier. I can't tell if that's because something is on their minds or they're merely mentally prepping for the day.

"Those of you who have been here a while should remember Bradyn," Elliot says, gesturing to his older brother.

"Who?" Another ranch hand, Leon, calls out with a grin.

Bradyn offers a half smile and stands.

"He's rejoining us after being out for just over three months. Bradyn runs the show most days, but since he's been gone awhile, we have to make sure he remembers how to do this."

Everyone laughs, and Bradyn's gaze briefly rests on me.

I swallow hard.

He looks away. "I'm glad to be back," he says. "I'm looking forward to getting to know those of you who are new here, and I'm ready to work alongside the rest of you again. Thanks for not letting the place fall into shambles while I was gone." He steps back again.

"It's going to be a great day," Elliot says as he sticks his notebook into his back pocket and removes his baseball cap. "So let's pray and get this day going."

Everyone stands—including Bradyn—and bows their heads. I'm not entirely sure where I stand in the faith department. With everything I've seen, I'm just not so sure there's more to this life than what's in front of us. But I bow my head anyway.

"Lord, we thank You for this day. For bringing Bradyn and Bravo home safely as well as granting us the strength we needed to keep this place running without them. Please guide us today so that the work we do is solid, productive, and is for the betterment of this ranch and those who rely on us. Watch over us as we head out, Lord, and please bring us all back safely. I ask this in the name of Jesus. Amen."

A chorus of "Amen" fills the barn, and the six other ranch hands currently employed by Hunt Ranch all head over to the stall of their horse of choice so they can start prepping the animal for the day.

Bradyn is talking to Elliot, both of them huddled in the corner. After a brief conversation, they separate. Unlike the other Hunt brothers, Bradyn doesn't hang out in the barn with the rest of us, likely because Rev is already saddled and tethered outside the barn.

And since I also prepped Midnight prior to this meeting, I have the perfect opportunity to head outside where she's tethered, too. Maybe if I can catch him before—Arthur steps in my way. "Hey."

"Hey."

"It's going to be a short day today, huh?"

"Looks that way." I offer a friendly smile then try to step around him.

"Yeah, should get a decent amount of downtime today."

"Definitely. I already saddled Midnight, so I'm heading out. See you later." Without giving him the chance to block me again, I rush out of the barn, moving as quickly as I can without being too obvious.

But by the time I get out there, Bradyn is already riding away on Rev.

"I told you he was going to take his horse back."

I glance over at Elliot and smile. "Yeah, he was quick to stake claim to him first thing this morning."

Elliot laughs. "He said you were up here thinking someone was trying to steal the horses."

"When I gave it any actual thought, I realized what a foolish idea it was." Elliot has always been easy to talk to. He's clearly the most social of the brothers, and conversation has always flowed between us.

"Still thoughtful though. But maybe next time, you give one of us a call so we can meet you up here just in case."

I smile and pat his dog, Echo, on top of the head. "Fair enough."

"See you out there," he says then heads back into the barn.

"See you out there," I reply quietly then climb on

Midnight and glance in the direction Bradyn rode off in. I could follow now, catch him before anyone else gets out to the pasture, but is that really such a good idea?

I turned down his friendly offer this morning, setting what I was hoping would be very clear boundaries in the process. Which is what I wanted, right? Boundaries? Distance?

Then why does my stomach feel like a pit as I stare off after him?

# CHAPTER 6
# BRADYN

"Bradyn Hunt. I have to say it's good to see you." Conner Matthews, the owner of Pine Creek Café, reaches out and shakes my hand. He's owned this place for nearly fifteen years alongside his wife Talia. They moved here two decades ago, and the rest is history.

"Good to see you, too, Conner. How's the family?"

"Jessie got engaged," he says. His oldest daughter had just turned twenty-three right before I left.

"Really?"

"Really. I'm feeling old these days."

I laugh. "Adam is a good guy, though. He'll treat her right."

"He is, and she's happy, which is all that matters." He smiles. "You want your usual?"

"Three months away and you still remember?" I take a seat in a corner booth.

He laughs. "You've eaten here so much over the years it's branded into my brain."

"Fair enough. The usual is good, thanks."

"Anytime. Talia will be right out with your water." He heads back around the counter and into the kitchen while I shrug out of my jacket.

The café is lean tonight with only a few other tables taken. One with a group of teenagers laughing and happily chatting about their day, and the other with Mandy Bell, the town's librarian, and Betty Elliot, the owner of our local coffee shop.

I'm honestly surprised Lani isn't over there with them since the three of them have been thick as thieves since elementary school.

"Here you go, honey." Talia sets a glass of water in front of me and steps back. "It's good to have you back in town."

"Good to be back."

"You doing okay?" she asks, eyes narrowing on me.

"I'm doing good, thanks for asking."

"Always. You boys are like family. It's tough when you're gone."

"Hard on us, too," I admit.

She smiles softly and pats my shoulder. "You are some of the best men I know." The bell rings over the door, and

Lani walks in. She offers Talia a wave then turns back toward the door and smiles.

Sammy steps in, her hair loose around her shoulders and curled softly. She's traded out her ranch attire for a pair of leggings and a long cream sweatshirt that hangs nearly to her knees. She surveys the diner and stalls on me.

Our gazes hold, and I am completely unable to tear my eyes away from her even though, on some level, I know I should probably wave or smile or do something—anything —to stop myself from staring at her like she's the last piece of pie on the planet and I'm a starved man.

Then Lani turns and waves before crossing toward me, dragging Sammy in tow.

"Hey there, big brother." She slides into the booth, and Sammy slides in beside her, keeping her focus anywhere but on me.

"Hey, how's it going?" I say, finally regaining the ability to speak. Who is this woman that she has me behaving like a lovestruck teenager?

"Good. Since you guys wrapped up at the ranch early, I convinced Sammy to come out with me. We're headed over to the movies after this. Of course, I had to drive all the way over there since she doesn't believe in cell phones." She nudges Sammy with her shoulder, and she grins in response.

Going to a movie here in Pine Creek consists of attending the small community theatre where they've set up a projection screen. They only show movies on the week-end, and everything they show has been out for months, if not years.

"Fun. What are they playing tonight?"

"*Angels in the Outfield*."

"A classic," I reply with a smile and a quick glance at Sammy, who now has her gaze trained on a menu Talia dropped off.

"That's what I told Sammy. But she hasn't ever seen it."

At the mention of her name, Sammy looks up.

"You've never seen *Angels in the Outfield*?"

"I haven't," she replies. "Though I hear I'm in for a treat."

"It's one of the best."

Lani looks at me. "You should come with us."

"What?"

"Yeah, why not?" Lani looks at Sammy as though searching for confirmation.

"I don't mind," she says, though I can see the hesitation on her face. I just can't tell if it's because she's feeling the same sort of attraction I am or if she genuinely doesn't care for me. Though I can't imagine it being the latter given I haven't known her but a day.

"I don't want to intrude on girls' night."

"Oh, stop." Lani waves her hand. "You're not intruding on anything. Unless you have a date or something?"

"What?"

"A date. Do you have a date?" Lani glances around the diner. "Are we taking her spot?"

"No, no date. I just didn't feel like sitting at home tonight, and since Mom and Dad are having their weekly dinner for just the two of them, I thought—"

"That you would eat with your little sister and her new friend then go with us to the movies as our chaperone. Much appreciated, Bradyn." She beams at me, and before I can respond, Talia steps up to the table.

"Evening, ladies. What can I get for you?"

"I'll have a cheeseburger with everything, barbeque sauce on the side, and onion rings, please. Oh, and a sweet tea."

"You got it. How about you, Sammy?"

"Uh, I'll have the club sandwich and fries, please. And a water."

"You got it." Talia takes the menus and heads back to place their order.

"How was work?" I ask Lani, hoping to keep the conversation light because Sammy looks about ready to bolt out of the diner.

"It was good. Had a full day of appointments then headed over to Mrs. Kinsley's to drop off the prescription I'd called in for her."

Mrs. Kinsley has been bedridden for the past six months after a nasty fall in her shower. She broke her hip in two places and fractured her wrist. As her doctor, Lani has gone above and beyond to make sure she's taken care of until she's back on her feet.

"How's she doing?"

"Good. She said to tell you hi."

"Tell her hi back the next time you see her."

"Will do," Lani replies.

The bell dings over the door again, and Lani glances over her shoulder as Gibson Lawson walks in wearing his sheriff's uniform. He heads toward the counter, and Lani's smile spreads.

"Let me out a sec. I want to say hi."

Sammy slides out so Lani can slip out of the booth; then she takes her seat as I watch my sister head over toward the deputy.

She's had a thing for Gibson since they were in high school, but neither of them ever had the courage to do anything. Then she went off to school and he stuck around town. He'd gotten married about three years out of school, but the marriage didn't last long before she left town with a musician, leaving Gibson to pick up the pieces and pay off all the debt she'd taken out in his name.

It was nasty, and the town rallied around him to offer any support he needed. It's sad, but I think that divorce is the reason he never asked Lani out even after she returned to town.

When Lani laughs, I turn my attention away from them,

not wanting to intrude on my sister's moment. "So, uh, how are you liking working at the ranch?"

Sammy shifts those gorgeous blue eyes to me. "I like it a lot."

"Have you always had an interest in animals? Or did you grow up on a farm?"

"Just an interest in animals," she says. "Never was lucky enough to spend a whole lot of time around them growing up."

I nod, unsure how to proceed when her answers are very curt and don't leave much room for conversation. Finally, because I can't stand awkwardness when a conversation might clear things up, I lean in. "Listen, did I do anything to upset you?"

She looks genuinely surprised. "No. Why would you think that?"

"I don't know, you just seem standoffish with me, that's all."

"I don't really know you," she says. "And I'm not much of a small talker."

"Fair enough." I lean back. "As long as I didn't do anything."

"You didn't, I promise."

"Good."

She offers me a tight smile then turns her head to look outside. It's dark, so aside from the streetlamps, she's not seeing much. But in the glass, I can make out her reflection, and her eyes are speaking volumes.

She's haunted. By what, I'm not sure, and I'm not nosy enough to try and find out. My rules are simple—if it doesn't affect the ranch, I don't need to know. And so far, it's not affecting the ranch even though she's clearly got a hold on me.

"Sorry." Lani returns to the table, sliding in beside Sammy. Since the booth we're in is rounded, she's forced to scoot closer to me, though she remains a good two feet away.

Something about me unnerves her. I just wish I knew what it was.

# CHAPTER 7
# KENNEDY

Bradyn Hunt seems to be the complete package.

He's handsome.

Kind.

Interesting.

Opens doors.

And loves his little sister. Since we ran into him in the café, Lani not only talked him into letting us crash his quiet dinner and tagging along with us to the movies, but she also got him to do the snack run while we went in and grabbed seats.

As much as I wanted to sit on the opposite side of him, Lani had saved him a seat directly next to me, forcing us to sit elbow to elbow during the movie. What I saw of it was great, at least, though I'll admit most of my attention was on the fact that Bradyn and I kept accidentally brushing hands when either of us went for the popcorn.

I can still feel the heat climbing up my arm, radiating from where his hand brushed mine.

"So what did you think?" Lani asks as we step out onto the sidewalk.

"Huh?"

She grins at me. "The movie. Did you like it?"

"Oh, yeah. I thought it was great. Definite classic."

"Right? I told you." Lani links arms with me.

She's such a force of positivity. Honestly, she reminds me a lot of a friend I had in college. My thoughts darken with the weight of memories better left buried, so I force a smile and try to keep my head on straight.

*Stay focused, Kennedy.*

"Do you want ice cream?" she asks.

"It's, like, thirty degrees outside," Bradyn argues.

"It's never too cold for ice cream. Sammy?"

"Uh, sure. I'm good for whatever."

"Yay. Mint chocolate chip, here we come." Lani guides me ahead, and Bradyn falls into step behind us. Even though I can't see him, I can feel his gaze on me. Heat climbs up the back of my neck even as unease settles in my gut.

Is he trying to figure me out? Or is he just feeling the same type of attraction I am?

As we approach the small ice cream shop, which also doubles as the town's bakery, Bradyn rushes around to open the door, his long legs effortlessly eating up the strides between him and the building.

He holds it open, and we step inside.

The teenager working the counter grins at Lani. "Hey there, Doc. What can I get you?"

"Mint chocolate chip, please," she says.

"You got it." He starts scooping. "And you?" he asks me.

"The same." I'm not even sure I like mint chocolate chip as I've never had it. I always go for cookie dough. But every decision I make seems like it carries enough weight it could crumble the world around me, so sometimes it's easier to just follow along than risk saying too much.

*You like cookie dough? How cool, me too. Where did you grow up?*

Contrary to what I told Bradyn, I've always been super social and a serial oversharer. Before, that didn't matter as I didn't have much to share. Now, though—the chain around my neck feels heavier as the past tries to sneak up on me again.

*Not now, Kennedy.*

"Here you go, ladies." He offers me my cone, and Lani takes hers. "For you, Mr. Hunt?"

"Bradyn," he corrects. "And I'm good, Chance, thanks."

"No problem. That'll be five even."

"I got it," Bradyn offers, stepping in front of us and offering the kid a twenty.

"You didn't need to do that," I say quickly, feeling completely uncomfortable with the favor. I know he's only doing it to be kind, but his family has already done so much for me, and they don't even know who they're letting sleep on their property. It feels wrong to take anything else.

"I don't mind."

"Thanks, brother," Lani says and heads toward the door. I follow her, and Bradyn heads out after us, once again holding the door. "See, if you eat ice cream when it's not a thousand degrees outside, it doesn't melt as fast."

"But your tongue freezes twice as fast," Bradyn replies.

Lani chuckles. "You think you have all the answers."

"Just most of them."

Their adorable sibling back-and-forth has made me insanely jealous that I never grew up with a sibling.

"Here I am." Lani points to her car. I head for the passenger seat.

"Are you heading back to the ranch?" Bradyn questions.

"Yeah, why?" Lani asks.

"I'm headed back there too. I can drive you back, Sammy, if you like. Then Lani can just head home."

"Oh, good idea. Is that okay, Sammy? Do you mind?"

Deer in the headlights, that's me. Either accept the invitation to be driven home by my boss, whom I am incredibly attracted to and can never hope to have a relationship with, or risk hurting his feelings and insist Lani drive me home so I can have distance.

Decisions, decisions.

"Sure, that would be great, thanks." I step away from the car and head back up onto the sidewalk.

Lani looks between me and Bradyn then back to me. "Are you sure? I can drive you out."

"Totally fine." I smile. "Thanks for the fun night. It was really great."

"Anytime. See you tomorrow! Love you, Bradyn!"

"Love you too, Lani."

She beams at us then climbs behind the wheel of her car and heads out.

"I'm right over here." He gestures toward his truck, which is parked right in front of the café.

We walk in complete silence as I finish the ice cream, even though it's the last thing I want to do. We pass a trash can, so I toss my napkin inside then wait as Bradyn opens the passenger side door of his truck for me.

As soon as he shuts the door, I realize what a mistake this was.

His scent is everywhere. Pine and leather, a heady combination that has my blood pumping. He smells just as good as he looks, something I'd been somewhat able to avoid because I wasn't basking in his personal space as I am now.

"Sorry if I caught you off guard by offering," he says as he climbs in. "I just thought it would be easier for Lani since I'm headed that way anyway."

"No, it's fine. Thanks for the ride."

"Anytime." He fires up the truck and backs out of the parking spot then heads down the street.

Fifteen minutes.

I have to make it fifteen minutes without saying anything that might lead to more questions.

I can do that.

Right?

"So how is it managing two jobs?" I ask, figuring that if I keep the conversation on him, I might be able to avoid any direct questioning myself.

"It's tough at times. But having my brothers onboard definitely eases the stress."

"You all work together, right? Not just on the ranch."

"Right. We rotate who takes the jobs—unless there's one that requires a specific skill set."

"You all have skill sets?"

He grins. "We do."

"Can I know what they are?"

His smile falls just a bit, but he hides it well by glancing out his window. "Tucker is great with computers, Dylan is stealthy, Elliot is great with locks, and Riley could charm information out of a turtle."

I laugh at the comparison. "How about you?"

The amusement on his expression falters again. He's got secrets, too. "I'm good at reading people and situations."

"That must come in handy." Even as his declaration that he's good at reading people sets off a spike of fear, I keep the conversation as light as possible. He hasn't read me so far; that must mean I haven't given him much to go off of. Good.

"It does. Sometimes it's a bit of a curse though."

"I get that."

He offers me a quick smile. "How about you? What did you do before coming here?"

*Uh-oh.* "I was in college." *Stick close enough to the truth, and he won't be able to tell I'm omitting.*

"Yeah? Quite a change coming here."

"It was. But I needed to get away, so I've been traveling for a couple of years. Staying in different places and trying to find peace." I turn my attention out the window as we turn off the highway and start down the gravel road leading up to the ranch. "I don't know if I ever will though," I say softly.

"Find peace?"

I sigh. "Yeah. It's a hard thing to find."

"Not if you know where to look."

"And where is that?"

"I find mine in my Bible." He says it so simply, so confidently, that I can't help but stare at him. He glances over and smirks. "I take it that's not what you thought I would say?"

"No," I admit. "It's not."

"There is nothing that can bring you peace quite like God's word."

"I wouldn't know."

"No?"

I shake my head. "I'm not sure what I believe."

"A lot of people aren't," he replies and pulls the truck to a stop in front of my cabin. "If you ever want to talk about it, I'm around."

"Thanks. I'm okay though." I open the door and climb out. Bradyn does, too, meeting me in front of the truck. "You don't have to walk me up."

"I know, it's habit." He shoves his hands into his pockets. "Thanks for letting me tag along tonight. I had fun."

"It was fun," I reply, grateful that for once I can speak the whole truth. "Maybe you can tag along the next time they're showing a movie your sister is horrified I've never seen before."

He laughs. "I'd like that." He turns to head back toward his truck but pauses at the door. "Good night, Sammy."

A smile spreads over my face. "Good night, Bradyn."

# CHAPTER 8
# BRADYN

I'd seriously hoped Sammy would be up and at the barn first thing this morning just like she was yesterday. Unfortunately, that's not what happened, and I ended up spending the morning cleaning horse stalls while I mentally went over every second of last night.

It really was a great night.

The best I'd had in a while.

Seeing Sammy outside of the ranch meant I got to see a woman who smiled often and laughed at Lani's jokes. Even a few of mine. Though she's still guarded, I'd gotten to see more of her personality by the time I'd dropped her off.

And by the time I got home, I'd come to the conclusion that I desperately want to know more about Sammy Lewis. Maybe take her to dinner one day, just the two of us.

I dump the final wheelbarrow and head back into the barn to remove my gloves and take a drink from my bottle of water. Bravo is stretched out just inside the breezeway, his belly up in the air, body in a crescent shape as he snores happily.

Oh, to be a dog.

"Hey, I thought I might find you here." Elliot steps into the barn. He spent a good portion of yesterday ordering food for the animals. Then, because the delivery trucks were down, he and Riley did a run first thing this morning to pick it up.

"Just trying to kill some time before dinner. How's it going?"

"Not bad. We got all the bags unloaded. We're about to head over to the church for service."

"Service? What time is it?" I check my watch, shocked to see that it's nearly ten in the morning. "I completely lost track of time. Sorry." I set my gloves aside and retrieve my phone and water bottle from the shelf near the tack room.

"No worries. Want us to wait for you?"

"Nah, that's all right. I'll get cleaned up and sneak in the back."

"Sounds good. See you there."

"*Hier,* Bravo," I call out. Bravo jumps up and follows me into the UTV. As we make the drive up to my house, my attention is stolen from the road momentarily as Sammy crests the hill on the back of Midnight. She sits high on the horse's back, a baseball cap pulled low over her face.

She sits like she was made for the saddle, and seeing it only cements the budding feelings I'm carting around for her. I just wish I knew how long she planned to stay so I'd know exactly what I'm getting myself into.

Eventual heartbreak? Or something more permanent?

---

"BRADYN HUNT. It's good to see you back in town," Pastor Gabriel Ford greets as I leave the pews and head out into the fellowship hall.

"It's good to be back," I reply, shaking his offered hand. I've met with the pastor on more than one occasion when I've been struggling with the weight of a mission, and he's always there to listen and guide.

He's a good man, one I've known since I was a kid. His daughter, Melody, graduated the same year I did.

"If you need to talk, my door is open."

"Thank you, sir. I appreciate it. How is Grace? Melody? The grandkids?"

"All doing great. Grace went over to Melody and Huey's place this morning to sit with the baby. He had to work, and Melody's not been getting a lot of sleep with having a teething baby and a toddler."

"I'm sure Grace is loving every moment of that."

He beams at me, his gray eyes shining with joy. "You know she is."

More people start filing in behind me, so I shake his hand again and say my goodbyes then head out into the mid-morning sun. It's warmer today, though not by much, and if the weatherman is right, temperatures will be plummeting again tonight. Just in time for the nasty storm headed our way midweek.

I'm just about to open the door to my truck so I can head home and get back to work in the barn when I spot Sammy heading into our town's small office supply store. Before I know it, I'm abandoning the truck and heading across the street.

I really shouldn't follow her in here. It's her private business after all, but the desire to see her again is so strong I'm walking into the store before realizing I have literally no reason to be here.

Sammy is standing in front of an assortment of postcards, studying the collection with the same scrutiny one might expect to use when diffusing a bomb. I start to turn away, but she happens to glance up at the same time and see me lingering near the entrance.

*You're doing this, Hunt.* Not like I have a choice now. If I left, it would be weird.

Her gaze darkens when she sees me, and I have to force myself to smile. What is it that she has against me?

"Oh, hey," I greet.

"Hey."

"Afternoon, Bradyn," Jerry Davidson, the owner, greets. "What brings you in here today?"

"Uh, I needed to get some stationary."

"You got it." He guides me over to a shelf directly across from the postcards. "Here is what we have. Anything in particular you're looking for?"

"These are fine." I grab the closest stack, not even bothering to look at it before I do.

"Sounds good." He takes the stack then heads to the counter, right as Sammy is also ready to check out. Jerry scans the back of the stationary pack then sets it on the counter. "That'll be twelve-sixty."

I reach into my pocket and pull out my wallet then pay for the stationery. It's only then that I lift it and realize I just bought twenty-two pages with kittens in the letterhead.

"Cute stationary," Sammy comments.

"It'll do the trick." I glance down at her postcard momentarily, just long enough to see a beautiful background of bluebonnets. "Need one? You can send a personal note along with the postcard?"

"That's okay. I'm partial to dogs myself." She smiles, and I can't help but return it.

"I can love them both."

"No judgment here," she replies.

"That all, Sammy?" Jerry asks as he takes her postcard.

"That's it. Thanks."

"Anytime. Hopefully, you can get it out before the storm hits."

She nods. "Thanks. I hope so, too."

He takes the money she set in front of him then offers her a few quarters back. "See you next week."

"See you next week." She smiles before heading for the door, but I beat her there, holding it open.

"Weekly office supply visits, huh?"

"It's thrilling, what can I say." Once we're on the side-walk, she looks me up and down. "You're dressed nice for an afternoon of errands."

"Church," I reply, pointing to the chapel across the street.

"Oh, yeah. It is Sunday, isn't it?"

"It is." She starts walking, so I join in, noting her truck parked a few spots away. We're there before I've even managed to come up with anything else to say, and as Sammy unlocks her door, I'm kicking myself for going into the store to begin with. "See you later?"

"See you later." I offer her a wave then watch as she drives off before crossing the street toward my truck.

Much to my dismay, all of my brothers are standing there, waiting for me. Elliot arches a brow. "Needed kitten stationary?"

I unlock my door and toss the pack into my truck.

"I saw Sammy over there, too," Riley offers.

"Curious, isn't it?" Tucker adds.

"Can't a guy buy kitten stationary in peace?"

"Not when that guy is practically shooting hearts from his eyes," Dylan says. "Though I will say, hearts and kittens do seem to go together."

"I am not shooting hearts out of my eyes."

"No?" Riley leans back against my truck. "That's certainly what it looked like to me. What about you, Tucker?"

"Looks to me like our big brother has a crush on Sammy."

Heat creeps up the back of my neck. "She's just interesting is all."

"Hey, we think it's great," Elliot says.

"You do?"

"Yeah. Sammy is great, and you're you, so why wouldn't we be happy?"

"I just get a 'you're you'?" I snort. "Flattering."

He shrugs. "I speak the truth. Want to grab some lunch before heading back to the ranch? I'm starving, and Mom is heading over to Mrs. Kinsley's house."

"Sure, I could eat."

"Great." He pushes off my truck and starts back across the street toward the café. I fall into step with my brothers, my thoughts still on Sammy. She'd said last night at dinner that she left college to travel. Based on her tone, I assumed she either lost contact with her family or didn't have anyone left.

Yet, the postcard says something else, doesn't it? And if she sends one weekly, that's having regular communication, yet she doesn't own a cell phone, and there aren't landlines in any of the cabins. Maybe postcards are her only way of getting in touch with family? Or maybe she's estranged?

I can't imagine anyone ever turning their backs on her, but people have done stranger things. Still, it's one more mystery surrounding a woman who has captivated me from the moment I laid eyes on her.

# CHAPTER 9
# KENNEDY

"Hey, Sammy." Arthur steps up onto my porch, though he remains on the second step rather than coming up all the way.

I'm sitting in a rocking chair, enjoying the peanut butter and jelly sandwich I made for myself along with a mug of steaming hot elderberry tea. "Hey, have a good day?"

"Yeah. Not as good as you did."

"What does that mean? We had the same day." I take a bite.

"Yeah, sure." He runs his hand over the back of his neck, expression frustrated. "Listen, if you didn't want to go out with me, you could have just said so."

"What are you talking about?" I set my sandwich down, defenses slipping into place now that I note his irritated tone in addition to the expression on his face.

"You told me that you didn't want to date anyone, yet

you were out last night with Bradyn Hunt. What is it, because he's rich? The boss? You just jumped at that opportunity."

I practically lunge out of my chair. "I don't know what you think you saw last night, Arthur, but I was not on a date."

"Yeah, okay, which is why he drove you home last night," he scoffs. "Don't lie to me, Sammy. It's not attractive."

"First of all." I take a step closer, jabbing my finger out. "I don't care whether or not you find me attractive. Second, even if I were seeing Bradyn Hunt, it would be none of your business."

"Sure it wouldn't. I'm just the guy whose feelings you jerked around."

"Feelings? What? How did I jerk your feelings around?"

"You lied to me!"

The door to a cabin opens, and one of the other hands steps out. An older man with a handlebar mustache who's worked here for over a decade. "Everything okay out here, Sammy?"

"It's fine, James," he snaps.

"I didn't ask you," James retorts. "Sammy?"

"I'm okay, James, thanks." I offer him a smile, but he hesitates before retreating back into his cabin. As soon as he's gone, I cross my arms. "Look, Arthur, I don't owe you an explanation. You asked me out, I said no. End of story."

"Why did you say no? I don't have enough money for you?"

Fury envelops my blood, boiling it in my veins. I rip the jacket off of my chair and march past Arthur down the stairs, sandwich forgotten.

"Wait! Sammy, I'm sorry." He jogs after me then grips my arm.

I swing, not even thinking before I do. My fist cracks into his nose, and blood spurts out. He stumbles backward onto the ground and screeches in pain. I just stand there, staring at him as he scrambles to his feet.

"You hit me! I think you broke my nose!"

"You grabbed me. I don't like to be touched."

"I can't believe you hit me." He takes a step away from me, likely afraid I'll hit him again.

"Look, I'm sorry. I didn't mean to hit you."

Then he turns and rushes into his cabin, blood dripping from his hands. I remain where I am, unsure if I should go after him or not. Trouble. I just caused trouble. Does this mean I'll be put out? Thrown off the ranch? It was in their contract that we don't resort to physical violence with anyone here on the ranch.

What if they throw me out? I have nowhere to go. And I'm getting tired of running from place to place. Panic begins to creep up my spine, chilling the fury that had been in my veins only minutes ago. So, before Arthur can get to them and tell a different story, I start toward the main house.

I'm just reaching up to knock when the door opens, and Bradyn nearly walks right into me.

"Sammy, what are you—" His expression falters as his gaze lands on my raised fist. A fist that is red and has a smear of blood on it. "What happened?" He steps out of the way, and I move into the warm house.

"I'm sorry. I didn't mean to do it. He was just making me so angry and—"

"Sammy, honey, good to see you," Ruth greets.

Brayden cuts in, "Mom, can we use Dad's office?"

Her face goes serious. "Of course, go on."

"Come on." Bradyn gestures down the hall, so I head past him, stopping at an open door that looks like it goes into an office. As soon as we're inside, he shuts the door then moves around me to lean back against the desk. "What happened?"

"Arthur."

"Kidress?"

I nod.

"What about him? Did he do something to you?" Bradyn's face turns beet red, and his hands clench into fists at his sides.

"No. I punched him."

Bradyn stops and leans back against the desk. "Why?"

"He was hurt and therefore saying all of these stupid things. Then when I tried to leave, he grabbed my arm. So I swung. I'm sorry, I know the ranch has a no-violence policy, but I'm not sure what happened. I just saw red. If you have to fire me, I understand, but please consider granting me a second chance."

Bradyn studies me. "I'm not going to fire you, Sammy, but I need to know what Arthur did to provoke you. If it was a threat or you were worried he'd hurt you, I won't allow him to remain here."

"No, he didn't threaten me. He was just angry, that's all."

"About what?"

How much to tell him? I decide to stick with all of it since it was likely overheard by James, anyway. "Arthur asked me out a couple of days ago. I said no because I'm not big on dating right now. He was fine until he saw me arrive home with you last night. He accused me of dating you because you're wealthy then said a bunch of other things that angered me. I tried to walk away. When he grabbed my arm, I snapped."

I expect Bradyn to be furious that Arthur made such an accusation. I expect him to laugh at the very idea of dating me. Instead, the handsome cowboy simply stands up and moves around me to open the door to the office. "Let's get you some ice."

"Ice? You're not going to lecture me or write me up?"

"Why would I?"

"Because I probably broke his nose."

Bradyn chuckles. "It sounds like he tried to make us both look like fools by accusing you of being after money and me being gullible enough to date someone after my money. And it sounds like you were simply defending yourself when he put his hands on you. I don't see any reason to write you up."

"Really?"

"Really." He smiles. "Now, let's get you some ice, and I'll call Lani to swing by on her way home so she can check in on Arthur's nose."

# CHAPTER 10
# BRADYN

"All right, that'll do it." I straighten and roll my shoulders then step back and examine the gate we just rehung. It hadn't been fully down, though it was sagging enough that it was only a matter of time.

"Looks good." James, the ranch hand who's lived and worked here the longest, lifts the box of tools and carries them over to the UTV. He sets them in the back before getting into the passenger side while I climb behind the wheel.

I was supposed to be bringing Arthur Kidress out here since, out of everyone, he needs the most hand-holding when it comes to performing tasks around the ranch. Honestly, even without what happened last night, I'm about ready to fire him.

The man just has no attention for details. Mainly, the

rule of leaving the gates exactly as you find them. If it's open, leave it open. Closed? Secure it behind you. His inability to do the latter led to a few of the cattle getting loose earlier today and us having to round them back up.

But last night was just icing on the cake.

Seeing Sammy wild-eyed and afraid she was going to lose her job unlocked an anger in me I don't know that I've ever felt on the home front. Of course, we wouldn't have fired her for that.

Self-defense is self-defense.

When I'd told my dad about it this morning, even he'd been ready to fire Arthur. But I'd promised her last night we wouldn't do that. Unless things get worse. If he doesn't back off and stop putting his hands on her, he's out. Period.

"Let me ask you something, James." I pull away from the gate and start heading back to the shop.

"Go for it."

"What do you think of Arthur Kidress?"

James snorts. "I think he's a snot who didn't have enough structure growing up."

"So you don't like him?"

"Not at all. He's lazy. Most of us have to go behind him and finish up whatever he'd been supposed to be doing because he lacks any kind of pride in his work. He's a passerby."

Passerby is a term we use for people who won't be

staying long at the ranch. Those who clearly have no pride in their work and therefore have no reason to stick around.

"He's got a mouth on him, too," James adds. "Mostly muttering under his breath, though I think that'll change now that Sammy took a swing at him." He chuckles. "Girl has a mean right hook."

The pride in his voice makes me smile.

"What about Sammy? How do you feel about her? Right hook aside."

"She's great. Hardest worker here. Besides me, of course." He winks. "She's up first, in last, and always leaves the gates the way she found them."

I chuckle. "Ranch rule number one."

"Ranch rule number one," he repeats. "She's quiet... keeps to herself most of the time."

"Think she's a passerby?"

He considers. "She's a hard one to read. Doesn't speak much about her life. I get the feeling she left something behind she doesn't want to revisit."

I get the same feeling. That, and she's hiding something. Though I keep reminding myself that it's none of my business unless it affects the ranch.

"I'm glad she's at least working out so I don't have to fire two hands."

"You planning on getting rid of Arthur?"

"Possibly. Keep it between us though."

"Lips are sealed, boss."

We're just pulling up to the shop when Arthur strolls out. He glances our way, and I get a look at the black eyes he's sporting as well as the bandage on his nose. Lani wanted to have it reset last night, but he wouldn't let her anywhere near him. Now, it looks like he'll have a slightly crooked nose until either he gets it fixed or puts his hands on Sammy again and she hits him from the other side, knocking it straight.

I park the UTV and climb out. "You get the stalls cleaned out?" I ask him.

"Sure."

"Sure?" I try not to pull out the boss card often, but the blatant disrespect has anger roaring to life inside me.

"Want to try answering that again?" James questions.

"You asked if I got the stalls done. Yes, I got the stalls finished. I was just about to head home and take some more meds for this massive headache I have. If, of course, that's okay with you?"

He's trying to get a rise out of me, which makes him an idiot. I don't have to bite. And I won't. "Fine by me. Feel free to take the rest of the afternoon if you want it."

Arthur heads off in the direction of the cabins, muttering something under his breath. I just let it slide. No reason to get all worked up over someone who is proving every single day that he doesn't need to be here.

If it weren't for Sammy, I'd have fired him already. But she'd been adamant that I don't fire him because of her, and even though I have valid reasons without that, it's exactly how it would look.

"Hey, boss." James taps me on the shoulder, and I turn as Sammy, Elliot, Tucker, Dylan, and Riley all ride toward me on horseback, Rev saddled and running beside Sammy.

Adrenaline surges in my system. "What is it?"

"Some cattle got loose. They're on the road now. Sheriff Gray called it in. We need to go wrangle them up."

"Got it." I head over toward Rev and take the reins when Sammy offers them to me. "Which pasture?" I ask as I climb onto my horse's back.

"Three," Elliot says.

I look down at James. "Load up some fencing equipment, take Leon, and go find out what happened."

"What about Arthur?"

"Leave him to tend to his nose," I reply.

James nods. "On it, boss."

We take off riding, guiding the horses down the road and toward the highway so we can cut the cattle off.

As we ride, I go over all possible scenarios. A predator could've driven the cattle through the fence; it's happened before.

A tree could've taken the fencing down, or a gate could've been left open.

And if it's the latter, not even Sammy can save Arthur's job.

---

"Who would have cut the fence?" Sammy asks as we survey the damage.

"A couple of years ago, we had some teens sneak onto the ranch to see if cow tipping was a real thing. They cut the fence then, but we'd caught them quick and haven't had any issues since."

"Could be a new set of teens," Riley replies.

Thanks to the still-soft dirt from the last storm that came through, I study the tire tracks in the mud. Someone parked near our fence, got out, and cut the wires. Boot prints head into the pasture, though they stop about a quarter mile in. "I don't think this is teens."

Following the prints again, I stop where they turn back around. Standing where the intruder stood, I try to put myself into his position and see what it is he was looking for.

"What are you thinking?" Elliot questions.

"I'm not sure. Seems strange that they didn't go any farther in." I study the trees in the distance. They just stood here, out in the open. Were they spooked maybe? Or just someone who doesn't mind trespassing as they're trying to get close to a cow? We've certainly had our fair share of those before.

"We'll get the fence patched back up," James offers.

"Good. We'll drive the cattle back toward the closer

pasture. We needed to do it in preps for the storm anyway."
I turn my attention to the sky, noting how dark it's gone in just a matter of a few hours.

While the storm isn't quite here yet, it's looking like we may end up with some rain tonight. Better to have the cattle moved before it hits than have to try and drive them the rest of the way through deep mud puddles.

# CHAPTER 11
# KENNEDY

Freshly showered and completely exhausted, I lie back on the bed and just remain still for a few moments. I really should get up and get something to eat, but doing that requires energy, and I'm fresh out of that.

Between chasing the loose cattle down, herding them toward the pasture closest to the house, the evening milking of the dairy cows, and rubbing down the horses after the ride, I'm not even sure how I managed to find the strength to shower.

Though it felt really, really good.

It's nights like these I'd love to go sit outside on the porch and breathe in the fresh air, but I'm too afraid Arthur is going to use that as an opportunity to harass me all over again. I've managed to avoid him most of the day, but that'll change if he corners me. And based on how furious

Bradyn was last night, I'm not sure a broken nose will be the biggest of Arthur's problems should he choose to grab me like that again.

There's a knock at my door, and I groan.

I really don't want to get up.

Another knock.

Keeping my firearm close, I force myself to get out of bed and head over toward the door. After peeking out the peephole, I set my firearm in a kitchen drawer and pull open the door for Lani.

"Hey, I brought food!" She steps inside with a white bakery box seated on top of a pizza box. It smells *amazing*.

"Did you read my mind? I was just thinking about how hungry I am."

"Seems like I showed up just in time then," Lani replies and sets the pizza on the counter. She heads toward the far cabinet and retrieves two plates then offers me one.

I've only known her a short period of time, but it feels like we've been friends a whole lot longer. Which is honestly great. Aside from the fact I'm going to have to leave one day, and she'll never know why.

It makes me think of—*No, Kennedy.*

"What kind of pizza did you bring?" Shoving thoughts of the past down, I check the box and nearly groan with delight when I see double cheese and pepperoni staring me in the face. "This looks fantastic."

"Gio's," Lani replies. "He's the best."

"Definitely the best." I put a piece onto my plate then head over toward the two-seater table where Lani is already sitting and take the chair across from her.

Lani bows her head. "Lord, we thank You for this food we are about to eat. We thank You for bringing us through today and allowing us this time to spend together. In the name of Jesus, Amen."

I open my eyes and take a bite. Salty cheesy delicious-ness dances on my tongue. "This is so good."

"Best pizza in the south. I'm convinced. So how was today?"

"It was long."

"How's your hand?"

I hold it up. "Not too bad."

Lani takes my hand and inspects my knuckles. "You wouldn't even know these were nose-breaking knuckles."

I smile and take another bite of pizza. "I feel so bad."

"He shouldn't have put his hands on you."

"No," I say. "But I hardly think my hitting him was an appropriate response."

She sets her pizza down and takes a drink of water. "Why did you hit him?"

"What do you mean? I told you, he grabbed my arm."

"Sure, and I'm not saying he didn't deserve it, but why did you hit him? Did he do something else, too? Back you into a corner?"

How do I tell her it's because I've been stuck in fight

mode for the last two years? How do I explain to my new friend that the reason why I hit first and ask questions later is because, the one time I didn't trust my gut, everyone I loved died?

"Just instinct, I guess. Something I need to work on."

She doesn't respond, just takes a bite of pizza. "How did Bradyn take it?"

"What do you mean? Didn't you talk to him?"

"Sure, but I got the muted big-brother version. I want to know how he took the news live. Come on, Sammy, spill."

"He was angry. Wanted to fire him."

"He should've fired him. I'm actually surprised he didn't."

"I asked him not to."

Lani grins. "Interesting."

"What's interesting?"

"Oh, just that he didn't fire him."

"Why is that interesting?"

Lani takes another bite then swallows it down with a swig of water. "Bradyn is very black and white in a lot of ways. This ranch is one of those things. He doesn't let things slide here. He's more than willing to give someone a chance, even a second chance a lot of times. But Arthur putting hands on you? On top of his lack of performance in his actual job? Those are both grounds for firing, yet he let him stay. All because you asked."

I try not to read too much into that. The last thing I need

is Lani feeding the delusion that Bradyn Hunt might actually be interested in me. Especially when nothing can come of it. "I'm sure he just felt bad for me. I was pretty panicked that he would fire me."

"Maybe." But Lani doesn't look convinced. "Do you like my brother? As a boss, of course." She grins, letting me know that's not how she meant it at all.

"He's great to work for. And with. All of them are."

"But Elliot's not who you went to when you broke Arthur's nose. You went to Bradyn when any of them could have handled it for you."

"Bradyn's just who answered the door. I went to your parents' house."

"Uh-huh. All in God's timing." Lani grins.

"What is *that* supposed to mean?" Frustration gnaws at my earlier exhaustion.

"I just mean that it's interesting how Bradyn was at my parents' house at the exact time you arrived."

I take a bite of pizza. "You're not going to let this go, are you?"

"Sure, I will. One day." She grins. "So, what were you planning to do tonight before I crashed your solo party?"

"Crawl into the kitchen and make something to eat. Then probably have some tea and do some reading."

She glances at my bedside table. "The Bible?"

"What? Oh. No. That was my mom's." I get up and

tuck it into the bedside table before returning to finish my pizza.

"Sorry, I didn't mean to pry."

"It's okay. I just had it out because I was looking for something."

"What?"

"A psalm my mom used to read out loud occasionally. It popped into my head last night, and I was looking for it because I can't remember anything but the first two sentences."

Lani finishes off her water. "What are the sentences? I've been studying the Bible ever since I was old enough to talk. I might be able to help."

I consider letting her in on this. It's personal, which is typically on the *no* list of conversation topics, but since I can't see what it would hurt, I recite words my mother spoke more times than I can count. "God is our refuge and strength, always ready to help in times of trouble."

"Ahh, yes. That's a good one." She stands. "May I?" she asks, gesturing toward the bedside table.

"Sure."

Lani crosses the small cabin and retrieves the Bible then heads back. She sets it down, completely ignoring the faded blood splatter on the worn leather Bible. I've tried so hard to get it out, but nothing works. It remains there, branded onto the cover like my grief is tattooed on my soul.

"Here it is," she says. "Psalm 46." She offers me the

Bible, and I take a look at the words printed in black and white.

"'So we will not fear when earthquakes come and the mountains crumble into the sea. Let the oceans roar and foam. Let the mountains tremble as the waters surge.' That's the one. Thanks."

"Anytime. That's cool that you have her Bible."

"Yeah. Helps me feel close to her."

"Do you want to talk about her?"

*Yes.* "No, I'm okay, thanks. I'm all about leaving the past in the past." *Especially since not doing so could lead to me being discovered.*

"Fair enough. Here if you change your mind." She cleans up our plates then brings the bakery box over to the table.

"What's that?"

"Dessert," she replies with a grin then removes the cover of the box, revealing a perfectly delicious-looking assortment of cookies. Everything from frosted to chocolate chip.

I select the latter. "So tell me about that deputy."

"What deputy?" Her cheeks redden. "Oh, you mean Gibson?"

"If he's the one you were chatting up at the café the other night, then yes."

She grins. "That obvious?"

"Most definitely."

She groans. "He's the only one who won't pick up on it. We went to school together, and I always had such a thing for him. He was cute, smart, kind...but we were just friends. I thought when I got back from school, maybe things would change, but he ended up marrying Kleo Yarring." She makes a frustrated expression.

"I'm guessing you didn't like her."

"She was awful. And after they'd been married a year, she left him for a musician she'd been having an affair with since even before they were married."

"That's horrible."

"It was. By the time I got home, he was so heartbroken that he could barely hold a conversation. I've been trying to keep close enough that, maybe when he's open to it, he'll see *me*. You know?"

"I know." I offer her a smile. "He'll see you."

"Maybe. Hopefully before I start going gray," she jokes. "I want a family. It's one of the main reasons I haven't started my house yet."

"Started your house?"

"Our parents gifted us each an acre to build our house on. My brothers have all finished theirs, but I've been holding off because the last thing I want to do is live in a big house all by myself. My apartment is bad enough as it is."

Given the amount of time I've spent alone over the last couple of years, I completely see where she's coming from.

"Your brothers weren't worried about that?"

She snorts. "No, but after getting home from a mission, they enjoy the solitude. Bradyn came home last year and spent an entire week alone."

"A week?"

She nods. "I'm still not sure what happened. None of them talk in any detail about what they're doing, but whatever it was, was bad. I hated it for him. He stayed in his house and prayed his way out of the hole."

"I imagine they deal with a lot of bad stuff."

"Yeah, I wouldn't know for sure, but that's where I'd place my money, too."

Lani begins talking about Gibson again, but my thoughts linger on Bradyn. I can't see him locking himself in the house, especially since, the day after he was back, he'd asked me to join him on an early morning ride.

What happened that shook him so much he didn't want to leave his house?

My gaze drops to the still-open Bible. After what I went through, I can barely look at it. So how does Bradyn maintain his faith even in the face of everything he deals with?

# CHAPTER 12
# BRADYN

The last couple of days have gone by in a blur as we prepare for the storm, and by the time we finished prepping for it, I was exhausted.

If only my brain would settle down long enough for me to get some sleep.

A fire crackles in the hearth before me, bright orange and yellow flames dancing while they fend off the chill that even my heater can't seem to touch. It's been a cold winter, colder than in recent years. And the storm that hit just over an hour ago still rages on, deepening the chill.

While I don't mind the cold, I'm definitely more than ready for the warmth of spring. Bible open to *Job*, I go back to reading through the trials and tribulations God's faithful servant suffered through. I've read this particular story in the Bible countless times, and every time, I notice something I missed before. A message that was embedded in the text that finally sinks in.

And nights when I can't sleep, this is the only way I can pass the time without completely losing my mind in the past. The devil loves to trap me there, taunting me with mistakes and pain.

Especially on nights like tonight when I'm plagued with exhaustion and the wounds are still so fresh.

I set my Bible aside and head into the kitchen to make some chamomile tea. Here's hoping Mom's old remedy will do the trick tonight. Otherwise, I'm not sure how I'll function tomorrow.

Given the amount of ice we'll likely be dealing with come morning, I need to be at the top of my game. Especially if I plan on working with Arthur any. Which, after seeing him actually start doing a decent job the last day or so, I've decided to do.

Maybe I can get him on the right track.

Either way, it's going to be a long day of breaking ice out of water troughs and cleaning stalls.

Bravo raises his head from where he's lying on the couch beside me. His ears perk up, and he tilts his head to the side.

Something crashes down outside. It's distant, and if I'd had anything but the fire going, I likely wouldn't have heard it. Abandoning my electric kettle, I head over toward the front door and pull it open.

The moment I do, I know something is wrong.

Beside me, Bravo lets loose a whine.

Even from my house, which is a few miles away and out of sight from my parents, I can see smoke billowing up into the night air.

I rush toward the hall closet and pull on my boots and jacket, grab my beanie, and sprint out onto the porch. Bravo tries to follow, but with how cold it is, letting him out in the snow for an undetermined amount of time could be detrimental to his paws without the booties I don't have time to put on.

"*Bleib*," I order. *Stay.*

He lies down inside, and I close the door to keep him in before making the mad dash through freezing rain to the UTV. As I race down the path, I have to maintain a careful speed since some of the water has already frozen.

The closer I get, the thicker the smoke. As I crest the hill between my parents' house and mine, my stomach turns into a pit. Flames are licking the sky, shooting up from the barn. Chaos ensues as the ranch hands are frantically trying to free the horses.

My phone rings. "I see it," I tell my mother.

"Your brothers just got here," she says into the phone.

"I'm nearly there." I end the call and pick up speed, moving as quickly as I can without sliding down the icy hill. Since my house is closest to my parents, it's not unusual for my brothers to stay with them whenever there's a particularly nasty storm heading our way. It's a precaution for them and the animals.

And thank God for that.

Arthur has Midnight on a lead and is rushing the wide-eyed, terrified horse out of harm's way. Elliot is doing all he can to guide Juniper, our newest rescue mare, away from the flames as she stares back at them, so terrified I can see the whites of her eyes even from a distance.

"How many horses are left?" I yell toward my dad, who's standing the closest. He rushes over to me, wearing pajamas, a heavy jacket, and boots. Freezing rain beats down on us. It slicks my clothing to my skin and the beanie onto my head.

"Your mother called the fire department. They're trying to get out here, but we're not the only ones who called for help. Tree took down the power line," he says, gesturing toward the pole that once stood on the other side of the barn. "My best guess is it sparked when it hit the barn." He shakes his head. "I can't believe this is happening."

"The horses?"

He's in shock; I can see it all over his face. But the barn is coming down any moment, and we need to make sure it's empty.

"Right. Sorry. We have seven out."

"Seven? We're missing three."

He nods. "Three of the horses got out, thanks to the damaged paddocks. Rev is one of them," he adds quickly.

"They're not in the fire?"

He shakes his head. "Stalls are empty."

Thank God. It's unfortunate that they're out in the storm, but if we can get this fire out, we can go after them at first light. It's far too dangerous to go out right now. Not until the fire is under control and this rain lets up. They're better off seeking their own shelter in one of the run-ins scattered throughout the pastures.

Tucker rushes forward, his cheeks red and ash-stained. "Sammy's not back." He coughs.

"What do you mean, she's not back?" The blood in my veins chills, and not because of the storm around us.

"She went after the runaway horses on foot. Leon tried to stop her, but he just got back. Said they lost each other somehow."

"She's out there alone?" Dread coils in my belly as I look off into the distance. She couldn't have been dressed in protective clothing. Nothing warm enough to brave a few hours out in the ice.

He nods.

The rain lets up just enough that it's not pounding down on us.

What's left of the roof crashes down, and sparks fly into the air.

"Get all of the horses into the east barn. Get them settled and fed. Make sure there aren't any injuries needing tending ASAP." I head toward the UTV parked off to the side.

"Where are you going?"

"To get Sammy." I climb into the UTV and fire it up. Lights illuminate the barn, highlighting that the entire thing will have to be rebuilt.

"Here." My father tosses me a med pack they must have pulled out of the barn before the entire thing went up. "Stay safe. We'll head out after you as soon as we get the horses settled."

"Want backup now?" Elliot asks, rushing over.

"No, I'll get her. Make sure the horses are safe."

He nods. "We told her not to go. She took off after them anyway."

Anger heats my veins even as the rain continues to chill me to my bones. "Get everyone else inside and warm as soon as the horses are situated," I tell Elliot. "If I'm not back in an hour—"

"Come find you. Got it."

Thinking of all the ways this could go horribly wrong, I take off down the path that leads around the barn and toward the back pasture. Thankfully, the UTV's roof is covered, but both doors are wide open, giving the freezing rain a perfect chance to pierce the side of my face like needles.

I drive slow, knowing Sammy is on foot, but as the

storm picks up steam again, I lose all visibility. Adrenaline kicks in.

If I don't find her, she's going to freeze to death out here.

Why in the world would she go out alone? It's insanity!

*God, please let me find her.*

I stop the side-by-side just in front of some downed fencing. It's fresh, that much I know since I rode through all of our pastures before the storm hit. Grabbing the emergency flashlight we keep inside all ranch UTVs, I step out into the rain and, using the flashlight and the headlights from the vehicle, study the fence.

Blood and hair are stuck to the wire. Horses must have taken the fence down out of fear. Dread coils in my stomach as the need to find both Sammy and the injured horse grows stronger.

Muddy hoofprints continue into the pasture. Rushing back toward the vehicle, I retrieve a pair of fence clippers so I can take down the rest of the fence and get the vehicle through when the thing dies.

Rain hammers down on me.

"No. This cannot be happening." I get in and try to fire it back up, but the engine won't turn over. It's completely dead, leaving me stranded. "You have got to be kidding me." I pocket the pliers and the flashlight then head out on foot.

I should go back for help. For another UTV. But if I do

that, I'm wasting time getting to Sammy. She couldn't have gotten much farther than me, so instead of turning back, I press on. My cheeks sting, and I can't feel my toes, but I keep pushing forward.

And then the beam of my flashlight hits a loafing shed, and I see Sammy inside, crouched in front of a downed animal, her hands moving swiftly in and out of the medical bag beside her. Two other horses are inside as well, both huddled in the corner, trying to get as far away from the storm as possible.

Shifting my direction toward them, I slow down just enough that I don't frighten the already terrified animal. *Rev.* His eyes are wide, his nostrils flared. He tries to get up, so I quickly kneel down at his head, pressing both gloved hands down onto his wet neck.

As my beam of light rests on the injuries, she removes the small pen light she'd been holding in her mouth and sets it to the ground before returning to her work. "I've got you, boy," she tells him. "I'm not interested in your lecture right now, Mr. Hunt. Feel free to hit me with it later. Right now, I'm busy."

*Mr. Hunt.* I swallow down the furious words I want to throw her way, just grateful that she's okay. Refocusing my attention from anger—for now—I scan Rev's body. There are no burns on his body—thank God—but his leg is covered in lacerations that Sammy has already cleaned with iodine. The brownish-red liquid stains his white hair, and as she works to bandage the ones she can, I note the way her hands are steady.

The way she moves without thinking.

Was she a veterinarian before she came here?

As she works, I remain silent, trying not to let myself be too concerned with the storm outside as it continues to gather steam. The sleet is coming down so hard I can't see past the edge of the overhang above us.

Fixing Rev's injuries is only part of the problem now.

Getting out of here is going to bring a whole other wave of problems. I might be able to get Sammy back to the side-by-side and try to get it going, but doing so could lead to hypothermia for both of us should we get lost in the storm. I know this ranch like the back of my hand, but when you can't see twelve inches in front of you, it's easy to get turned around.

And if we leave, get turned around, and end up farther away from the main house, my brothers won't be able to find us.

Staying here as the temperatures continue to drop presents the exact same problem, though it keeps us in one spot long enough to either be found or wait the storm out until it dies down enough that we can safely make the journey back to the side-by-side.

So, what do we do?

"Okay, that's the best I can do right now," Sammy says as she stands. I release Rev's neck and the horse thrashes to his feet. Keeping the injured back leg off the ground, he moves away from us the best he can.

"Now do I get to lecture you?" I snap.

She turns toward me, fight in her eyes. "He was hurt. I helped him."

"At the risk of your life and mine."

"You didn't have to come after me!" she yells.

"I don't make it a habit of letting my people wander off in a freezing rainstorm alone."

"So you'd rather your horse be in pain? Die? His injury might not have been life-threatening, but for all I knew it could have been," she snaps.

"Oh, you knew he was injured then?"

"Yes. There was blood outside of his paddock. I grabbed the med bag and went after him because he needed me. He was hurt, scared, and bleeding." There's something in the frantic tone of her voice. Buried pain, a memory she's trying to suppress, maybe. Whatever it is, it shuts me up.

"You shouldn't have run off alone. It was foolish."

"PJ followed after me."

"He went back to the barn."

"Well, that's not my fault."

I let out a breath in frustration. "If you had waited for me, we could have gone together."

"You're here now."

"Except the UTV is dead, and now we might freeze to

death." I shake my head and survey the storm outside the shed.

"Look, I—" She hisses in pain, and I whirl on her, all anger draining from me in an instant as I take in the sight of her favoring her right leg.

"You're hurt."

"It's just a sprain," she insists. "I tripped over the downed wire."

But even as she says it, I'm already kneeling down at her feet and lifting the leg of her flannel pajama pants. Blood has crusted to her skin, thanks to a gash about three inches long on her shin. "You're cut, too. Come over here and sit." I guide her carefully away from the horses just in case they get scared. Last thing I want is to add a trampling to tonight's bingo card.

Then I rush back over and grab both the med bag Dad gave me and the one she had. After opening it up, I clean the area with iodine and wrap it with white gauze. "You said your ankle is sprained?"

"I don't know. Maybe. I can't put much weight on it."

"You shouldn't have gone after them. The horses could've waited until the morning."

"Rev could have died."

"He would've been fine until we could get to him."

"Maybe. Maybe not. I wasn't going to risk it. Not when I didn't know how badly he was injured."

"No, you'll just risk your own life even though you're no good to them dead."

Her jaw tightens, and I sense she's holding back. Whether it's out of respect for me as her employer or something else, I'm not sure. But she clenches her hands into fists at her sides. "Fine. But I'm not sorry for what I did."

I glare down at her. "You will be if it kills us."

# CHAPTER 13
## KENNEDY

W hy did he follow me? Why didn't he just stay back? I knew it was a risk running out here, but I just didn't think much about it past that. The animals needed me, and risking my own life didn't seem like that big of a deal, but with Bradyn out here? What if he freezes to death? Or gets sick?

I take in what I can see of him given the flashlight beam illuminating the loafing shed. The dark strands of hair peeking out from beneath his beanie are matted to the side of his head. His cheeks are bright red, his gaze full of frustration. His stormy expression rivals the one that chased us into this small shelter.

"We can't head out yet," he tells me, tone clipped. "Especially since you can't walk."

"Agreed." I lean back against the far wall of the loafing shed. "If you just give me a minute, I'll be ready."

"You need longer than a minute," he snaps.

He leans down in front of the medical bag I'd taken from the pile of salvaged supplies we'd grabbed out of the barn once the horses were out. Rummaging through it, he withdraws a fire starter kit and a small zippered pouch.

"Here." He tosses me the pouch without looking in my direction.

I take it and unzip it, surprised and relieved to find an emergency thermal blanket inside.

Bradyn moves to the far side of the shed then takes some of the old straw on the ground and pushes it into a pile, carefully ensuring he leaves a gap of dirt around the outside of the pile. Then, he crouches down and prepares to strike a match to the bottom of the fire starter kit.

"Is that such a good idea? Won't the flames scare them after what they went through?"

He glares up at me. "It might, but we don't know how long we'll be here, and freezing to death seems like a bigger risk at the moment." Without waiting for a rebuttal, he strikes the match, and it crackles to life as he sets it in the straw pile.

The horses snort, but they don't run.

Bradyn sits down near the fire, his back close to the wall of the shed, so I open up the thermal blanket and set half over his shoulders as I slide down the wall and scoot in closer.

We sit in silence with only the sound of the raging

storm around us. The wind howls as rain slams into the sides and roof of the shed.

"We're lucky the wind is blowing in the other direction," I say. "Otherwise, this wouldn't do us any good."

He doesn't respond.

I tuck my knees up to my chest as the rest of the adrenaline leaves my system. Cold settles around me, and I start to shiver despite the fire. My body convulses, the shivering getting so bad my head begins to pound right alongside it.

"Come here." Bradyn separates his legs and pulls me between them, hugging me back against his strong chest. He pulls the blanket out from behind him and places it over me then rubs his strong hands over my arms.

I can't even form the sentences required to remind him he could freeze too.

The fire continues burning, but I know it won't remain that way for long since there's only so much straw in this shed.

Minutes tick by, and finally, the shivers begin to slow just enough that my entire body isn't convulsing uncontrollably. Bradyn shifts, leaning fully back against the wall of the shed, though he keeps me pressed against his strong chest. Heat begins to spread through my body. Not a lot but enough that I can feel the beat of his heart against my back.

"Th-th-thanks," I stammer.

"Yeah." He wraps his arms around me and holds on, giving me as much of his warmth as he can, even as I can feel him shivering right alongside me. "I would have gone out after them too," he says. "Though I would have taken ten minutes to get dressed in warmer clothes first."

"Which would have been smart," I reply with a half laugh, my body still shaking.

"It's admirable, though, what you did. Thanks for going after the horses."

"Here's hoping help arrives before we freeze to death."

"We'll survive," he says. "I told Elliot to wait an hour, which is likely almost up. They'll be headed out soon. You just have to hang on until then."

---

"You did a number on your leg, Sammy," Lani says as she finishes bandaging me up. "Seriously. What were you thinking?"

"That the horses needed help." I stare over at the floral wallpaper of the guest bedroom Mrs. Hunt insisted I be placed in once we got back. I haven't seen any of the brothers, just her and Lani. I'm desperate to know if Bradyn was hurt at all or if Rev's leg has been tended to by an actual vet.

But so far, any time I try to ask questions, they tell me to keep focused on myself for now. That everything else will be just fine.

"Without X-rays, I can't know for sure if it's broken, but—"

"No X-rays," I say quickly. I can't let them put me in a system. Any system. Even if it's a hospital. If they do, the careful backstory I crafted will fall apart. All it would take is someone looking too closely. And right now, I can't even run.

"Well, then, all I can do is tell you to keep it wrapped and stay off of it for the next couple of days. If it's not broken and it really is just a sprain, you should be able to start putting a little bit of weight on it in about forty-eight hours. But just some, don't go crazy."

"When can I get back to work?"

"Honey, don't you worry about that," Mrs. Hunt says as she pats my uninjured leg.

"I need to work, though. I need—"

"You need to rest," Mrs. Hunt interjects. "Don't you worry about a thing until you're healed. Your job will still be here. For now, you can stay here so we can keep an eye on you."

Dread coils in my stomach. The things in my cabin—I need them. "I can't stay here. It's too much. Please, just let me return to my cabin, and I promise that I'll rest up."

"Nonsense. We'll have one of the boys bring your stuff up. This is the best place for you."

"I—"

"I'll just go and make you something to eat. We're

having beef stew for dinner. Something to warm everyone up." With a final smile, she leaves Lani and me, shutting the door softly behind her.

Lani snorts. "She's always done that."

"Done what?"

"Steamrolled when she goes into protective momma bear mode." Lani closes her med bag and stands. "You're lucky you didn't lose any toes out there."

"Is Bradyn okay?"

"I haven't talked to him yet, but I'm sure he's fine. My brother could walk through the very fires of hell and come out unscathed. Has a time or two." Her gaze darkens just a bit, those bright-blue eyes she shares with her mother momentarily turning stormy.

"I'm sorry I put him at risk."

Lani waves her hand. "If it hadn't been you, he would've gone out there anyway. Granted, a lot more prepared than he was, but it's just who he is. It's who all of them are."

"He's a good man."

"Good as they come. But don't tell him I said that. I have an annoying little sister reputation to keep up. Even now in my thirties."

I smile. "Fair enough. Your secret is safe with me."

"Good. All right, well, I'm leaving you in good hands. Call if you need me, but I think you'll rest up just fine. Ibuprofen and lots of fluids. I'll have Mom bring another ice pack up in about thirty minutes. You should be icing it off and on."

"Thanks, Lani."

"No problem, Sammy. See you later." She waves and starts to head out but pauses to peer out the window and groans. "Ugh, Sharon is here. I knew it was only a matter of time before local media decided to show up."

*Local media. The news.* Fear claws at my chest, and I have to fight to push it down. I'm in here. Tucked away in this house. No one can see me. Not a single camera will be able to capture me in here, which means—

"Look at her, walking around down there like she owns the place." Lani clicks her tongue. "That woman is a menace just waiting to sink her claws into one of my brothers. Excuse me while I go deal with her." Lani offers me a quick smile before ducking out into the hall.

I have to fight the urge to get up and hop down to my cabin to gather my things. Truth is, even if I wanted to leave, I couldn't go anywhere. Not on a hurt ankle. My best bet is to remain right where I am, tucked away on this Texas ranch, surrounded by military heroes. If ever there was a safe place to lie low, it would be this place, right?

# CHAPTER 14
# BRADYN

"You are so brave," Sharon says with her lined eyes wide and full of false concern. I can see through the mask, though, have been able to ever since we were in high school. Still, it doesn't stop her from trying to make me her next husband.

Not that I'm judging. Her personal life is none of my business. I'm just not biting on that line, no matter how many times she tries to cast it out.

"I did what anyone else would do."

"You went out into an ice storm to save horses and one of your ranch hands."

"Yeah, well, anyone would have done it."

She makes notes on her notepad then looks up at me. "Arthur Kidress said that the female ranch hand was injured. What's her name? Sammy, right? What injury? Can I speak to her?"

In a small town like this, any news is newsworthy. A fire at Hunt Ranch will likely make the front page, giving Sharon one heck of a byline. But there's no way I'm letting her use Sammy for clout. "We keep our employees private, you know that." It's bad enough Arthur mentioned her at all. Especially when we have a confidentiality agreement with all of our employees. *One more strike against him.*

"Can I speak with her?" she asks again.

"I'll have her call in if she wants to talk to you."

"Oh, come on, Bradyn." She pouts. "For old times' sake? I would love to get this story." She bats her false lashes at me, and even though I'm agitated that she thinks I'd fall for the act, I force a smile.

"No, sorry, Sharon. If she wants to talk to you, she'll reach out."

"Okay, fine." She laughs and playfully smacks my arm. "Always with the secrets. You would think we hardly knew each other."

*We do hardly know each other.* "Sorry, Sharon, it's the nature of my business. Thanks for stopping by."

"Anytime, honey. You know that." She flirtatiously bats her eyelashes, really making sure she drives the invitation home.

I turn to leave, but I don't have to look behind me to know she's following. Bravo is padding along beside me, not paying her any mind. I have to say, the fact that he doesn't have to deal with her makes me momentarily jealous that I'm not a dog.

Elliot, Tucker, Riley, and Dylan are nowhere to be seen, likely avoiding Sharon like the plague she is. Which I know is not a very kind way to look at her. But given that she rotates which of us she's trying to land, her lack of genuine affection and simple desire to bear the Hunt surname makes her unwelcome on this ranch.

"Bradyn!" I stop and turn to the right, breathing a sigh of relief when I see Lani moving toward me, her gaze narrowed on Sharon, who's still behind me.

"Hey, Lani."

"Sharon," she clips. "If you don't mind, I need to speak to my brother. In private."

"Oh, well, if it's about the damage, I should be a part—"

"No. You shouldn't." Lani's sweet smile is laced with venom as she wraps her hand around my wrist and tugs me away. Bravo follows happily, tail wagging.

"Call me if your ranch hand wants to talk!" Sharon calls out.

I don't respond, just let Lani drag me into the house and slam the door behind us. Elliot, Riley, Dylan, and Tucker all look up from where they're sitting on the couches. My dad, looking just as guilty, grins sheepishly from his recliner.

"Cowards, all of you," she accuses.

"Hey, don't look at us. It's Bradyn she's really after," Tucker replies.

"Then why are you hiding?" she asks.

"Because now that Bradyn is back, she finally stopped coming after me," Elliot quips. "And I'm not interested in rekindling her affections."

Rolling my eyes, I remove my boots and head into the kitchen to grab a glass of water. "Thanks for the rescue, sis."

"No problem." Lani sets her bag down. "One date eons ago, and she's still trying to sink her claws into you. I know we're supposed to forgive, and I'm not holding a grudge exactly, but the idea of letting her anywhere near you after what she did makes my skin crawl."

Years ago, I'd had a crush on Sharon. I was home-schooled my entire life, and she was the head cheerleader. Beautiful, seemingly confident, and we'd met at church camp. When I'd finally gotten up the courage to ask her out, she'd agreed. Our relationship lasted all of a month before I found out she'd been cheating on me with Billy Granger, who ended up being her first husband.

It was messy, and even though Lani was only twelve at the time, she'd been out the door, ready to get vengeance for my broken teenage heart.

She's always had a fiery soul, and if she'd been open to it, I would've had her join the Search & Rescue team. But

God has a different plan for her, and she found her calling in the medical field, helping people heal.

"It's not worth the grudge," I tell her truthfully. "But I appreciate the backup."

"Yeah, well, anytime." She smiles. "Sammy's doing okay, by the way. I don't think her ankle is broken, but she won't let me take her in for X-rays."

*Curious.* "Why not?"

She shrugs. "Won't say. Money, maybe?"

"Maybe. I'll head up to talk to her. Remind her that the ranch will cover all medical expenses for employees injured during working hours."

"Well, don't be too pushy. I don't think it's anything more than a sprain. And the laceration on her shin has been stitched, so it should heal up nicely. Still, I need to remind you that you both are really lucky neither of you froze to death." She arches a brow.

"Yeah, I know."

"Next time, maybe don't go running out in the middle of a storm."

"Tell Sammy that. She's the reason I went out."

Lani arches a brow. "First of all, I already did. And second, we both know that, even if Sammy hadn't gone after the horses, you would have."

"I would've gotten changed first. Grabbed supplies." Again, she arches a brow. I chuckle. "Fine, I'll be more careful next time."

"That's all I ask." With a beaming smile, she retrieves her med bag and heads toward the door. "I've got to get back to the clinic for my afternoon appointments. Call me if you need me, okay? Love you!"

"Love you too!" I call after her as she leaves the kitchen and heads out. I hear her give the others a hard time for hiding from Sharon again; then the front door closes.

I've just finished my glass of water when my mom comes into the kitchen. "Hey, honey! You hungry?"

"Not really," I tell her. "I was just about to go check on Sammy."

"Good. I took her some food, so you can make sure she eats it. She's not happy about being in the guest room." Her brow furrows. "That girl. Stubborn as they come."

"Why isn't she happy about being in the guest room?"

"Says she doesn't want to be an imposition. It breaks my heart to think she believes she could ever be one."

My thoughts drift back to what she said in the barn yesterday morning. That she and Rev had bonded over traumatic pasts. Is that what's causing her insecurities about us caring for her? Her childhood or a past relationship?

"I'll go talk to her."

"Good. Thanks. And please take her this too. Maybe she's in the mood for something sweet." She plates a piece of pie from the leftovers we had after dinner last night then offers it to me.

"Done."

"Good. Dinner is at seven tonight."

"Sounds great." Pie in hand, I head up the stairs and down the hall. The guest bedroom door is closed, so I pause a moment and take a deep breath to steady the nerves in the pit of my stomach.

I can still recall how it felt to hold her in that shed, and the desire to wrap my arms around her again has only grown with every passing hour. The only reason I didn't come sooner is because I can't seem to shut down this need to see her. To talk to her. Which I'm starting to think is a problem. I'm falling hard and fast, and I'm a man who likes my feet on solid ground. At least until I know whether or not the feelings are reciprocated.

Before I can change my mind and recruit Elliot for the pie delivery job, I raise my fist and knock.

"Come in," Sammy calls out.

I gently turn the knob and step into the room. The curtains are open, so the room is full of vibrant light from the bright sun outside. Sammy is lying on the bed, covered by a thick floral comforter, except for her injured leg, which is wrapped and propped up on a stack of pillows.

Her foot is bare, and her bright pink toenails make me smile just a bit. That is until I get a look at the lush honey-colored waves of her hair falling over her shoulders.

She's stunning.

Breathtaking.

"Hey," she says. "How is Rev?"

*That would be her first question.* I smile and set the pie down on the nightstand. "This is for you," I tell her. "My mom sent it up in case you wanted something sweet. As for Rev, he's doing just fine, thanks to you. The vet came and saw him earlier and said that, had you not gotten to him when you did, he could've ended up lame. So thanks."

"No need to thank me."

I take a seat in a high-backed chair in the corner of the room. "I do need to thank you. Especially with how frustrated I was that you were out there."

"You weren't wrong. It was foolish to run out unprepared. I have a habit of not thinking through decisions sometimes. I just run."

Because I sense there's a lot more to that than she's willing to discuss, I opt for a subject change. "How are you feeling?"

"Better. But I told your mom I really should go back to my cabin."

"Why the hurry? Is the room not comfortable? I could—"

"No, it's fine. I just—I don't want to be a burden."

"You clearly don't know my mom," I reply with a smile. "You're making her day by letting her take care of you."

"Still, I do okay on my own."

*Who hurt you?* I can see it all over her face. Body language is a specialty of mine. It's one of the reasons I'm so good in the field and why I excelled in interrogation when I'd been stationed overseas.

This woman has been hurt…badly.

The more she lets her mask slip, the easier it gets to see.

"No one doubts that," I tell her. "We'll get you back to the cabin as soon as you're on your feet. I can go get your stuff for you if you'd like."

"No. That's okay. Thanks, though." She's frustrated but relaxes back against the pillows again.

Awkward silence settles around us, so I lean forward and clasp my hands together. "Lani said that you didn't want to go get X-rays? The ranch will cover medical expenses for all of its employees injured during working hours. So if that's what you're worried about—"

"It's not," she interrupts. "I just, sorry, I just don't like hospitals."

"Okay, well, if you decide you want to go get checked out, I could take you."

She smiles, and my heart flips in my chest. *So beautiful.* "Thanks, I'll let you know if I change my mind."

"Sure thing."

More silence, and she shifts her attention toward the open window. I take a moment to study her profile in the sunlight, my eyes greedily drinking in the sight of her as she closes her eyes and soaks in the ray of sun sneaking in through the window.

"Well, I should get back out there. We're sifting through what's left of the barn."

She turns back toward me. "I wish I could help. Maybe if I had crutches—"

"No," I tell her. "Just rest, Sammy. I promise your job will be here for you when you're better."

# CHAPTER 15
# KENNEDY

R ain pelts me from all sides as wind whips the drenched strands of my hair. My clothes are plastered to my skin, and my bare feet slap against the wet pavement. Blood pours from my forearm, but I do my best to maintain pressure on the wound.

I just have to survive long enough to make it to the boat. As soon as I do that, I can leave this place and sail somewhere they'll never find me. Somewhere not even the devil himself can hunt me down.

Who am I kidding? He'll always find me. Tonight is merely an example of that. The marshals tried to hide me, but he found me, and now they're dead.

They're all dead.

I choke on a sob. Crying will do me no good now. Later I can grieve, but right now I have to stay focused. If I die, everything I know dies with me.

*My frantic dash toward freedom does nothing but buy the feds enough time to fully close in on him. If I can do that, then I stand a chance at living to a ripe old age. Otherwise—I shove that thought away because it's no help to me now.*

*I trip, my toe splitting open against a crack in the pavement. Pain shoots up my leg like lightning, momentarily obliterating the burning agony of the gash in my forearm. I whimper, my knees slamming into the ground as I go down. Asphalt bites into my skin, and even though I know I should keep running, I can't bring myself to stand.*

*Knowing they're not that far behind me, I try to hide myself as best as possible by crawling behind some boxes in the alleyway I'd chosen. In hindsight, I might have been able to get help if I'd stayed on the crowded street. But doing that would only put anyone who offered me aid in danger. And I can't let anyone else die because of me.*

*The body count is already too high.*

*Clutching the wet Bible beneath my shirt, I tuck my legs up as best I can and lean back. Just a minute. I need just a minute to catch my breath.*

*A door opens behind me, and an old man peers out. I do my best to remain still even as the freezing rain has soaked straight through to my bones.*

Please don't see me.

Please don't give me away.

*A steely gaze levels on me. "This is not a place to sleep, girl," he snaps.*

*"I'm not trying to sleep. I promise. Just resting. I'll be gone soon."*

*Yelling echoes in the distance, though it grows closer.*

*They're closing in, and they won't hesitate to kill this man just for looking at me.*

*"Please, sir, I'll go. Just get inside." I stand, but my legs turn to jelly, and I fall back into the hard wall.*

*The stranger must notice the blood saturating the front of my shirt because his gaze narrows further on me before raising in the direction of the angry voices. He reaches for me. "Get inside, girl."*

*"No." I shake my head. "You have to get inside." Tears sting my eyes as I try to move away from the building, but my legs won't cooperate. Every step I try to take sends me falling right back into the wall. Rain hammers the ground, the storm above picking up speed.*

*"Inside. Now." He reaches forward and pulls me inside then shuts and locks the door. I look down. My toe is already drenched in blood, a stark crimson against the white tile I'm standing on.*

*"You're making a mistake. You need to put me back outside. Please."*

*The man says nothing, just takes my hand and pulls me toward an office chair situated in front of a computer. He takes the Bible from my hands and sets it on the counter* beside me. It takes me a moment to gather myself enough to actually look around, but as I do, I note comfortable-looking animal cages with two wide-eyed dogs staring back at me, both of them with their legs wrapped.

A glass-front refrigerator sits on one wall, prescription bottles filling its shelves. A bookcase stands beside it, also full of medication, and as I glance around the room, I note there are medical supplies organized carefully throughout the entire space.

The man retrieves a clean towel from a cabinet and grabs bandages, a bottle of cleaner, and a small sterile bag from a shelf then returns to me. "Let me see your arm."

I hesitate for only a moment before I hold it out. The gash is deep, and blood continues to drip from the jagged wound. He wraps it in the towel. "Keep this pressed to your chest to apply pressure," he orders. I do as he says. "What's your name?"

"K—" I start but stop myself. "Sammy," I reply, using the nickname the marshals gave me instead of the one my mother gave me at birth. A name I haven't gotten to use in over a year. Maybe one day. If I survive this.

He pulls a short stool over and sits down. "I'll let the lie slide, Sammy. What happened to you?"

A buzzer rings, and I jump. He turns over his shoulder and glances at a security camera. My blood turns to ice in my veins as I take in the black-and-white image of Jexton and Bruiser, the two men they sent after me. The image may *be grainy, but I can see the harshness of their murderous gazes.*

*My stomach twists into knots so hard I can barely breathe.*

*"You have to let me leave," I insist, panic setting in. "I can sneak out—"*

*"You're going to bleed out if you try to go anywhere," he says, gesturing to the already-soaked towel pressed against my arm.*

*"They're going to kill you," I whisper, tears rolling down my cheeks.*

*The man's expression hardens. "I'm not that delicate." He stands and crosses over toward the security monitors then presses a button on the side. "Can I help you?"*

*"We're looking for my sister," one of the men replies, his tone a façade of worry. "She fell and hit her head, so she's disoriented and confused. We think she could be a danger to herself and others."*

*"I am so sorry to hear that. Did you try the police station? They're right down the street. There's a hospital two blocks over too."*

*"We're headed there next. Please, sir, can we come in and just take a look around? She might have snuck in somehow."*

*"I'm sorry, but I'm locked down for the night. It would have been impossible for anyone to have snuck in without my knowing it."*

"*Please, sir,*" he insists, tone more frustrated now. "*Can we just come in for a moment? Look around?*"

"*Normally, I wouldn't have an issue with it, son. But tonight, I have two animals who are very sensitive to strangers and are barely clinging to life as it is. I'm afraid I cannot risk them hearing you enter and losing their minds.*" The man forces a soft sigh. "*But if I see anything, I'll be sure to contact the authorities. I hope you find her safely.*"

One of the men glares up at the camera, a challenge in his gaze. Can he sense me in here? Does he know that the stranger is lying? I hold my breath, waiting for him to use the brute strength he's known for and kick in the door. "*I appreciate that,*" he replies then reaches into his pocket and withdraws a business card, holding it up for the camera. "*Here's my number. Please call me first. She'll panic if she feels cornered.*" He leaves it in the mailbox near the door.

"*Understood. Good luck. I pray you find her.*"

I don't breathe again until they're no longer in the camera frame. The man rushes over to me and sits back down on the stool then removes the towel from my arm.

"*We need to contact the police,*" he says quickly.

"*No,*" I say, frantic. "*They have officers on his payroll. Please. I need to disappear. Just for now. I know who to call.*" The thumb drive hanging around my neck has never felt as heavy as it does now.

*It carries the weight of two more lives now.*

*"You can't go anywhere yet," he says.*

*"I can't stay here. They'll come back."*

*He uses a large syringe to draw liquid out of a container. "This is going to hurt." He grips my arm and depresses the plunger until liquid hits the wound. I suck in a pained breath and do my best to maintain my breathing as the liquid washes away the blood and dirt from the injury.*

*The man assesses the injury then reaches up onto the silver tray to pick up a vial and another syringe. He withdraws the liquid. "This will numb the area enough that I can close it, okay?"*

*I nod, tears in my eyes. The pain is severe, but I remember what my mother used to tell me when I got hurt.* "We can do anything for ten seconds, right, Dee?" *she'd say. And somehow, I always knew she was right.*

*He injects the medicine, and I keep my eyes closed as I feel the tugging of thread around my injury. Breathing through it, I remain perfectly still, all the while trying to make sure I do my best not to pass out as the adrenaline I've been carrying bottoms out.*

*"All done." His hand leaves my arm, so I open my eyes and stare down at the neatly stitched line going from my wrist up to just below my elbow.*

*"It was big."*

*"I'd say so. You're lucky you didn't bleed out." He rises*

*from the stool and pushes the metal tray with blood-soaked gauze and tools off to the side then washes his hands in a deep sink.*

*"We need to tend to your feet, too," he replies. "But I need fresh supplies. Give me a few."*

*I stare down at my dirty feet. They're crusted with dirt and blood, and now that the pain in my arm has ebbed away just a bit, I can feel the stinging pain shooting through my foot and up my leg from the toe I basically split open.*

*The man sets a stainless-steel tub of water at my feet along with a tray of clean gauze and bandages. "I don't think you need stitches here, but I won't know until they're clean. Put your feet in here."*

*"I'll get it dirty."*

*He arches a brow. "I'm counting on that."*

*"But these supplies cost you money."*

*"Girl, I've already stitched up your arm; what's a bit more?" Instead of waiting for me to do it, he lifts my injured foot and gently guides it into the bin. I hiss in pain as the liquid hits my injured toe. "Yikes, no stitches, but you did a number on it. If you're squeamish, don't open your eyes."*

*I'm not, but I keep them closed anyway.*

*It's easier to hide the tears that way.*

*I'm not sure how long he works on my foot, but it feels like forever before he's wrapping it in a bandage. "All done."*

*I open my eyes as he's lifting the pan of filthy water and dumping it into the sink. The man places his tray of soiled tools and gauze beside the sink then washes his hands and returns to the stool in front of me.*

*"Why did you help me?"*

*"Because you needed it."*

*"But you didn't have to help me. You risked your life. If you'd have known—"*

*"I still would have done it."*

*Tears blur my vision. "I don't even know your name."*

*"Cillian," he replies.*

*"Cillian."*

*He nods and crosses his arms. "Now, how about you tell me what's going on so I can see just what I've gotten myself into?"*

*The tears come hot and fast, my shoulders shaking as the weight of everything comes crashing down on me. Gentle arms come around me, and Cillian offers me a firm hug, holding me close as I cry.*

*"Easy, girl," he coos. "You're safe now. We'll get you help."*

*"We can't," I tell him as I pull back, finally managing to get control.*

*His brow furrows. "You said no police, but what about the FBI? Surely someone—"*

*"No. He has people everywhere. It's how they found me.*

*Anyone at the FBI that's good is already doing everything they can. If I go to them, he'll find me again."*

*"Who? Who is after you, girl?"*

*I can't tell him.*

*I know I can't.*

*So I don't.*

*"Then tell me your name. Your real name," he adds. "You can tell me."*

*The reward for me is likely going to be a high one.*

*For my own safety, I have to keep my mouth shut and hope that, if Cillian is truly a good man, he'll understand my need for privacy.*

*"Just Sammy," I say.*

*He doesn't try to hide his frustration, but he doesn't press, either. "What were you doing bleeding in my alley, girl?" He stands and reaches for his phone. Panic shoots through me, and I push to my feet, hopping over toward him.*

*"No. Please stop. Don't call anyone. You can't."*

*"Someone is hurting you. We need to report it—"*

*I close my eyes, my throat constricting. "I told you. You can't call. No one can know I was here. Please. If they find me—"*

*Slowly, he lowers the phone. "What will happen if they find you?"*

*I answer without hesitation. "They'll kill me."*

I COME AWAKE SLOWLY despite the nightmare. Tears have dried and crusted to the sides of my eyes already, but it's not anything I'm not used to. The nightmare is one I've had nearly every night for the last two years, and it's showing no chance of slowing down.

Truth is, I work myself so hard all day because, if I'm exhausted enough, sometimes I can manage a full night of uninterrupted sleep. Unfortunately, lying in bed all day is not conducive to exhaustion.

I reach over and turn the lamp on then swing my legs over the bed. After grabbing one of the crutches Lani left for me, I hop my way into the bathroom. Every movement hurts, but since it's not quite as bad as yesterday, I'm taking it as a win.

After splashing some water on my face, I take a minute to study myself in the mirror. My eyes are red from crying and sleep, and my cheeks are streaked with dried tears. Unfortunately, it's not an uncommon look for me.

After making my way back into the bed, I leave the crutch beside me and throw the comforter up over the top of my leg. I literally cannot sit in this bed all day today or I will go crazy.

Straight bonkers.

Closed spaces for long periods of time do that to me.

Someone knocks on the door.

"Come in," I call out.

The door opens, and Bradyn sticks his head in.

My heart hammers in my chest as my stomach does somersaults. Why, oh why does he have to give me the butterflies?

"I saw your lamp come on as I was making my way up for breakfast. You doing okay?"

"Yeah. Just woke up." As he opens the door further, the delicious aroma of coffee and frying bacon fills my lungs. My stomach growls.

"I was actually going to see if you wanted to come down to breakfast. I can help you down the stairs, but then you can get out of this room. I imagine, even with as lovely as it is, you might be losing your mind a little."

I smile. "You would be right."

"I also spoke with my mom, and after I promised to make sure you were eating and well cared for, she's agreed to let you return to your cabin."

Hope shoves the attraction out. Back in my space. Near my things. Near the one thing that carries the weight of my freedom. I can't believe I took it off before going out into the storm. It was foolish and a mistake I'll never make again.

"Really? I mean, I don't need you checking in on me; I'll be fine."

"I know you don't, but I did promise to hand deliver

food twice a day. If you're okay with that? She'll also be by to make sure you're resting."

I get the feeling that if I told him no, he'd respect it. But I also really don't want to tell him no. Momma Hunt's cooking is spectacular, and not having to worry about feeding myself twice a day would be nice. Especially since I don't see myself getting to the store anytime soon. "Food delivery would be great."

He beams at me. A genuine ray of sunshine that would have the sun itself jealous. "Great. I'll step out for a few minutes. Just call out when you're ready to venture down the stairs." With a final smile, he steps out and shuts the door softly behind him.

I waste no time as I throw the covers off of me and eye the jeans and shirt folded up on the chair in the corner.

I could try to put them on.

I'd probably be successful.

But the thought of falling on my butt makes it not worth the try. So, I grab the crutches and opt to come back for them. Instead, I slip my unwrapped foot into my boot then make my way over toward the door.

When I pull it open, Bradyn turns to look at me. His gaze darkens just a bit before he smiles. Warmth spreads through me, turning my stomach into a pit of butterflies yet again. "I'll have to come back for my jeans when I'm able to get them on without a struggle," I tell him with a smile. "Until then, sweats will have to do."

He chuckles. "I can bring them to you with the first food delivery."

"Sounds good, thanks." I use the crutches to get out of the room then eye the stairs. Somehow, they looked less intimidating as I was literally being carried up here by Elliot the first time. Then again, I'd been freezing cold and somewhat out of it then. "I'm not sure I can do this easily, and scooting down on my butt might be a bit more than my pride can take at the moment."

Bradyn laughs, and the rich sound envelopes me in warmth. "While I spent many years scooting down on my own butt, I get it. Here." Without waiting, he grips my arm, plucks the crutches out, and scoops me into his arms.

He does it so effortlessly that it makes me feel like I weigh practically nothing.

And even though I know I should, I don't fight it because it feels amazing to be held in his strong arms. "Thanks. This is much better."

He chuckles. "I'll come back for the crutches, but let's get you breakfast before Tucker and Dylan eat it all."

"Both my empty stomach and I thank you for that."

We move down the stairs easily, and by the time we get to the bottom, I can already hear the brothers arguing back and forth. It's all friendly jesting and makes me smile. I would've loved to grow up with siblings.

Instead—my thoughts darken, and I have to actively shove them out of my mind to avoid being pulled under.

"I'm just saying that you should pick up the slack a bit more, Dylan. I can't be the best looking and the hardest working of the two of us," Tucker says.

"What a burden that must be," Riley replies with what I imagine is an eye roll.

We emerge into the dining room, and all gazes shift to us. Color floods my cheeks. Why didn't I think this through? Why didn't I insist he put me down at the bottom of the stairs? I must look absolutely ridiculous being carried through their house in sweats!

Ruth enters the room. "Oh good! You got her down here safely! Come and sit, honey. You must be starving. Get the girl a chair, Riley. Bradyn can't do all the work."

Riley gives us a grin before he stands and pulls out a chair for me. "Here you go, Sammy. You can sit right between me and Elliot. Break the tension a bit."

Elliot snorts and shakes his head. "They've been going at it since mom let Dylan have the first pancake."

# CHAPTER 16
# BRADYN

As soon as I've set Sammy down, I head back into the kitchen to make her a plate. I can hear her out there chatting with Elliot, and it makes me a bit jealous. Which, of course, is ridiculous. But there it is.

Jealous because my brother seems to have an easier time finding words around her than I do.

"She looks tired," my mother comments as she comes into the kitchen. "I hope that bed was comfortable enough."

"I'm sure it's just her leg bothering her," I reply as I pile some eggs onto her plate.

"Maybe."

I finish putting a few strips of bacon onto her plate then turn. My mother is watching me curiously, a smile on her face. "What?"

"Nothing." She shakes her head but continues smiling.

"What is it?"

"You two just make a nice pair, that's all."

"What?" My cheeks heat. "I barely know her."

"I knew the moment I met your father that I wanted to marry him."

"We're not all you and Dad," I reply with a snort. "Besides, Sammy works for us."

"As far as I know, there are no Hunt laws about falling in love with a coworker."

"*Love*? Again, I'm forced to repeat myself, I barely know her."

"Uh-huh." She continues smiling though, and because I know that continuing to press will only make me look even more guilty, I head out into the dining room to deliver Sammy's plate.

Just as I'm entering the room, she starts laughing at something Elliot said, and I can't keep my own smile from spreading. She looks *right* sitting here at my family's table. Like this is where she belongs.

*God, please help me here. I need to know what to do. How do I make this woman open up to me?*

"Here you go," I say as I set her plate in front of her.

"Thank you. This looks delicious, Mrs. Hunt."

My mom beams at her as she sets a tray of fresh biscuits down in the center of the table. "I'm so glad. Here's hoping it tastes just as good." She takes a seat.

"Morning, everyone," my father announces as he takes his seat at the head of the table. "Good morning, Sammy."

"Good morning, Mr. Hunt. Thank you for letting me join you all this morning. And for allowing me to stay."

"Anytime," he replies with a smile. "Shall we?" He holds out his hands, taking Mom's and Elliot's. Elliot reaches for Sammy, who hesitates just a moment before slipping her hands into his and Riley's.

I hold Riley's hand while Dylan and Tucker finish off the loop with Tucker taking my mother's hand.

We all bow our heads.

He clears his throat. "Heavenly Father, we thank You for this meal before us, for the roof over our heads, for our health, and for every moment You grant us here together. Please bless this food we put into our bodies and guide us through today so that we may do Your will. I ask this in the name of Your Son, Jesus Christ. Amen."

We all unlink hands the moment the "amens" have been spoken, and everyone begins eating. My gaze continually finds Sammy across the table. I just can't help it. I'm drawn to her in a way I've never been drawn to anyone.

As though she's the light that will drive out the darkness in my soul.

"Busy day today, Ruth?" my father asks.

"Not too busy. We'd postponed the bake sale until Sunday morning before service, so I'll be re-baking some of the goodies that wouldn't keep those few days. Then I promised Sally Henderson that I'd swing by and help her with the quilt she's been working on. There's a stitch that's giving her a fit."

"Wonderful. Give Sally our love. And, if those goodies won't keep—"

"I already set them out on the counter for all of you to enjoy," she interrupts.

"You know us so well, Momma," Tucker says with a smile.

"So, so well," Dylan adds.

"How about you, Bradyn? Anything with the business yet?"

I shake my head. "We've got a couple files to sort through, but nothing that's catching our attention just yet."

"And ranch business?" he asks. Since he's been what he likes to call 'retired lite' for the last three years—ever since he broke his hip in three places getting thrown from the back of a young gelding—I handle the bulk of ranch business. He puts his opinion in and offers help when I need it, but otherwise, he stays out of it.

Instead, he helps my mom around the house or volunteers his time in town, doing odd jobs for those who can't.

"I'm headed to the lumber mill this afternoon to grab supplies to start rebuilding the barn. Elliot is meeting with the vet so she can take a look at Rev and check his progress. Riley, Tucker, and Dylan are taking the ranch hands out into the pastures to check all the fencing; then they're headed over to Piney Drive Ranch to help with some damage they took from the storm."

"Good, good. I'm glad you're helping Dan. He's had it rough these last couple of years." The tone turns somber as we all recall the accident that took his wife and left him to manage the ranch alone.

"We'll get him taken care of," Riley says.

"What can I do?" Sammy takes us all by surprise by speaking up.

We all shift our attention to her. Wide crystal-blue eyes shift around the table nervously.

"Honey, don't you worry about that. You need to rest up," my mom tells her.

Sammy's lips flatten in frustration. "There has to be something I can help with. Please. I promise to take it easy, but I'll go crazy just sitting around staring at the same four walls."

"There's nothing wrong with taking it easy while you heal," she retorts.

Riley snorts.

"And just what is that supposed to mean, Riley Jude?"

"Nothing, Mom. I was just remembering that emergency appendectomy you had when you were supposed to be taking it easy but decided the laundry couldn't wait."

My dad throws his head back and laughs. "Yes! And then the woman pulled three stitches loose and got angry that we made her leave to go get them closed back up!" Everyone around the table joins in his laughter.

Even Sammy looks delighted to have the attention off of her for a moment.

My mom shakes her head, though her expression is amused. "Yeah, well, I don't see you complaining that you always have clean socks."

He leans over and presses a kiss to the side of her head. "Never, my love. We appreciate everything that you do."

"It's true, Mom. You're the best," Riley quips.

"Yeah, yeah." She beams at him.

"Why don't you go with Bradyn to the lumber yard?" Elliot offers, returning the conversation to Sammy. "It's about an hour one-way, so having the company wouldn't be such a bad thing."

I swallow hard, my amusement from the conversation mere seconds ago vanishing. In its place is something far more dangerous…hope. Why didn't I think to invite her?

She turns to me. "Would that be okay? I can help with directions or make a list while we're driving."

*Beyond amazing.* "Sounds good. I'd love the company." Somehow, despite my excitement at the idea of sharing the trip with Sammy, I keep my tone level.

My earlier prayer about my desire to have her open up to me pops back into my head, and I can't help but wonder if this is His way of answering it. *Thank you, God.*

She smiles. "Great. I'll need to head over to my cabin and change first, but then I'll be ready to go."

"I still think you should rest. Keep your foot up," my mother says.

"I promise to be careful," Sammy promises. "I'll elevate as soon as we get back."

"Okay, I'll hold you to that."

---

AN HOUR LATER, I'm parking my truck in front of Sammy's cabin. The other ranch hands have already left for the day, out handling chores before heading to Piney Hill Ranch, so it's completely quiet as I step out of my truck.

Feeling as nervous as a teenager picking up a girl for his first date, I make my way up to the front door. It's ridiculous, really. It's not even a date. And it's hardly the first time we've spent time together.

Yet here I am, stomach a pit of nerves, mind swimming with thoughts about the good that could come from this trip.

I'm just raising my fist to knock when she opens the door. She's wearing a pair of baggy black pants and a cream-colored sweatshirt that highlights the golden tone of her skin. Her hair's braided over her shoulder, and she's wearing a Hunt Ranch baseball cap. The same one that she was wearing that first day we met on the street.

She looks beautiful.

"Ready?" I ask.

"I am." Using the crutches, she makes her way out onto the porch. I note the chain around her neck, tucked into the front of her sweatshirt. I hadn't noticed it before, but since she tends to wear thermal shirts most days, that's not a surprise.

Dog tags? The chain certainly looks like the ones they issued to us. Is that her secret? Did she lose someone overseas? Or is she the soldier who served? It would certainly fit her.

"Here, let me help you." I rush forward and offer her help getting down the steps then move around the truck to open the passenger side door.

As soon as she's settled into the truck, I take her crutches and slip them into the backseat then head around to the driver's side. Once I'm behind the wheel, I offer her a quick grin. "Ready?"

"Let's do this." She reaches into her pocket and takes out a slip of paper. "I looked up directions, and I think if we take—what?" she asks when she glances up and catches me grinning at her like an idiot.

"You looked the place up?"

"Well, yeah, I said I would help with—" She trails off, closes her eyes, and lets out a laugh. "You've probably been going to this place since you were old enough to walk. You don't need directions, do you?"

"No," I reply. "But I think it's great that you printed them out. Your attention to detail is something I admire."

"Admire?" She snorts. "You barely know me."

"I'm a good judge of character." I put the truck into drive and head down the road that will take us off of the ranch.

Sammy's fallen completely silent, her gaze fixed on the landscape out the window. I get the sense that the mood has shifted between us, though I can't quite figure out why.

"I hope you don't think I was mocking you or anything. I really do appreciate you taking the time to look it up."

"What? Oh, no, I know you weren't. Sorry, my mind is just elsewhere."

"Everything okay?"

"I'm glad to be out," she replies, completely avoiding the question. *Interesting.*

Is it her past that has captured her attention now? Whatever it is that brought her to our doorstep?

Pain?

Memories?

A bad relationship?

"Glad I could be of service." I clear my throat, trying to decide how to start more than a surface-level conversation. I really want to get to know her, but so far, she's thrown up roadblocks every chance I get. "So what brought you to Texas?"

She looks over at me curiously. "What makes you think I wasn't born here?"

"Your accent," I reply. "Certain words you say have a different inflection."

"Then exactly where do you think I'm from, cowboy?"

I grin at her before returning my gaze to the road. "I'd say the West Coast. Maybe California? Oregon?"

"You're good, Bradyn, I'll give you that." She smiles. "I was born in Oregon, though I spent a good portion of my life in California."

"Then I have to ask again; what brought you to Texas?"

"A friend of mine told me about this town. He said he'd stop here whenever he was driving into Dallas. I was looking for a change in scenery, so I came here."

"And loved it so much you decided to stay?"

"For now," she replies with a smile then shifts her attention back out the window.

Those two words hang in the air between us. Truth be told, most of our help doesn't move on unless they're relocating for family, looking to settle down, or they retire. So even though the idea that she's just here as a temporary stay had absolutely crossed my mind, I'd just dismissed it. Now it seems my fears are confirmed.

"You move around a lot?"

"I like to travel."

It's a lie. I can tell in her tone that she's not being

honest, but I drop it because it's her business, not mine. I'm desperate to know, though. Desperate to get to know the woman beneath the walls she so carefully hides behind.

# CHAPTER 17
# KENNEDY

This was a mistake.

We're not even thirty minutes into the drive, and I've already given him more information than anyone else I've crossed paths with since the marshals were killed. I take a deep breath. *Get it together, Kennedy. This man could be your enemy if he ever finds out the truth.*

"How about you?" If I redirect the conversation, maybe we can move past the awkward silence at my clipped answer.

"What about me?" he asks.

"You were obviously born and raised here in Texas, but you left to join the Army. What made you return?"

"This is home," he replies. "I love this town and the ranch. Coming home was always part of the plan."

"What about the traveling you do now? I don't know

much about it except that you were off saving the world. Do you still do contractor work for the government?"

Something in his gaze darkens. "Something like that," he replies.

More awkward silence.

Both of us have walls, and neither of us seems willing to let the other see what's behind them. "Did you go to college after the service?"

"No. Never felt the desire to spend time behind a desk."

"Had enough of it by graduation, then?" I ask.

He laughs. "Never had to. We were homeschooled our whole lives."

"Really?"

"Yeah, it was great. We got to do our schoolwork in the first part of the day, were done by lunch, then spent the rest of the afternoon running around like wild children on the ranch."

I smile. "Seems we have some solid ground, cowboy."

He glances over at me and arches a brow. "Oh, yeah?"

"I was homeschooled too," I tell him honestly. "Both of my parents worked from home, so we got to spend a lot of time together." My throat burns with emotion, and I try to swallow down the fresh wave of pain.

"Eventually, if I get lucky enough that God blesses me with a family, I'm hoping I get to offer my kids the same type of life I had."

His words tug at my heartstrings.

If God is truly listening, I hope He grants Bradyn his desires. I may not know him well, but if anyone deserves a family to love, a wife to hold, and children to raise, it's this man right here.

"I'm sure it'll happen for you," I tell him with a soft smile. Then, after a few more moments of awkward silence, I clear my throat. "Well, this conversation got heavy. How about something lighter? Do you like music?"

"I do."

"What kinds?"

"Country, but I listen to a lot of Christian rock, too."

"Christian rock? That's a thing?" I ask, arching a brow.

His grin would've knocked me right down if I'd been standing. "You ever heard of Skillet?"

"I know what a skillet is."

Leaning forward, he grabs his phone from the cup holder and tosses it to me. "Code is 0214. Unlock it and open up the music app. It's the top playlist."

---

WITH EVERYTHING NEEDED for the barn rebuild ordered and on the schedule to be delivered tomorrow, our task list for the morning is done. It's definitely bittersweet knowing this outing is nearly over, even though every moment I spend with Bradyn Hunt, I like him more. What's not to like?

He's handsome, strong, smart, and I watched him quite

literally load a bunch of stuff into the back of an elderly woman's car when he saw she was struggling.

Which means we might as well go ahead and add kind to that list, too.

We haven't spoken a whole lot since stopping to eat, though, and the silence is deafening. "So Skillet is a cool band. I never would've thought Christian rock was a thing."

He laughs and plucks a fry off of his tray. "They're my favorite. Saw them in concert a few years back. Elliot and I were in Lubbock, and they had a show, so we popped in. Was a great show."

"That's awesome. I've never been to a concert. Hope to go one day, though."

"Really? Never?"

I shake my head. "I was relatively sheltered."

"Well, maybe we can go one day. I'd love to see them again."

Does he realize he essentially just asked me out? Or was it just a friend thing? Either way, my heart leaps at the thought of spending more time with him, even as the pit in my stomach reminds me it's impossible. "Maybe."

"Do you have any siblings?" he asks.

"What?" That sick feeling returns.

"You know all about my family. I was just curious." He eats another fry.

"Um. No. I had a friend who was like a sister, but she isn't with us anymore."

"I'm really sorry to hear that."

"Thanks. You and your family all seem really close," I reply. "Even Lani."

He grins. "Yeah, we're all a tight-knit bunch. Though my brothers do tend to drive me and each other crazy from time to time. Lani handles us all effortlessly."

"I definitely get that feeling. She's great."

"She is. Our lives got immensely better after she came along."

The way this family loves each other makes my heart ache for the knowledge that I'll never have that. If I'm ever lucky enough for this nightmare to end and I end up getting the chance to have a family of my own, I'll never get to take them to where I grew up. They'll never see where their mom came from or have grandparents on my side they get to be spoiled by.

My heart sinks as my throat burns with emotion. *Bury it, Kennedy. It'll do no good now.* "Well, this is the best burger I've ever had." I pluck another fry from my tray and eat it.

"I always stop here on my way back from the lumber yard because no one makes a burger like Earl." He turns and waves at the man standing in the window of the food truck.

He waves back then returns to prepping an order for two people standing near the trailer.

"What's on the plan for the rest of the day?" I ask curiously, hoping it's something I can partake in too. The idea of returning to the ranch and going our separate ways is less appealing than it was just this morning.

"I'm going to take a look at everything they got done at the ranch then head over to Piney Hill to see what I can do to lend a hand."

"Do you guys always do that? Just offer help whenever it's needed?"

"We do."

"Why?"

"It's what God calls us to do," he says simply. "We're supposed to serve others."

"That simple."

"That simple," he replies. When I don't immediately respond, he finishes eating another fry then asks, "You seem skeptical."

"I am. A little. I didn't grow up in church, and the idea that there's a greater purpose to all of this seems a little far-fetched to me."

"Why is that?" There's no judgment in his tone, just genuine curiosity.

"I don't know. There's a lot of bad stuff that happens in this world. I'm sure you saw some of it when you were overseas. Doesn't really fit the idea that we were all created and are loved, does it?"

He's quiet a moment, clearly processing what I said. Then he wipes his hands on a napkin and takes a drink of his tea. "There were moments where I thought to myself, 'Why is He allowing this to happen? Why not stop these things from ever taking place at all?'"

"Exactly. How can you continue to have such faith when the world is full of so much darkness?"

"Human nature is to sin. We live in a world that's full of it, and the further humans get from God, the worse it gets." He sits up straighter on the bench seat of the picnic table we're sitting at. For a moment, the only sound around us is the steady buzzing of the propane heater beside us. "But every time I've gone to God in prayer and asked Him why these things were happening, I have the same verse pop into my mind, along with this overwhelming sense of peace in the knowledge that, one day, there will be no pain."

"What verse?"

"Proverbs 3. 'Trust in the Lord with all your heart and lean not on your own understanding,'" he replies. "We will never be able to fully understand or comprehend God's plan for each and every one of us. But there is a plan. Sometimes we must suffer, but in that suffering, we find a well of faith we never knew was there. God is in everything; we only have to seek Him."

"It just seems out there," I reply. "I'm sorry, I don't

mean that to be offensive. I just— Things have happened in my life that made me feel very alone. And I'm not sure how to open my heart to that."

"Pray," he replies. "Open your heart to Him, and He'll lead you where you need to be."

"That sounds too easy to be true."

He chuckles. "I can promise you that there's nothing easy about it. But it's certainly worth it." His cell rings, and he pulls it out of his pocket and puts it on speaker so he can eat another fry. "You're on speaker," he says. "What is it?"

"You seen the news yet?" Elliot questions through the phone, his tone frustrated.

"No. Why? The ranch make headlines?"

"Something like that. I was surprised to see that you let her talk to Sharon."

Bradyn sits up a bit straighter, his expression darkening ever so slightly. "What do you mean? Who?"

"Sammy," he replies. "The two of you are all over the front page."

# CHAPTER 18
# BRADYN

I f ever there was a day I might actually lose the leash I've put on my temper, it would be today. I told Sharon that I wanted employees to be kept quiet. I specifically told her that, unless Sammy wanted to speak with her, she was not to be included in the article.

And what happened?

The woman somehow managed to get an immense amount of information—far beyond what I told her—on the fire itself, and the damage, as well as the full scoop on Sammy—her injuries, what happened that night, and a photo of her that was clearly taken from a distance sometime before even I came back home. The green magnolia trees in the background serve as proof of that.

I glare down at the newspaper in front of me as I try to decide how I want to proceed. Sammy was furious when I told her. Even angrier when she saw the image printed of her in the newspaper. She'd insisted on going home and barely spoke the entire ride back.

Which just makes me even angrier. Whoever fed Sharon this information ruined what was turning into a great trip.

Someone knocks on my door. "Come in," I call out. The door remains unlocked as it usually is. Bravo raises his head as Dylan comes in, looking just as cruddy as I feel. "It was Arthur," he says. "They had dinner last night, and she sweet-talked him into providing not just the photograph but all of the information, too."

"He's fired." He was already on thin ice, and I have a zero-tolerance policy for providing any information to anyone outside of this ranch unless I've given explicit permission.

It's in all the contracts our new hires sign and something I refuse to bend on.

While we don't have secrets here, I want to avoid drama or fallacies from being spread about this place. And keeping our employees tight-lipped is the best way to do it.

"Already done. He's packing his stuff as we speak."

"Good. Thanks."

"You looked a little close to a lit fuse, so I figured I'd handle it for you. Sammy okay?"

"She was relatively quiet on the drive back, but I know she's mad."

"I would be, too. Guy made her sound like a helpless damsel in need of rescuing. Sammy isn't like that at all."

"It's just part of the many things I'm angry about." I cross my arms and lean back against the counter. "I told Sharon to drop it. That, unless Sammy wanted to talk to her, there was nothing anyone else had to say."

"You going to deal with her?"

"There's not much I can do. I already sent off an email to the editor of the paper, letting them know that Hunt Ranch does not appreciate what was printed, nor do we endorse it, but what's done is done. This is hardly the first time we've had a news story printed about us we didn't care for."

"You're not wrong there."

It wasn't too long ago that an employee we'd fired for being abusive toward our horses went to the news and told them that Hunt Ranch was a hazardous place to work and that he'd been fired for no reason. The article was a complete fallacy, of course, and given that everyone in town knows it, there wasn't a ton of backlash. But that was the straw that had us tightening up our hiring process.

This ranch is the largest in the area, and the last thing we need is to end up a target for someone looking to make a name for themselves.

"It wasn't a bad article, at least. Aside from the way she portrayed Sammy, of course. That was pathetic."

"Sharon loves to tear people down," I remind him. "It's

what she's always been good at." I rub my hands over my face and sigh. "Okay, so Arthur has been fired. He'll be gone by morning. That's one problem taken care of. The email to the editor has been sent, and while I don't expect anything to come from it, I can only hope they'll be more cautious. And as far as Sharon goes, we keep her off the property. I don't want to see her anywhere near this ranch. We can't risk her getting wind of the details linked to the Search & Rescue side of things because once she does—"

"Operating off the record will get a lot more difficult if there are any photographs of us out there linking us to specific cases. I got it. She stays off the property."

"Then that's all we can do."

"What about Sammy? She was really upset?"

"Yeah. She was. I'll talk to her. Mom called and said she'd have dinner ready by seven. I'll take Sammy hers."

Dylan nods. "How'd today go, by the way? How was your outing?"

"What do you mean?"

"Don't play dumb with me."

"We had a good time. Sammy's a good worker."

"She's gorgeous, too. And kind. Smart." He's fishing, but I don't intend to bite.

"Sounds like you're interested."

He laughs. "Nah, I like her fine, but not the way you clearly do."

"As I told you before, I barely know her."

"You should know her better after the drive today. Or did you keep your foot in your mouth and not actually ask anything of value?"

I glare at him. "We had a great time until—" Another knock at the door. "Come in."

Elliot opens the door. "We have company."

"Who?"

"Some guy in a black SUV. Asked to speak with you directly."

"Did he say who he was?"

Elliot's expression says it all. Whoever this guy is, it's not good news.

"I'll head up now. Dylan, check in with Riley and see if Arthur called in a suit."

"Will do."

"Do you really think he called a lawyer?" Elliot asks as we head for the front door.

"It wouldn't be the first time." I roll my shoulders. "Bravo, *heel.*" The dog jumps up and follows me out the door, keeping close by as we make our way toward my truck. Dylan jumps onto a four-wheeler and takes off toward the cabins while Elliot gets behind the wheel of his own truck.

"Something feels off about this," he says before closing his door. "I can't pinpoint why, but something feels off."

"Let's find out what he wants," I tell him. "Then we'll see if there's something to worry about." I wait for Bravo to jump in then climb in behind him and shut my door. Given the nature of our company, it could be someone needing us.

We're word of mouth only, so if that's why this guy is here, he'll know one of our other clients, too. But somehow, I seriously doubt this guy is here to ask for our help. I'm not sure how I know, but I just do.

Call it discernment, intuition…whatever it is, I have a pit in my stomach.

The drive up to the main house doesn't take too long, but by the time I've put my truck into Park, I've managed to pray my way out of coming into this impromptu meeting on the defensive.

A black SUV with tinted windows sits in front of my parents' house. Two men wearing dark suits stand just outside of it, and even though their eyes are covered with dark sunglasses, I can feel their gazes on me as I get out of the truck.

Bravo jumps out with me, and as we get closer, his body language shifts from happy puppy to attentive working dog. He doesn't like them.

And I trust his intuition over even my own.

I make my way into the house to find both of my parents sitting at a table with a middle-aged man wearing a black button-down suit. The slight bulge beneath his left arm means he's armed, too.

My mom gets up when she sees me. "Bradyn, this is Klive Newart." He stands and offers me his hand.

"Mr. Newart," I greet. "Bradyn Hunt." I shake his hand, noting the way he squeezes as a form of intimidation. If only he knew I'm not intimidated by any man who walks this earth.

"It's great to meet you," he replies then releases my hand and takes a seat. "I was just telling your mother here that she makes the best sweet tea in the country."

My mom blushes. "Well, I don't know if that's true, but I appreciate the compliment."

Dad has yet to say anything, so I momentarily let my gaze travel to where he sits at the end of the table, noting the stiffness of his posture. He doesn't like this man either. "Come on, Ruth," he says. "Let's leave them to this meeting." He doesn't spare another glance at the man as he takes my mom's hand, though he offers me a look that speaks volumes. *Be careful.*

I take a seat, and Bravo sits beside me, his gaze trained straight ahead at the stranger. "What can I do for you, Mr. Newart?"

"Right to the point, then?" he asks with a laugh. "I like you, Mr. Hunt."

"Bradyn," I correct. "And I don't see the point in beating around the bush."

"I'm not a fan of that, either," he says. As he reaches into his jacket pocket, Bravo lets loose a low warning growl. "Just grabbing a piece of paper," he tells us with a smile that's dripping with venom. "My employer is looking for someone, and we think you might be able to help."

"Who recommended you?" It's not typically the first question we ask, but given Bravo's reaction combined with my own gut feeling, I need to know who sent this man my way so I can determine whether or not he can be trusted.

"My employer didn't say," he replies.

"Then who is your employer?"

Klive smiles, but there's no kindness in it. "My employer must remain anonymous. At least until you accept the job. Then you can sign an NDA, and we'll go from there."

"Then we don't have any business here." I stand, and Bravo gets to his feet. The other man doesn't move, though.

"I'm afraid I must insist on anonymity."

"And I'm afraid that I must insist on declining this job. I don't work for people I don't know, and I won't accept the job without knowing who's offering it."

His expression turns even more frustrated. "He's looking for his daughter." He sets a photograph down on the table, and I stare down at the young woman in the picture. Leaning forward, I take it from the table, that pit in my stomach turning into a full-on canyon.

Her hair color is different, darker than the strands of sunshine pulled back into a tight ballerina bun. But those eyes—I'd recognize them anywhere. Even though they're dull compared to the real thing.

Sammy is staring back at me, her expression unreadable. Both hands are folded in her lap, and she's wearing a pink skirt and a pink suit jacket. The background is neutral, clearly a photo studio of some kind.

"Who is your employer?" I ask again, setting the photograph down as I mask my expression. Until I know the entire situation and get a chance to talk to Sammy, I'll betray nothing.

"Senator Alexander Brown," he replies in frustration, clearly realizing that, unless he starts answering my questions, I have nothing to say. "That's his daughter, Olivia. She's been missing two years and is believed to be in grave danger."

"Was there a call for ransom?"

"No. She was just gone one night, and he hasn't seen her since. We heard no word from anyone, and no one made the claim that they'd seen her."

"Then what makes you think she's still alive?"

"Because of this." He lifts a newspaper from the table and tosses it toward me, Sammy's picture face-up. It's grainy, of course, given that it's an article, but clear enough that someone looking for her will draw conclusions. "This woman works here, right?"

"You believe that the daughter of a senator is being held

captive on this ranch? Is that the accusation you're throwing my direction?"

"Of course not. I'm merely suggesting you aren't fully aware of the people on your staff."

"The woman that works here is named Sammy. She's been employed here for a month, just like the article states."

"We're considering the possibility that she ran away and has been in hiding. If that's the case, using a pseudonym wouldn't be out of the question."

Every alarm bell in my head is screeching at full volume. There's something wrong here, very, *very* wrong. "I'm afraid that, if you're here to interrogate my employees, I can't help you. Have a good day, Mr. Newart."

"Just let me speak with her. If it's not Olivia, then there's no harm, correct?"

"*Sammy* was already interrogated enough. Which you would know if you read that article. She's injured, and I will not be putting her through any more stress, so you can check a box for your employer. I'm sorry his daughter is missing, and I truly wish you the best of luck in tracking her down." I gesture toward the door.

"She's precious to him." Switching tactics, he tries pleading.

"I'm sure she is, and if I believed that she was working here on the ranch, I would handle it."

"You find people, don't you? That's the nature of your business." When I don't respond, he keeps speaking. "You won't even give tracking Olivia a try?"

"I don't make the call alone. Leave the file, and I'll discuss with my partners then get back to you on whether or not we'll take the case."

"You don't know this woman," he insists, pointing to the newspaper. "If she hasn't been working here long. She could be anyone. It's really not that difficult to get onto this property. She could be right under your nose, and you wouldn't even sense the threat until it was too late." The underlying threat does not go unnoticed by me. Bravo lets loose another warning growl as the man takes a step closer to me.

"I miss very little, Mr. Newart. And I can assure you that I have everything here under control. But if it makes you feel better, I'll happily take your accusations to Sammy so we can all have a good laugh about it later. Now, if you'll excuse me, I have work to do, and you're currently standing in the way of that."

He glares at me for a moment, a clear challenge in his dark gaze. Then he drops the mask back into place and smiles. "I hope that you know your employees better than I do, Mr. Hunt." Reaching into his pocket, he withdraws a business card and sets it on the table. "If you happen to see anything, please give me a call."

I don't touch the card, nor do I lead him out of the house. Exposing my back to this man seems a dangerous game I've no intention of playing.

"I am sorry for your wasted trip," I reply. "I do hope it wasn't a long one."

"It was well worth it, Mr. Hunt," he says as he pulls the door open. "Have a great day. Tell your mother I really appreciated her tea. Hopefully, I'll be able to have some again someday." He heads down the porch toward his vehicle where one of the suits opens his door and the other climbs behind the wheel.

My dad steps out onto the porch as they're pulling out of the drive. "Something about that man was off."

"I agree."

"What did he want?"

"He was looking for someone." I turn to my dad. "When you hired Sammy, did she have any next of kin listed?"

"No," he replies. "I don't think so. We can check her employee file, though." He turns and heads into the house.

"I'll be right there. I need to check in with Dylan." Pulling my phone out of my pocket, I give him a call.

"Hey, what's up?"

"I need you to make sure that SUV leaves the property. It's top priority. Track him and make sure he doesn't double back."

"Headed to my truck now."

I end the call and wait until I see Dylan's truck pulling away from the employee cabins. He offers me a wave as he passes our parents' house, and only when I'm certain it's safe do I head inside.

# CHAPTER 19
# BRADYN

Sammy's file is a fake.

A very, very good fake but a fake nonetheless.

Tucker pieces together an email and sends it off to Elijah Breeth, a former Ranger turned private security specialist who works with my cousin Silas. Then he spins around to face my father and me.

"You had no suspicions when you hired her?" I ask Dad, who stands beside me.

"No. I asked her the typical questions and had her fill out the application."

"I ran the background check myself," Tucker offers. "But I didn't go very deep. Just the basic surface-level one I run for everyone we hire."

"You couldn't have known." Even as frustrated as I am that someone was hired under a false identity, I can't blame

Tucker. Deep background dives are standard procedure for our Search & Rescue business, but not for the ranch. Though they will be going forward. Another lesson learned.

The second we started pulling tax records—which *technically* we're not supposed to do—her identity fell apart. Sammy Lewis, as she put on her application, has never voted, paid taxes, or attended any kind of public school in the nation. The latter was not a surprise given she told me she was homeschooled, but she should still be somewhere.

And she's not.

"We'll get it figured out, son," my father says. "We'll sit down with her and figure it all out."

I take a deep breath and offer him a smile. "I know, Dad. I'm going to get some air." I head out of Tucker's home office and onto the porch. Bravo is with me where he's been ever since Klive Newart left.

We looked into him, too. Not only is he employed by Senator Alexander Brown, but he's also his son. Klive Newart is actually Klive Brown—something he failed to mention when he was here. Olivia Brown, the daughter in question, is his stepsister and was taken in when she'd been twelve and her mother passed away suddenly.

The articles called it a suicide. But I get the feeling there's more to all of this than I can find written in black and white.

Riley's been keeping an eye on Sammy's cabin for the

last hour, and Dylan returned as soon as the SUV hit the freeway, though I have him ensuring our security measures are fully in place. Tucker and Elliot escorted Arthur off of the premises hours ago, so that's at least one less thing we have to worry about.

My mom's car pulls up into Tucker's driveway, and she climbs out carrying a small bag. "Hey, honey."

"Hey," I greet as I make my way down the steps to give her a hug. "How are you holding up?"

"Just fine. I talked with God, and He calmed me as He always does." She smiles and hands me the bag. "Here's Sammy's dinner. I was going to take it down, but Riley told me I needed to leave it to you. Care to elaborate?"

"Once I know more, I will."

"I don't mind being left out of some things, but I care for the girl. If there's something going on—"

"I'll tell you about it." I kiss her on the head. "Right now, I need to talk to Sammy first."

My mom nods in understanding. "Very well. I'm going to head inside and grab your dad. There's enough food in there for you, too, if you want to eat while you talk."

"You're the best. Thanks, Mom."

With a final smile, she heads up the porch stairs, so I turn and open the door of my truck. Bravo hops in before me, and we head across the ranch toward the employee cabins. Riley is sitting in his own truck and rolls the passenger window down as I park beside him and climb out.

"No movement inside," he says. "She must have really been out of it when y'all got back."

"She was tired," I tell him. "And said she had a nasty headache starting."

"What was all that with the suit?"

"We'll talk later. I need to check on Sammy. Dad and Tucker know though, so if you want info before I can get it to you, check with them."

"Sounds good. You good here?"

"Yeah, thanks."

"Anytime, brother." Rolling up his window, he backs out and heads toward the main house, so I take the food and Bravo and head up to the front door.

I knock. "Sammy, it's Bradyn. I've got your dinner."

No answer.

I knock again. Is it possible she's sleeping? She did say her head hurt; maybe she laid down and—Bravo growls. A deep, threatening growl.

My stomach plummets as I set the soup aside and draw my firearm. "Sammy? If that's you, I'm coming in, okay?"

Still no answer.

Reaching forward, I check the handle. It turns easily, so I shove the door open. "*Such,* Bravo," I order. *Search.* He darts inside, and I follow, weapon at the ready. But from the moment I cross the threshold, I know I won't find her.

The place is tossed. Every nook and cranny searched. Her mattress has been ripped open with a blade, its stuffing all over the floor. Cabinets were left open, the dishes that were once tucked away inside now littering the countertops.

Someone was looking for something in addition to the someone I fear they found.

"Sammy?" I call out. *Please, God, let her be all right. Please let her be all right.* Even as I fear the worst, I make my way through the cabin, stepping into the bathroom and clearing the entire place before I lower my weapon and withdraw my phone.

"What is it?" Elliot answers on the first ring.

"Get the others and get to Sammy's cabin. Now."

"What happened?"

My heart thuds in my chest as I try to wrap my head around all that's happened today. "Sammy's gone, and someone tossed her place."

---

"I AGREE WITH TUCKER. Sammy is not Sammy," Elijah replies on speakerphone. "Though it's a great surface story —seriously, I commend whoever created it for her—once you really start digging, it falls apart."

"That's what we found too," Tucker replies. "I'm still kicking myself for not seeing through it."

"Don't," Elijah says. "I wouldn't have seen through it, either. Not without checking those tax records. I even ran her through a medical database, and nothing popped."

Which explains why she didn't want X-rays. Because she knew as soon as they put her in, the façade would crumble.

"Is she Olivia Brown?" I ask, though, in my gut, I know the answer.

"That's still not one hundred percent," he replies. "Especially since the photo you sent of Sammy isn't an exact facial match for an old newspaper article I found about the Browns."

"What do you mean?"

"I scrubbed the web for a photograph of Olivia Brown and couldn't find anything except for a science fair project she won in the third grade. The photograph was super grainy though, so it's possible that she is a match and the distortion can't give me a complete read."

"There are no photographs of her? She's the daughter of a public servant." Riley crosses his arms. "That doesn't make any sense."

"Someone removed her," Elijah replies. "And they did a good job."

"Likely after she was taken. My guess is they wanted to keep it out of the media," Tucker adds. "This is a mess."

"The guy who was here today didn't look like a political aide," my father interjects. My mother is standing beside him, her face pale, eyes wide. She's shaken, and it breaks my heart to see it.

"No," I agree, turning my attention back to the phone. If I can find her, I can fix this. I have to find her. "He was the senator's son. Olivia Brown's stepbrother."

The expressions on my brothers' faces harden.

"Something stinks here." Tucker crosses his arms. "And the only person who can answer anything for us is missing."

"Thanks, Elijah. You'll keep digging?"

"Always," he replies. "Check in with you if I find something."

After ending the call, I shove the phone into my pocket. "Tucker, did you find anything on the security camera footage?" I ask.

"Not a thing. We didn't pick up anyone in or out of her cabin. With the trees, there are some blind spots, but they're few and far between. Someone would have to have a map of the layout in order to get out unnoticed."

"Or have worked here and have a great memory," I consider.

"You think she mapped out the security cameras?" Riley questions.

"I think she was hiding from them." My thoughts run loose over the course of what she said earlier today. She'd said she was settled 'for now' and that she moved a lot.

"When you're on the run, the first thing you do is carve out an exit strategy."

"You're going to look for her, aren't you?" Elliot asks.

"She's in trouble, and I intend to find out why." I take the photograph Tucker printed of Sammy and stick it into my pocket.

"Are you sure you should go? Don't you do rotations so you have time to get your mind right?" my mother asks. "I don't want you running out there so soon after you just got back. What if you're not ready to be back in the field?"

"I'll be fine, Mom. I promise." I can't tell her that I stay ready. That there's never been a moment in my adult life that I wasn't prepared for war. Because if I tell her that I can't ever find rest, it'll break her heart.

She just stares back at me.

"Even though we all knew her longer, Bradyn spent more time with her. He has the best chance of finding her," Elliot offers.

My mom nods. "Just be careful. Something about this feels wrong."

"I agree, but I need to know if she ran or was taken. Someone was in her cabin, and we don't have footage of that either. It's possible someone managed to dodge the cameras."

"It's possible." Riley shakes his head. "Or she tossed the place to cover her tracks."

"You want me to leave her out there?"

"No, of course not," Elliot replies. "But rushing out without a plan isn't smart either."

"I'm not rushing out without a plan. Bravo and I will go after Sammy while you all make sure no one gets onto this property without you knowing about it. Whatever you have to do, fill those blind spots with something."

"That would require cutting down trees," Riley says.

"Then do it."

My brothers fall silent a moment.

"What's got you spooked?" Elliot questions. "There something you aren't telling us?"

"Not spooked," I reply. "Just cautious. Klive made a couple comments today that sounded an awful lot like threats, and I'll take no chances. As soon as I catch up with Sammy, we'll come back here with some answers. Until then, we need to make sure we have our bases covered."

I get to my feet, and Bravo falls into step beside me.

"Are you sure you don't want backup?" Elliot asks.

"No. Bravo and I can cover good ground. I want all hands on deck back here just in case something goes wrong." I start toward the door.

"Wait!" my mother calls out. She rushes forward and wraps her arms around me in a hug. Pulling away, she cups my face just as she did when I was a child.

"I have to track her down and make sure she's safe."

Nodding, she releases my face. "I know that, honey. You be safe too. Okay? I don't think Sammy is wrapped up in anything bad. At least, not that's her fault, she's far too sweet for that."

"We'll get to the bottom of it," I promise her, careful not to add to that feeling. Truth be told, I think Sammy might just be the missing Olivia Brown. And I think she's been on the run. The reason is still a mystery to me, but I intend to find out as soon as I get the chance.

I just have to get to her before they do.

---

THIRTEEN HOURS and two states later, I'm pulling my truck into a rest stop. As I turn off the engine, I note the black sedan that pulls in right after me, parking a handful of spots to the right of me even though there were plenty right up near me.

At first, my tail was a black SUV. Then, once I hit Tulsa, it dropped off, and a white van took its place. This particular sedan caught up to me in Little Rock. But I intend to lose it here.

Climbing out of the truck, I step aside and call Bravo forward. After clipping his leash onto the vest that reads *working dog*, I let him jump out, grab my bag, and make my way into the rest stop. The bus station in town told me that Sammy booked a one-way ticket to Springfield, Missouri, claiming she needed to see her sick aunt.

So, Springfield is where we're headed. I'm just hoping

we're the first to track her down and that we get there before she makes her next move.

As I always do when Bravo is with me, I get some weird looks. And since I didn't see the driver or passenger of the sedan get out, I make my way up to the young guy working the cash register.

He's likely mid-twenties and looks far more bored than I think I ever have in my life.

"Hey, my truck broke down, and I was wondering if there's a bus station near here? I need to get to Memphis."

"Man, that's a bummer. But yeah. There's a station about a mile up the road. They have a lot of routes they run, so you might find some luck."

"Great, thanks."

"No problem. Cute dog."

I glance down at Bravo, and he tilts his head as he looks back at me. "You hear that, bud? You're cute." I look back at the kid. "Thanks for the tip." After reaching into my wallet, I pull out a hundred and slide it over the counter. "If anyone asks about me, tell them I went in another direction."

He grins and takes the bill like I just handed him the world. "You got it, man. No questions."

I head toward the back of the rest stop and slip through the kitchen which, thanks to the early hours, isn't operating right now. The back door doesn't have an alarm notice, so I take the risk and push it open, peering outside before taking Bravo all the way out.

The grass is tall behind the gas station, so we move quickly and silently, using the still-dark morning to shield us from unwanted attention.

By the time the tail realizes I'm not coming out, Bravo and I will be on a bus and hopefully closer to Sammy.

# CHAPTER 20
# KENNEDY

"Thanks so much." I take the key and shove it into my pocket then use the single crutch I managed to bring with me to make my way back out of the office and toward the stairs. I stare at them, intimidated by the sheer height I'm about to have to climb with only one good foot.

I'm already exhausted from the travel, dirty from having to slip off of the ranch on what equates to pretty much a single good foot, but it's the idea of a hot shower that has me putting one foot in front of the other, using the rest of my strength to make my way up the steps. Normally, I insist on a low-level motel room, but they were booked solid except for one room on the second floor.

The next motel isn't for another fifteen miles, and since the bus station doesn't open until six tomorrow morning, I'm out of options.

By the sheer force of my desire to rest, I make it to the top.

My ankle is throbbing. I haven't had the chance to take any pain meds since I left Hunt Ranch sixteen hours ago. Sixteen hours on three different buses, all while I try to outrun a past that seems hell-bent on taking me out.

I can't believe she put my photograph in the newspaper. I can't believe Bradyn let her. Why would they give her that image? Why allow it to be run without my permission? I hadn't even known it was being taken.

Anger burns through my veins as I unlock the door and shove it open to reveal a mildewy-smelling room with two double beds, an old block of a television, and a bathroom. The red-and-gold floral comforters likely haven't been replaced in decades, but I can at least hope the sheets are clean.

After ensuring the door is locked up tight, I prop a chair beneath the handle and peek out the window. The parking lot is dark, and there's no movement, so I find it in me to relax just slightly.

I got out before they found me. That is if they're even still looking.

I toss the crutch down and half-hop into the bathroom. Of course they're still looking. They'll never stop looking. I'm enemy number one, and I'm not even entirely sure why. The shower comes on with a groan, and there's a few seconds of delay before the hot water hits the bottom of the dingy-looking bathtub.

It's not much. But it'll do tonight.

Someone knocks on the door.

My heart jumps. I leave the water on then withdraw my firearm and limp toward the door.

Another knock.

Is it possible they caught up with me? That I didn't slip out of Pine Creek fast enough?

Another knock.

Adrenaline pulsing through my system, I peek up into the peephole on the door, only to find myself staring at someone I'd already told myself I'd never see again. *How did he find me?*

"I know you're in there, Sammy. Open up so we can talk."

My first instinct is to pull the door open. But as I'm reaching for the handle to do just that, another thought hits me. What if he's part of it? What if somehow I ended up on the doorstep of someone with ties back to the very people I'm trying to avoid?

"Sammy. Whatever you're wrapped up in is big, and I can't help if you don't let me in."

"How do I know I can trust you?" I call back.

"If you don't already know that you can, then I can't help you."

If he wanted to hurt me, he's had plenty of chances to do it already. He quite literally knew where I slept, and then there was that whole ride home from the café, and the car trip to the lumber yard. At any moment, he could've followed through with what they've been trying to do for the last two years.

Yet he didn't.

Bradyn Hunt was nothing but kind to me.

My thoughts drift back to Cillian. He'd been kind to me too. And he'd nearly paid the ultimate price for it. The same price as all the others did. But I'm so tired of running alone. Of hiding. Of barely living. I'm just—so, so tired.

"Sammy." The way he says my name undoes me. So even though it might be the biggest mistake I've ever made, I unlock the door and pull it open, though I maintain the hold on my weapon.

His expression is hard, his eyes narrowed as he looks me up and down, momentarily focusing on my firearm. "You planning on shooting me?"

"That depends."

"On what?"

"Why you're here." Stepping aside, I allow him and Bravo to enter my room. The dog's ears are perked forward, his focus on inspecting my room thoroughly. After he's looked through the entire room and peeked into the bathroom, he comes back and sits at Bradyn's side.

As soon as he does, Bradyn shuts and locks the door

then sets a black tactical backpack onto the floor directly beside it.

"Care to explain how you found me?" I ask.

"It's what I do," he replies. Silence settles over us again. He's furious, even angrier than he was when he'd found me during that storm. "Care to explain why you ran, Olivia?"

*Olivia.* I haven't heard that name in years, and it's an instant punch to my gut. The USB drive around my neck feels heavier at the mere mention of the one who gave it to me. Anger sings through my veins, even as every worry I had that he was a part of this thing vanishes.

Because if he were a part of it, he'd know there's no way I could be Olivia Brown.

"I'm not Olivia."

"No? You sure look a lot like her. And the suit who showed up at my ranch yesterday certainly thought you were."

I stiffen. "Who was it? Who showed up?"

"A man named Klive Brown."

My entire body goes rigid, and I can feel the blood drain from my face. Stumbling back, I drop down onto the bed, sitting at the edge while I try to regain my rational thinking. *He did find me.* That means it's only a matter of time before—"Did he hurt them? Are they okay? How did you get away?"

"They're fine. He didn't hurt anyone. Breathe, Sammy."

"I have to go. Now." I push up and limp into the bathroom to shut off the water.

As soon as I turn around to head back into the main room, I run into a hard body blocking my way. Large hands go to my shoulders.

"Easy."

"If you found me, it's only a matter of time before they do."

"First off, I'm exceptional at what I do, which is how I found you. Second, I shook the tail they put on me already. Now, I do agree we need to move, but you need to relax for a second. Okay? Tell me what's going on."

I take a deep breath as Bradyn releases my shoulders and steps back. And because my ankle feels like it's on fire, I take a seat on the edge of the bed closest to the bathroom, leaving my gun on top of the mattress beside me.

Bradyn leans back against the desk across from me while Bravo lies by the front door.

"You said you're not Olivia Brown."

"No." I meet his gaze. "Olivia Brown is dead. She was murdered two years ago, along with three U.S. Marshals and both of my parents."

Emotion flicks over his expression before the hardened soldier mask returns. "Then why is it Olivia's stepbrother accused you of being her?"

"Because they can't admit that she's dead. Doing so would raise too many questions." Tears burn in the corners of my eyes as I reach down and rub my ankle. "The main one being that they didn't report her missing two years ago."

"Hang on." Bradyn heads over toward his pack and kneels, his back to me. Without his gaze focused on me, I can fully appreciate the way it feels to have him here. I've spent so many years relying only on myself. Focusing only on keeping my head while I survived day-to-day.

Can he really help me?

*"It's what I do."* I may not know exactly what the brothers do on the side, but is it possible he'll have contacts that can be trusted? People not on Brown's payroll?

Pills rattle in a bottle as he carries them over to me, along with a bottle of water. "It's not much, but—"

I nearly weep at the sight of the blue-and-white Advil bottle. "It's perfect. Thank you." Popping the top, I take two gel capsules and drink down the entire bottle of water he handed me.

"I figured you might be hurting when I found you. Not that I could tell how much you took with you, but I assumed the load was light."

"What do you mean?" I set the empty bottle beside me as he leans back against the desk.

"Your cabin was tossed. So unless you did that to throw us off—"

"I didn't," I interrupt. They were so close to me. I haven't been gone a full twenty-four hours and they've already tossed my place? "I should have moved on weeks ago. It was a mistake to stay as long as I did."

"Then why did you?"

"It was the first place that felt like home in a long time," I tell him truthfully.

The silence between us stretches on. "So, the son of a senator is pretending you're his sister. Why?"

"He had her killed." The nightmare from two years ago comes rushing back in a solid wave of pain. Bradyn remains silent while I collect myself. "Olivia was my room-mate in college. We'd roomed together our freshman, sophomore, and junior years. She came back from spring break looking like she'd spent the week in hell." I remember her wide, red-rimmed eyes and the way she'd been constantly checking over her shoulder. "When she finally opened up to me, it was just to say that she'd seen things she wasn't supposed to and that she'd grabbed proof before running."

"Proof of what?"

I shake my head then reach into my shirt and withdraw the drive I've worn ever since she died. "She never told me. Just that she had it and had contacted the authorities. They showed up that same night and took us both into custody."

"What happened next?"

"It all moved really fast. My parents were brought in

and placed in protection as well; since the marshals were worried that they'd be used as leverage against me."

"But you didn't know anything."

"Apparently, that didn't matter. Klive thought I did, so I was a risk. Olivia was never the same. Whatever she saw—it changed her."

"What happened after you were taken into custody?"

"They interviewed us separately then placed us in witness protection along with my parents. The four of us were in a safe house always monitored by three marshals."

"Why didn't they confiscate the thumb drive?"

"No one knew she had it. Olivia kept it a secret from everyone—including me—until the night she died." The images come rushing back. The blood. The bodies. People I loved. My family.

"I'm sorry, Sammy," Bradyn says gently. "I imagine it's painful, but I need to know everything if I'm going to help."

"Kennedy," I whisper.

"What?"

I lift my eyes to meet his bright hazel gaze. "My name is Kennedy. Kennedy Angelina Smith." I can't stop the soft smile that spreads across my face. "I haven't gotten to say that in years."

"Kennedy."

It's ridiculous, but just hearing him say my name, my *real* name in that deep, gravelly voice is comforting. And it feeds that flame of desire I've carried for him since that very first meeting.

"It's not a good story."

"I'm not unfamiliar with pain," he replies then reaches forward and brushes a strand of my hair out of my face. It's that gentle touch that gives me the strength to dive headfirst into the darkest night of my life.

# CHAPTER 21
# KENNEDY

A fire crackles in the small fireplace, casting the tiny living room of the cabin in a soft orange glow.

Olivia is staring at the window even though the curtains are so thick you can't see anything through them. Her blonde hair is back in a tight braid, her eyes just as hollow as they were that first night she came back from spring break.

"Yahtzee!" Brietta announces, her short, black hair swaying as she does a little victory dance in her chair. She's won the last three rounds, and I know she's trying to keep our morale up, but we're slowly losing it a bit more each day.

I can still appreciate her attempt, though.

"I was close," my dad says as he pushes his glasses back up on his nose.

*"You were close last time, too,"* Mikey replies with a grin.

*"I was,"* my dad insists then shoulder-bumps me. *"Tell him, Dee."*

*"He was close,"* I say and try to fake a smile of my own. It's been three weeks trapped in this house. Three weeks of sitting here, unable to do anything or even see the sunshine. My mom's been in a depression since the start of week two and barely says anything all day.

She just sits in the corner quietly, clutching her Bible to her chest.

*"Everyone needs to get to bed,"* Vincent announces as he stands. He didn't play the last round with us, his own mood faltering today. He's been a bit off since this morning. *"It's late, and tomorrow might be the day we all get to get out of here."*

It's been the same hopeful statement every single day since we arrived.

Tomorrow might be the day we get out of here. What a joke. No one will even give my parents or me any clear answers as to just what is going on, and Olivia's certainly not talking about it. She's barely said anything to me in a month.

*"Come on, Dee, let's get you settled."* My dad stands and wraps his arm around me. I give in to the hug, breathing in the scent of his familiar embrace. Getting to

*spend more time with my parents has been the only good that has come out of this whole nightmare.*

*And hopefully, soon, we'll be able to go back to our normal lives. I haven't had the chance to tell them that I've decided to take a semester off from college so we can be together outside of this place. Maybe we can go to the lake. Spend some time fishing.*

*"You doing okay?" he asks me as soon as we've waved good night to everyone and headed down the hall toward the room I'm sharing with Olivia. We pass the closed door of the room he and my mom are in, and I long to push inside and curl up next to my mother.*

*"As good as I can be. You?"*

*"Doing okay. I never thought I'd be ready to get back to work, but here I am."*

*I laugh. "That's how I feel about studying."*

*"What a pathetic pair we are," he replies with a gentle squeeze. "I love you, kiddo. You know that, right?"*

*"I do. Always."*

*"Good." He leans in and presses a kiss to my forehead. "See you in the morning."*

*"See you in the morning."*

*After changing and brushing my teeth in the bathroom attached to our room, I head into the bedroom to see that Olivia is lying in bed, staring up at the ceiling. The room is dark except for the small nightlight near the bedroom door.*

*I pull the covers of the small twin bed back and lie down, clutching them to my chest.*

*"Do you think things will ever be normal again?" I ask aloud.*

*"No," Olivia replies.*

*Before I can respond and beg her to just tell me what's going on, someone yells just outside of our room. Olivia jumps up, and I do the same. A gunshot booms through the room, and I cover my mouth on a cry.*

*Olivia's expression turns terrified, and she lunges for me.*

*My mom screams, and my blood turns to ice.*

*"Mom!" I yell and rush for the door.*

*Olivia grabs me around the waist and pulls me back. "You can't help them. Not now."*

*"Let me go!" I try to squirm free. I have to do something. Anything.*

*Heavy boots thud down the hall.*

*Olivia pushes me into the closet and rips a chain over her neck. She shoves it into my hands. "Do not let them get this. They're coming for me, okay? Not you. They don't know this exists, and you have to keep it that way. Wait until you find someone you trust. Someone who can help."*

*The door handle shakes.*

*"Hide, Kennedy. Please. I'm so sorry. I love you. You're my best friend." Her eyes fill. "Hide. Stay hidden. Then run as fast as you can."*

*I duck down into the closet and slip the USB drive over my neck. I'm too afraid to speak, to do anything but wait for this nightmare to end so I can get to my parents. Please don't let them be dead. Please.*

*Olivia shuts the closet door seconds before someone walks into the room.*

*"You?" she asks.*

*"Sorry, kid, it's not personal."*

*I jump and choke on a scream when the gun goes off and a loud thud echoes from the floor.*

*Holding my breath, I remain hidden in the dark until the closet door opens. Vincent looks down at me, his eyes cold. Blood is splattered over his clothes, and he raises his gun toward me. "This isn't personal, kid," he says. "But I needed the money."*

*I scream as a gunshot rings out. I expect pain but feel none, and when I open my eyes again, it's to see Vincent falling to the side, Brietta standing behind him. She lowers her gun and falls to her knees, clutching her blood-soaked chest.*

*"Brietta!" I rush out of the closet and fall to my knees, tears streaming down my face.*

*"You have to run, kid."*

*"I can't leave my parents, you—" I trail off as I look down at Olivia's body, her eyes frozen open. It all starts to set in.*

*She's dead.*

*They're dead.*

*Bile burns my throat, and I have to force it back down.*

*"There's nothing you can do for them now, honey." She reaches toward me and hands me a Bible. It's only when I see it up close that I realize it's my mom's. Then, she cups my cheek with one hand. "I'm so sorry we let you down. But you must run now. Run and wait until you find someone you can trust."*

*"I don't know where to go. I don't know what's going on." I sob, my shoulders shaking.*

*"You're smart. You'll figure it out. But he's already called them. They're coming, and if you're here when they get here—" Headlights pass through the crack in our curtains. "They're here." Brietta stumbles to her feet and locks the door then crosses the room and uses her elbow to break the window since they've all been sealed shut.*

*"I can't go. I don't know where I'm going. I have nothing." Panic sets in as the adrenaline surges once more.*

*Brietta grips my face with her hands. "Kennedy. Listen to me. You are going to climb out of that window, and you are going to make it. I will buy you time. Okay?"*

*I nod, even though I'm still not entirely sure what I'm even agreeing to. Everyone I know is gone. Where am I supposed to go? Who am I supposed to trust?*

*"Good." She retrieves the firearm she set on the nightstand and stands.*

*The front door opens. "He did a number on this place," a man says.*

*"Go," Brietta orders as she tugs the curtains farther out of my way.*

*"Bodies here!" someone calls out. "Looks like the brat's roommates' parents."*

*I climb up onto the nightstand. My leg is just barely swinging over the jagged edges of what's left of the window when someone tries the handle.*

*"I think someone's still breathing in here." The man laughs, and the door splinters. Brietta shoves me the rest of the way out of the window, and the glass rips my forearm open. I stifle a cry as I hit the bushes then bounce up and start running as gunshots ring out behind me.*

# CHAPTER 22
# BRADYN

"They chased me for a few miles. I managed to make it into a small town, and a veterinarian found me in the alley behind his clinic. He stitched me up and saved my life. I stayed there until they tracked me down the first time."

Tears stream down her face, and it takes everything in me to remain where I am and not rush to her.

I have to treat this like any other case, though, and its facts first, emotions second.

It has to be. Especially where she's concerned. I'm already too close as it is.

"As soon as I knew they were onto me, I took off, not wanting to risk Cillian's life. I moved every two weeks after that. Never staying in one place long enough for them to find me."

"Until you came to my ranch."

She nods. "I never meant to put you or your family at risk. It was Cillian who told me about Pine Creek. I never thought they'd track me down there. It's too small, too off the map. I was so tired of running." She closes her eyes, and more tears slip free. "It was the first place I felt safe. Like I could breathe."

"Because of who we are?"

"That's part of it," she admits. "I didn't find out until I was in town that you and your brothers were prior service —or that you ran your own company. Once I knew that, I assumed the security would be top-notch, and if someone came—"

"We could defend ourselves."

Her gaze darkens. "It's horrible. I know. I shouldn't have stayed. I shouldn't have risked it."

"It's not far off," I reply coldly. "Except for the fact that we have other employees with no training, as well as my mother, who has never even held a gun."

Her expression is full of remorse. "I'm so sorry, Bradyn. I was so angry at Olivia for dragging me into this. I imagine you hate me for doing the same to you. But please know I never meant to bring any danger to your door. Please know that."

"What's done is done. But we need to get back to the ranch."

She goes rigid. "I can't go back."

"We have to."

"I can't. He's already looked for me there. He'll come back. You need to go now. Leave me here, and I can disappear. You don't need to be involved."

"I'm already involved," I tell her. "The security there is great, and if I'm going to protect you while we figure out just what's going on and how to stop it, then that's the best place to do it."

"I got out," she insists. "Without you seeing. Someone got into my place without you seeing too, right? That's why you thought I tossed it?"

She's got me there. "That's currently being rectified," I tell her. "All areas surrounding our personal residences will be covered."

"It's not enough," she insists. "You don't understand who you're dealing with."

"It has to be enough," I growl. "Because I'm not leaving you to die in some motel room."

She pushes to her feet, wincing when she puts too much pressure on her injured foot. "You need to just go. Leave me to whatever comes next. I'm good at disappearing."

"I'm not leaving you." The fact that she even thinks I would is absolutely ridiculous.

"You're going to die. This isn't some storm where you come running after me, Bradyn. These men are killers. You have no idea what they're capable of."

I move in closer, getting within inches of her so I can make sure she understands just what I'm saying. "I know killers, Kennedy. I've walked alongside them, fought against them, and suffered at their hands. I can assure you, there is no man who walks on this earth that I fear. And I. Am. Not. Leaving. You."

"Why?" she asks breathlessly.

"Because I defend what's mine."

"You barely know me."

"I clearly don't know you at all," I admit. "But that doesn't change the facts. You worked for my family, and they found you because of a fire that happened at my ranch. I'm not leaving you to die."

"Then you should have thought about that before giving them my picture." The fire is back in her eyes, a fight that I first saw that night when she was tending to Rev's injury.

"I didn't give her your picture. Arthur Kidress did."

"Arthur? How did he get a picture of me?"

"Seems he had a torch for you and took it upon himself to grab a photo." I turn away, trying to beat back my own anger at her accusation. "Confidentiality is a clause in our contracts. You should have known it wasn't us who gave her that photo."

Her cheeks redden. "I should have," she admits. "I'm sorry."

"He's since been fired and escorted off of the property," I tell her.

She takes a seat back on the bed. "I can't believe this is happening again. It's never going to stop. The walls are

always going to cave in. I'm never going to be free of this."
She yanks on the thumb drive, but it remains securely on
her neck.

"Kennedy." Kneeling at her feet, I reach up and tilt her
face so I can see her eyes. "You're not alone anymore."

"All that means is one more body to add to the count."

"I'm not an easy man to kill," I reply.

"They're not easy men either."

"We're going to make it through this. You have to have
faith. Don't give up."

"Faith." She chokes on a laugh. "My mom had faith,
and look where that got her. Dead and buried without even
a funeral."

Kennedy's pain is still so fresh, her wounds ripped
right open again with having to tell that story. "I'm so
sorry for what happened to your parents." It's all I can say.
Explaining to her that God doesn't promise us a peaceful
life in this world will mean nothing right now. All I can
hope for is that, if I remain at her side, she'll see what
I do.

That He brought us together so I can do what I do best
and free her from these shackles.

———

"You good?" Elliot asks through the phone.

"For now." I lean out and peer through the window.

"But it's bad, Elliot. She's in deep and doesn't even know why."

"We can't find much either. Tucker ran those names you gave us, but all of it's buried. The marshals she mentioned are listed as KIA. But not anything else that we could find. It's all hidden behind security that even Tucker is having trouble cracking."

"Not surprised. If it's a senator involved, he'll have deep pockets and plenty of resources to pull from."

"We need to know what's on that thumb drive."

"I'll send you more details tomorrow, and you guys can come get us. I had to ditch my truck in Tulsa."

"Where?"

"Leave it where it is. I was being tailed, and they've likely got people watching it. We'll double back for it when this is all over."

"Sounds good. You sure you're okay?"

The bathroom door opens, and Kennedy limps out wearing baggy shorts and a black sweatshirt. Her hair is still wet, her eyes red and swollen from the tears I know she must have cried while hidden behind the closed door.

She's stunning even in her pain.

A sight to behold.

Light in the darkness.

"Yeah, we're good. I'll let you know if something comes up."

"Same. Love you, brother. Stay safe."

"You, too. See you soon." I end the call.

"Who was that?"

"Elliot. I gave him the list of names you gave me, and he looked into them."

"Anything?"

"They're working on it." No need to tell her that we've got a whole lot of nothing so far. "Feel better?"

"A bit." She limps over toward the bed and takes a seat on the edge of it.

"A shower always feels like a reset. Anytime I've been out in the field, it's the first thing I look forward to." I peer out the curtains again, scanning the parking lot for any sign of trouble.

"Olivia was a good person."

I turn toward her but don't respond.

The chances of Olivia not knowing what was going on in her home are low, but given that the senator wasn't her biological father, it's entirely possible he kept her out of it as a matter of self-preservation.

"She was one of the kindest people I ever met, and even as she was surrounded by bodyguards all the time, she never acted like the rich kid everyone thought she was."

"I'm sorry for your loss."

"You look like a man who knows how it feels to lose."

"Something like that." I shove the darkness down as it tries to resurface.

"Lani said, a couple of years ago when you returned from a mission, you locked yourself in your room."

"Did she." I take a seat in a chair by the door.

"She did. If you don't want to talk about it, I get it."

"There's not much to tell. I went after a missing woman and didn't make it in time."

Her expression turns sorrowful. "I'm sorry, Bradyn."

"I wasn't the one who lost my wife or mother. There's no need to apologize to me." It had been a horrific case. One that shook me to my soul and had me locked in my house for two weeks as I prayed my way out of the mental hell it threw me into.

"You still lost something, and for that, I'm sorry."

I don't respond, just nod, hating that, even after these few years, that woman's face still swims into view every time I close my eyes.

"Thanks, by the way."

"For what?" I question, forcing my gaze back to the sliver of window not shielded by curtains. I've been watching for any sign that they found us. Thank God there hasn't been one yet.

"Coming after me. Again."

How do I tell a woman I just met that I'll always come for her? That I feel so drawn to her that it doesn't matter she lied to me? All I want is to protect her from the monsters knocking at her door. Since I'm not quite sure how to find those words, I simply nod.

"Get some sleep."

"What about you?" She tugs the comforter down and slips inside, pulling it up to her neck and rolling onto her side.

"Don't worry about me. You get sleep, and I'll make sure the walls don't cave in while you do."

Her eyes fill, but she doesn't say anything. I reach over and turn off the lamp closest to me, and the room falls into shadow.

As Kennedy lies there silently, I do the only thing I can.

I pray.

*God, I need You. Please show me how to protect her. Please show me the path you want me to take because we can't do this without You. And Lord, help Kennedy. Soften her pain and help her find her way back to You. I ask this in the name of Your Son, Jesus Christ. Amen.*

# CHAPTER 23
# KENNEDY

"Kennedy, wake up."

I come awake quickly as Bradyn gently shakes my shoulder. The room is dark, so it takes my eyes a moment to adjust to the fact that he's hovering over me, his pack on the front of his body with mine hooked to a strap on the front.

"What is it?"

"A dark SUV just pulled into the parking lot. Two men got out. We need to go."

My heart begins to pound, and my body shakes with the force of my fear. We're trapped here. I knew this room was a bad idea, and I took it anyway because I'd been so desperate for a place to sleep.

I throw the covers off of me and get to my feet. "I need my clothes."

"We don't have time. They're in your bag, and I've got

it. I need you to get on my back. We have to move quickly."

"Bradyn, how are we going to get past them?"

"We'll figure it out, okay?"

But then someone knocks on the door, and our hope of a quick escape is gone.

"Get over in the corner," he tells me. "Stay down." He shoves my gun into my hand and helps me over to the back corner of the room.

He's going to die. Because of me. They all die. "Bradyn—"

He turns toward me. "Don't worry. It's going to be fine."

"Room service!" they call out from the other side of the door.

"Bravo, *fahs,*" Bradyn orders.

The door splinters, and Bravo attacks. Bradyn dodges a fist and slams one into the gut of his attacker. He shoves the man's hand up, and a gun goes off, sheetrock dusting down on top of him. Bravo yelps as he's flung into the wall, but the resounding growl from the animal is deafening.

Bradyn slams his face into his attacker, and the man stumbles back—then falls all the way out the door and over the railing.

"*Aus,*" he orders, and Bravo releases the man. Bradyn slams him into the wall then drops him to the ground. The man lies still as Bradyn searches his pockets, and I stare at my protector in a mixture of fear and fascination.

Soldiers masquerading as cowboys.

I always suspected it, but now I have confirmation.

It only took him and Bravo seconds to take down two armed men without firing a single shot. I don't even have time to fully process what just happened before Bradyn's turning toward me.

"Let's go." He shoves a wallet, keys, and a phone into his pocket. He crosses over toward me and drops down so I can get onto his back. "Keep your gun handy. I don't know for sure that there aren't more somewhere."

Moving so fast it might as well be like he's not carrying me at all, Bradyn goes down the steps and rushes toward the dark SUV. The body on the pavement missed a car, and with it being so dark outside, I can barely make out the shape against the asphalt.

Bradyn searches the inside of the SUV then deposits me in the passenger side and opens the back for Bravo. The dog hops in without a command, and Bradyn tosses our bags in after him then rushes over to get behind the wheel.

He fires up the engine and leaves quickly, all while I'm still trying to process what just happened. We were just attacked in an enclosed room—and survived.

Bradyn reaches into his pocket and withdraws his phone then holds it up so Face ID can unlock it before handing it off to me. "Tap Elliot's contact. He's at the top on the first screen. Then put it on speaker."

I do as he says. The phone rings, and a few seconds later, a sleepy-sounding Elliot answers. "Everything okay?"

"We were attacked in a motel room, and I need to know how they found us."

"On it." I hear some rustling. "I'll grab Tucker too. He can run security cameras in the area if you get me an address."

"An old motel off of I-49," he says. "Right outside of Harrisonville. Look it up."

"Missouri?"

"Yes."

"Sammy okay?"

Bradyn looks at me, so I clear my throat. "I'm okay."

Elliot breathes a sigh of relief. "Thank God. I'll get you some answers."

"Thanks."

"You should know they're watching the ranch."

My stomach plummets. If they're lingering there, it's because they think they'll catch me. And if they do—"

"There goes Plan A."

"You have a Plan B?"

"Always. But I don't want to risk it now. We stole their car, so we're going to have to ditch it. Make sure local PD knows they have two bodies to find at that motel. One dead, the other unconscious. Call it in so a civilian doesn't find them."

"On it. Stay safe, brother."

The call ends, and Bradyn shoves his phone back into his pocket. His gaze keeps shifting between the rearview mirror and the windshield, but he doesn't seem shaken. Just in problem-solving mode.

"Are you okay?" he asks after a few more minutes of silence.

"I'm not the one who fought our way out of that." I glance back at Bravo, who's sitting up in the back seat, staring out the window. "Is he okay?"

"He's taken much worse hits than that. But I plan to check when we stop. I asked about you." His gorgeous hazel gaze pins me in the seat. "Are *you* okay?"

"No," I reply honestly. "I'm so tired of running, Bradyn. I'm tired of constantly looking over my shoulder."

"We're going to figure it out." He reaches over and takes my hand and, without hesitating, links his fingers through mine. It's such a simple gesture, such a kind one, but it brings tears to my eyes and comfort to my weary soul.

It's silly, but I haven't held hands with anyone in years. It feels nice. Even as we're running for our lives.

AN HOUR LATER, we're exiting the highway and taking a side road toward a gas station. Bradyn releases my hand and parks the car around the back then shuts off the engine and climbs out. He reaches into his bag and withdraws a leash, clipping it onto Bravo's *working dog* vest.

"We're going to have to dump the car here and find another mode of transportation."

"Why?"

"If a senator is in on this, they'll likely have every law enforcement agency out there looking for this thing."

"Makes sense."

He nods and sets my small duffel up on the console so I can get my boots and clothes out. I unzip it, and the first thing I see is the Bible my mother clung to in her final moments.

A wave of anger and grief washes over me as I shove it to the side and withdraw my clothes. I've just gotten my boots on when Bradyn opens the door and helps me out. With one arm around my waist, he practically carries me to the restroom.

"Take Bravo inside. I'm going to go wipe down the car."

"Are you sure? You need him. What if—"

"I'd rather have him watching over you." He hands me the leash then waits for me to go inside.

"Come on, Bravo." The dog walks beside me.

The stench of urine fills my lungs, but given that I've

slept in much dirtier places over the last two years, I pay it little mind. When you're living day-to-day, the where doesn't matter so much as the resting part.

A few minutes later, I've managed to get changed back into jeans, a sweatshirt, and my boots. I pause at the mirror a moment and look at the woman staring back at me.

I look rough. Exhausted. Worn out. All of the things I'm feeling inside come rushing to the surface, and I grip the sides of the sink as the hold I've had on my emotions shatters in a public restroom somewhere in Missouri.

I've lost everyone that ever mattered to me.

Been pulled into a war that I have nothing to do with.

Risked the life of the first man who has ever really meant anything to me.

And for what? Some piece of metal that's hung around my neck for the past two years? Who knows if there's even anything on it? Or if it's too damaged to give any of the answers they're looking for?

But I know they'll never stop looking for me. If I stop running, they'll catch up, and then I'll be dead. I'd be lying if I didn't admit to myself that sometimes that doesn't seem like such a bad deal.

Then I wouldn't feel this pain anymore. This never-ending current of grief that continually sweeps me away.

Bravo whines, so I look down at him. "I'm okay, buddy. Sorry."

He cocks his head to the side then nudges me with his nose. It brings a smile to my face.

"Kennedy?" Bradyn knocks on the door.

"Sorry. Out in a minute." I sniffle and wipe my eyes. *Get it together, Kennedy.* Closing my eyes, I try to re-center myself on the fact that I'm not alone anymore. For better or worse, Bradyn has kicked the door in and joined me in this fight. Though, whether that's a good or bad thing has yet to be seen.

# CHAPTER 24
# BRADYN

"First step is finding out what's on that drive." I take a drink of my coffee.

"I've tried. It's locked down."

"I know a guy. Two, actually, but we can't currently get to one of them. Elliot says the ranch is being watched. They're working on getting rid of them, but it's not going to be easy. Especially since Brown has deep pockets."

I hate that I'm so far away and that there's nothing I can do right now. Nothing but hopefully make it to my "Plan B" before they catch up to us. Something that will be immensely more difficult if I can't find a way to Maine.

"Very deep," she replies. Kennedy has been relatively quiet ever since we walked into the diner. Her eyes are still red from the tears I heard her crying in that bathroom. It gutted me to hear her pain, and I'd walked away long enough to wipe down the SUV before returning to find her still deep in it.

How I wish I could help her heal. There's only One who can though, and she seems shut off from Him at the moment. My hope is that Elijah will be able to crack the USB drive when he and Jaxson Payne get here. They're flying into Kansas City, and we'll be meeting them at a motel down the street.

With any luck, they'll be able to get us some answers, and we'll finally know what we're up against.

Bravo is lying at my feet, catching curious and sometimes angry glances from the other diners. With his *working dog* vest though, there's not much they can do except glare.

"We'll get it figured out," I tell her.

"Refill, honey?" the waitress asks as she crosses over to our table.

"Yes, please. Thank you, ma'am."

"You are most welcome. How about you, sweetie?"

"Sure. Thanks." Kennedy offers her a half smile then turns her attention back out the big picture windows. She's watching the parking lot, completely and utterly on edge.

"Can I give him this?" the waitress asks then pulls a piece of bacon out of her apron pocket. "Snuck it from the kitchen."

I laugh. "He would love that."

"Ooh, yay. I love dogs." She drops the bacon down on the ground, and Bravo eats it happily.

"Thank you."

"You are most welcome." With a wider smile than when she first approached our table, she heads back toward the kitchen.

"You're great with people."

"What?"

"People. You make them feel comfortable."

"As opposed to—" I laugh, and Kennedy smiles.

"You don't intimidate. Though I'm sure you could if you wanted to."

I smile. "That's quite a compliment. I think?"

"It is. I've not known anyone like you. Your brothers are kind, too. But there's just something different about you." She looks so tired, so worn down that every smile must take everything in her. The fact that I'm at the receiving end of them makes me more grateful.

"I've always said I was the best Hunt brother."

She lets out a soft laugh then takes another drink of her coffee. "All of you are great." She clears her throat and directs her gaze to the steaming mug of coffee in front of her. "Your mom reminds me a lot of mine."

"Yeah?" I can see how it hurts her to bring her mother up, but I also imagine not being able to talk about her at all is just as painful. "Tell me about her."

Kennedy's eyes mist, and she crosses her arms on the

table, closing herself off just a bit to feel less vulnerable as she rips herself open. "She was great. Happy almost all the time. Loved to bake, and she'd sing while she did it. Occasionally, my dad would slip into the kitchen and put his arms around her just so they could dance together. When I was younger, I was mortified by it." She laughs nervously. "But as I got a bit older, I realized that that's what true love was, and I'd hoped to find it one day."

I don't interrupt to ask questions. I just let her speak and watch the way her eyes light up when she momentarily forgets that they're gone.

It makes me even angrier at the ones who stole the light from her. Who murdered the people Kennedy speaks so fondly of.

"My dad was an accountant, but he loved fishing. We'd go out at least once a month. Even after I got into college."

"What were you going to school for?"

"I wanted to be a veterinarian."

I feign shock, earning another half-smile from her. "You don't say?"

She laughs. "I know, I know, it's a shock. I was going to UC Davis. It's where I met Olivia. She was studying marine biology." Her expression falters. "We were like sisters from the moment we met. Or I thought we were."

Her hand instinctively goes to the USB drive hidden beneath her shirt. Part of me wonders if she hasn't been afraid to turn it in, not just because of the danger if she chooses to trust the wrong person but also because it's the last piece of her friend.

"Here you go." The waitress returns and sets our plates in front of us. "Can I get you anything else?"

"No, thanks," Kennedy replies. "This looks great, thank you."

"You're both very welcome. Just call out if you need anything." She leaves the table, so I wait for Kennedy to look up.

When she does, I bow my head and fold my hands. "Lord, we thank You for this meal You have provided us. Please let it nourish our bodies and give us the strength we need to get to where we need to go. Amen."

Kennedy doesn't say anything, though she starts eating as soon as I've finished.

"What is it exactly that you and your brothers do?" she asks after a few minutes of silence. "The town is pretty tight-lipped about it. That or they don't really know. I thought it might be contract work for the government, but now I'm not so sure."

"We don't work for the government, though at times, we've worked with them. We run a word-of-mouth search and rescue team. When people can't be found or things of importance have gone missing, we track them down."

"Really?" She raises her brows. "I guess that explains how you found me so easily."

"I'm good at what I do."

"Hopefully, you're just as good at staying hidden as you are at doing the finding."

I offer her what I hope is an encouraging smile. "The problem with hiding is that everything is eventually found. I'm not entirely sure what we're up against here, but once I am, I'll be better able to predict their moves."

---

IT'S NEARLY ten at night before Eljah is texting me to let me know he and Jaxson are standing outside the door. I check the peephole then pull open the door to a former Army Ranger and his former Marine coworker.

"It's good to see you again," Elijah greets as he shakes my hand.

"You too. Both of you," I say, releasing his hand and taking Jaxson's. "This is Kennedy Smith."

"Good to meet you, Kennedy," Jaxson offers.

We shut the door and click the lock behind us.

"You both too." She's sitting on the far bed with Bravo curled up beside her. It's where he's been since we got into this room. She's more relaxed when she's petting him, and I believe he can feel it too. Makes me love him even more.

"All right. Let's see what we can do." Elijah sets a laptop down on the table then holds his hand out for the thumb drive.

Kennedy stands and crosses over but hesitates before offering it to him.

"I'll give it back. Promise," he says, keeping his tone kind.

"Sorry. I've just been holding it for so long now it feels like a part of me."

"I get that." He smiles and takes the thumb drive then plugs it into his computer. After a few seconds, a completely black screen pops up with a passcode entry.

"This is as far as I could get. I was afraid to try too many different things just in case I locked it for good. You see that in the movies sometimes," she adds quickly.

"I'll get it open."

"Can I talk to you outside a minute?" Jaxson asks.

I look at Kennedy, who has already gone back to sit beside Bravo. "Are you okay?"

"I'm fine," she replies with a soft smile. "I've got my best boy here." She pets Bravo's head again, and he raises it to rest it in her lap.

"All right, call out if you need anything." I step out onto the dark walkway between rooms, and Jaxson comes to stand beside me.

"Whatever this is, it's big," Jaxson says. "I asked a buddy of mine at the FBI if he knew anything about Senator Brown, and he locked down really quick on the phone. He called me later from a new cell phone and told me that the man has been under investigation off and on for over a decade, but nothing could ever stick. Apparently, he has a lot of friends in high places, and any time anything is brought up, it disappears just as quickly."

"I assumed it was big when he managed to murder multiple U.S. Marshals, two civilians, and a witness, and it never made the news."

"He's going to bury anyone who comes anywhere near this. You need to be careful."

"I'm working on it." My gaze rests back on the door where Kennedy is. I can see her sitting there, petting Bravo, looking absolutely gorgeous and completely broken all at the same time.

How I long to be the man who puts her back together.

"She seems to be holding up," Jaxson says.

"She's strong."

He starts to respond but stops when Elijah opens the door and peers out. "You both are going to want to get in here."

# CHAPTER 25
# KENNEDY

"I'm sorry, I've had *what* chained around my neck for two years?"

"They're shipping logs. Though for what, I'm not quite sure. Everything is written in code, and without the key, it's useless."

"Useless?" I choke on the word. It's vile. Poison. How can it be useless when so many have died for it?

"Not useless," Elijah corrects. "We just need the key in order to decode it."

"What key? I don't have a key."

"It's not a key like you'd unlock a door," Bradyn explains. "It's a document that decodes the order in which the letters are arranged." I continue staring back at him as though he's speaking a foreign language. "Olivia didn't give you any hints as to what it could be? Did she say anything to you that sounded strange? Like she was trying to give you hints?"

"No. Nothing." Another blow. Another hit to my already worn soul. Why me? Why can't I be the normal girl? The one who gets to graduate college, fall in love, get married, and have a nauseating happily ever after like the ones you see in Hallmark movies?

"We'll figure it out," Bradyn says.

"See, you keep saying that, but every time I turn around, we're hitting another wall." The panic is setting in, and it's all I can do to remain breathing. *Useless?* This thing was supposed to be the key to everything.

It was supposed to set me free.

"There are no clues to what they're shipping?" Jaxson questions.

"No," Elijah replies. "They covered their tracks well. If they're killing for it, though—"

"It's bad." Bradyn crosses his arms. "Likely drugs, people, guns—maybe all three. But the other problem with this is that, since it's two years old, they could've changed the entire operation."

"So it really is useless." I shake my head. Why didn't she give me more to go off of? Or at least tell me there was an expiration date.

"It's unlocked," Bradyn says. "So that's one step done."

"Unlocked but unreadable," I reply. "Completely and

utterly unreadable." I close my eyes tightly and shake my head.

"Look, I copied the data, so I'm going to run it through a program, see if I can find some kind of pattern we can go off of." Elijah offers me a kind smile as he ejects the thumb drive and offers it back to me. Then he packs up his laptop. "We're going to head in and get some sleep. We're right next door if you need us." He taps on the door adjoining our rooms. "Just knock."

He and Jaxson slip inside and shut their side of the door. Bradyn closes ours then takes a seat on the edge of the bed directly across from me.

He looks tired, too. But still oh-so-handsome. His jaw is covered in thick stubble, courtesy of having not shaved in a few days, and his hair is a mess from running his hands through it so many times.

Is it bad that I long to do that? Run my fingers through it so I can feel the smooth strands for myself? If only to offer a distraction from this horrible nightmare I've found myself in.

"I'm sorry. I know I'm being pessimistic, but I've—" I trail off, frustration stealing my voice.

Bradyn reaches forward and takes my hands into his. The feel of the calloused palms against my skin sends shivers up my spine. I want those arms wrapped around me. I want him to hold me and tell me everything is going to be all right.

And better yet, I want to believe him.

"You've spent two years carrying the weight of a dead woman's secret around your neck."

Though his tone is gentle as he delivers those words, the heaviness of that simple statement crashes down on me.

He continues, "But what you see as a roadblock, I see as a clue. This is one more piece of the puzzle, Kennedy. One more thing slipping into place."

"Except we can't read it without a key. I don't even know where Olivia found that thing. How are we going to find a key?"

"It's a pattern that we're looking for, and we'll find it. Like he said, Elijah has a copy of the data encrypted on his laptop. He'll keep working on it. Maybe he can crack it without one."

"That's possible?"

"For men like him and Tucker, it is."

I nod, feeling a little flicker of hope settle over me. "And until then?"

"We go home."

That hope is dashed out at the mere thought of what happened last night happening to his family. "We can't go back. Don't you get it? Your entire family is at risk if I'm there. Every single person you love."

"Kennedy."

"No, Bradyn. You said it yourself; you don't know me

at all, so risking the lives of your family for me makes no sense."

"Except it makes every sense." He pushes off the bed and sinks down to his knees in front of me.

My breath catches as he takes my hand and presses it against his chest, right over his pounding heart. I can feel the beat of life moving through him, and through the panic, I focus on that and that alone.

"You came to my ranch for a reason."

"To lay low for a while," I reply.

"You were led there. Whether you want to believe it or not, I do. And I will fight for you until there is nothing left in my lungs."

"Bradyn—"

"Kennedy."

My eyes fill, making my vision of him blurry. I try to blink away the tears, but one slips free, and he reaches up to wipe it away with his thumb.

So strong yet so tender.

"So many people have already died for me, Bradyn."

"I won't be another one of them."

"If we go back there and anything happens—"

"I have a plan. They won't even know we're there. Do you trust me?"

"With my life." And I realize that I believe it. Bradyn Hunt will keep me safe; that much I know to be true. Why?

I have no idea, but he'll protect me. The question is: Who will protect him?

"You have so much confidence."

He grins. "I have so much *faith*. And I believe that God has a plan for us all. This is part of mine. *You* are part of mine."

"There's that word again. Faith." I want to believe like he does. I did for a while. But after what happened to my parents, to Olivia, how am I supposed to believe in anything good when I've gone toe-to-toe with darkness?

"There's that word again," he repeats. "Because, no matter what happens, no matter what trials we face, I know He's right there, walking through it with us."

"I wish I could believe that."

"Give it time," he replies. "You just might start to see."

---

IT'S NEARLY two in the morning when someone pounds on our door. I shoot up out of bed, adrenaline surging through my system, but Bradyn is already out of his bed and opening the door between our room and the one Elijah and Jaxson are sharing.

I get up and limp over toward him, grateful that I can put a bit more weight on my ankle this morning.

"What is it?" Bradyn asks.

"Proximity alarm," he replies then turns a tablet

around so we can see the screen. An entire team of what looks like SWAT is lining up in the parking lot. "I set them up before bed. My guess is they're here for you and her."

I've seen what Bradyn can do, and I imagine both Elijah and Jaxson are capable too. But I also know, without a doubt, that there's no fighting our way out of this.

*So what do we do?*

*Trust in Me.* Those three words come rushing to me like a freight train, though I have no idea what they mean.

Bradyn rushes into our room and starts shoving my stuff into my bag then clips the leash on Bravo. The whole thing is done so quickly that I barely have time to process what he's doing. "Get Kennedy and Bravo back to the ranch."

"What? No! What are you going to do?"

"Buy you time," he replies then tugs the blankets back up over the bed and tosses his bag on top so it doesn't look like anyone was sleeping there.

"Bradyn, they're going to kill you." Panic claws at my heart, suffocating me. This can't be happening. He can't be seriously considering staying here and letting them catch him.

"I'll be fine."

"If I can get out, then so can you. Come with me. Please." Tears stream down my cheeks as I grip his arm, trying to tug him toward the door.

But Bradyn is a wall that will not be moved. He reaches up and cups my cheek. "You have to go with them."

"You have to come too."

"If I'm not here, that room is the first one they're going to. This way, at least there's a chance."

"Bradyn."

"Kennedy." He leans in and presses a kiss to my forehead. "I'll find you, okay? I will make it back. Trust me."

"I don't want to go without you." Tears stream down my cheeks now. The idea of leaving Bradyn here to a fate that's not his own is killing me right where I stand.

"It's not me they want. They'll let me go."

"We're out of time, guys. They're at the bottom of the stairs," Elijah urges.

"Go. Get her to the ranch." Bradyn releases me, and Elijah tugs me into the room while Jaxson takes Bravo's leash.

Bradyn leans down and runs his hand over Bravo's head. "Be a good boy, Bravo."

"Bradyn—"

"Go," he says, keeping his voice low. "Please."

I back into the room, knowing that if I get caught in here, it'll make this sacrifice meaningless. If they get all of us, no one will know where to find us, and I'll have dragged three more men into the body count.

So, even though I don't want to, I go.

"Keep her safe."

"You have our word," Jaxson replies. "And we'll get you out."

"I know." He offers me one final smile then shuts the door. The lock clicks behind him.

A loud boom echoes like thunder, and muffled yelling fills my ears. I cover my mouth, choking on a scream as I imagine them attacking Bradyn, cuffing him, and hauling him away like a criminal when it's really me they want.

"Come here," Elijah orders. He takes my hand and tugs me over toward the small closet. Then, he hands me Bravo's leash and closes us both inside.

I'm immediately plunged back into that nightmare two years ago.

I can barely hear the sound of a knock at the door.

Nor can I make out the words spoken.

All I can do is wait for the door to open...and my life to end.

# CHAPTER 26
# BRADYN

"Well, well, Mr. Hunt. I have to say, this is not how I saw our second meeting going."

Klive Brown enters the interrogation room, and I tilt my head to glare up at him. I've been sitting here for two hours, waiting for him to arrive. All while I tried not to think too hard on the fact that they were searching the rooms, looking for Kennedy. All I can do is hope that Jaxson and Elijah were able to get her out.

"And just how did you see it?"

"Oh, I don't know. Maybe back at the ranch as I sipped some of your mother's delicious sweet tea."

"Sorry to disappoint."

"The day is young." He grins. "I bet she has a pitcher in her fridge right now."

He's trying to rattle me, but I don't let him see the hits landing.

"See, then we'd at least be comfortable when I tell you that the woman you've been harboring is wanted for murder."

"I don't know what you're talking about."

He tosses a photograph down on the table. The same one printed in the newspaper, only someone has enhanced it. "Who is this?"

"Sammy Lewis," I reply.

He glares back at me. "We can play this game all day, Hunt."

"I have no idea what you're talking about." When I was in Special Ops, I spent seven months as a POW in hostile territory, in a country that no one even knew we were in. I had no clue if someone was coming after me or if I'd ever manage to escape, but I held firm because my faith carried me through.

Stronger men have tried to make me crumble. But I built my house on an unshakable foundation.

This guy is one more in a long line of men who will not break me.

I just have to hope they get me out before he decides I'm more trouble than I'm worth. I'm not afraid to die, but I am afraid of being one less obstacle between them and Kennedy.

"Kennedy Smith," he growls, pointing to the photograph. "That's her name."

"I thought you said she was Olivia Brown. Your stepsister, if I'm not mistaken. Come on, Klive, your story's not quite checking out. What is it they say? The math isn't mathing."

He rears back and slams his fist into my jaw.

I spit some blood out onto the table then glare up at him.

His cheeks turn red. "Let's cut to it, okay? You were spotted with a woman matching this description, leaving the same hotel two men were later found dead at. I have you on murder charges, Mr. Hunt."

I say nothing. Just stare straight ahead at him because I know that, if they were to truly charge me with those, the men would likely be traced back to him. It's a bluff and one I've no intention of playing into.

Especially since only one was dead when I left. Cleaning up messes seems to be a Klive Brown special.

"Is that what you do for the senator? Clean up your daddy's messes?"

Klive's nostrils flare. "Mr. Hunt, we can do this the easy way or the hard way. Personally, I don't care either way."

I don't respond.

Klive continues glaring at me, his expression turning

more and more murderous with every second that passes. "Fine. Want to play tough?" He stands. "A few hours in a cell should loosen you up." He walks toward the door and taps on it. An officer opens it up, and two more come into the room.

My hands are unchained from the table, and I stand then place both hands behind my back so they can be hand-cuffed again. As we make our way down the hall and into what I imagine is a holding cell beneath the jail, I can't help but notice the lack of attention the other officers are paying me.

In fact, none are looking in my direction. Not even a glance. It's like they're going out of their way *not* to see me. Which means they don't want to be held liable for what happens if they do.

Fantastic.

We descend a set of stairs and reach the bottom of a windowless room with two large cells. One is empty. In the other are five muscled, angry-looking men, all looking at me like I'm the only thing standing between them and freedom.

"How many of these big fellas are on your Christmas card list?" I ask as they open the cell door, uncuff me, and push me inside.

"Do what you need to do to loosen his tongue, but don't kill him," Klive orders.

"So all of them then." I roll my neck. "Fantastic."

The first one charges—a large man with a neck tattoo.

He rips a small blade free and tries to jam it into my gut. I dodge to the side and grip the top of his jacket then slam him headfirst into the bars.

Another attacks.

A fist slams into my side, and I grunt but drop down and sweep out my legs, bringing my attacker down to the ground. Rolling to the side, I narrowly avoid a boot to the face. Then I'm back on my feet.

But my speed and size don't matter in here.

Not when I'm outnumbered in close quarters.

Neck tattoo grips my arm, twisting it just to the point of pain, while another holds my other arm, keeping me on my knees.

A third comes up behind me and grips my hair, ripping my head up and exposing my throat. Klive grins at me from the other side of the bars. Copper tang fills my mouth, but I don't let him see even an ounce of fear.

Because the truth is I'm not afraid.

"Let's try this again. Where is Kennedy Smith?"

I don't respond.

"We don't have to kill you right away. We can start by just taking a bit off the top." He nods to the guy with his hand on my hair, and he presses the blade against my ear.

"I wouldn't touch a single hair on his head if I were you," a woman calls out. Heels click against the concrete floor as a brunette wearing a light-gray pencil skirt and matching jacket crosses over toward me. Her hair is up in a tight bun, her lips painted a bright red.

I've never seen her before, but I can't say I don't applaud her timing.

"Who are you?" Klive demands.

"Mr. Hunt's lawyer," she snaps and reaches into her briefcase before pulling out a folded-up piece of paper. She hands it to Klive, who unfolds it angrily.

"You're from Boston."

"And?"

"How exactly does he have a lawyer from Boston?" Klive demands, a snarky grin on his face as though he just caught her red-handed.

She smiles sweetly, but it's dripping with venom. "I tell you what, Mr. Brown, you explain to me how you got an entire precinct to pretend you don't exist, and I'll explain to you how Mr. Hunt came to acquire a lawyer out of Boston. No? Don't want to play ball?"

He glares at her then back to me. "Let him out," he orders the officers.

"Fantastic," she says. "Come on, Mr. Hunt."

"This isn't the end of things," Klive calls out.

I stop and turn toward him.

"I'll find her, and there's nothing that will get in my way."

Because responding to his threat would only fuel his fire, I simply turn back around and follow the lawyer out of the precinct.

After getting everything they'd confiscated from me despite never actually booking me on anything, I climb into the passenger seat of a Kia Telluride while the mystery lawyer gets into the driver's seat.

"Mr. Hunt, it's a pleasure to meet you," she says, offering me her hand. "I'm Beckett Wallace. A close friend of Margot and Jaxson Payne."

I take her hand. "I'm glad to meet you, too. Have to say, your timing is impeccable."

She laughs and pulls out of the parking lot. "You looked like you held your own. At first, anyway."

I laugh. "I wasn't quite sure how I was walking out of that one."

"God didn't let my plane be late," she replies with a wink as we get onto the freeway.

"They made it out then?" It's a pretty easy parallel to draw given that the only people who could have called in a lawyer were Jaxson, Elijah, or Kennedy.

"They did." She tosses me a cell phone. "Untraceable. I've been told to have you use it instead of yours."

I don't hesitate before dialing Elliot's number. He answers on the first ring. "Hunt."

"It's Bradyn."

He mutters something to someone else. "Thank God, Bradyn. Where are you?"

"Beckett Wallace got me out. We're in her car."

"Jaxson told us she was headed out that way," Riley calls out. "But we were about to pull a full-on prison break if she couldn't get to you."

I glance over at the lawyer. "I don't get the impression she takes *no* often."

Beckett grins at me. "You'd be correct on that assumption. If I'm the *she* you're referring to."

"How is Kennedy doing?"

"Restless. Mom's hanging out with her at your place. It's the furthest from the road and the best protected."

I breathe a sigh of relief. She's alive. Restless I can deal with. Anything else would destroy me.

"Beckett is bringing you to an airfield where Elijah has a plane waiting. A buddy of his has a license, and he'll bring you back here. Then we can go from there."

"Thanks. Let her know I'll be there soon."

"Will do, brother." I end the call and offer the phone back to Beckett, but she shakes her head.

"All yours, cowboy."

"So what am I looking at going forward? With the arrest?"

"Nothing. They never pressed charges. There's not even a record of you being brought in."

"Then what was on that paper you handed him?"

"A fun little note letting him know that I'd own him and his boss if they didn't let you out."

"How so?"

"I have friends in high places," she replies, clearly unwilling to share. The secrecy doesn't bother me, though. Not when it got me out of what likely would've been an incredibly painful afternoon.

"Thanks for showing up."

"Of course. There's not a thing I wouldn't do for Margot. She and I have been best friends since childhood, and seeing her happy with Jaxson after that ex of hers destroyed her makes me indebted to him too. That, and I hate bullies who think they're above the law."

# CHAPTER 27
# KENNEDY

Bradyn's hardwood floors are going to have holes in them if I don't stop pacing, and yet, even knowing that, I can't make myself sit still. Elliot was here about an hour ago and told me that Bradyn had called and was boarding a private plane that will have him home by nightfall, but I'm still restless.

Especially because the sun has gone down and he's still not here.

*Please be okay.*

Even the dull ache in my ankle can't distract me from the fear gnawing at my chest. He should be here by now.

"Here, honey, drink this." Ruth offers me a mug of steaming tea, and I take it. Not because I want to drink it but because I need to do something with my hands. "Sit," she orders.

Again, I obey because I'm not sure what else there is to

do except continue to pace. His home is beautifully cared for. Gleaming wooden floors, pale gray walls, accents of yellow and blue. Ruth told me it's because Lani had her hand at helping all of her brothers decorate their homes so they wouldn't look like college dorms.

It made me smile.

The first smile I've had since Bradyn shut that door between us.

"How do you do it?" I blurt.

"Do what, sweetie?" Ruth questions then takes a sip of her tea and sets aside her crochet project.

"Live when they're out there doing what they do? I'm going crazy, and I barely know Bradyn. I can't imagine what it must be like as his mother."

Ruth smiles softly. "My sons go out into the world and bring hope to the hopeless. They spread the love of Jesus by serving others at their most vulnerable moments. When all feels lost."

"And that helps you sleep at night?"

"No." She laughs. "But it makes the sleepless nights worth it."

"My mother had faith like yours," I tell her. "This never-ending well of it. She was always there for anyone who needed her. Including Olivia. Anytime she'd needed help, my mother was there, aiding her just the same as she would have done for me."

"She sounds like a wonderful woman."

"She was." It feels so good to get to talk about her. To tell stories and stop pretending as though she never existed. It's a special kind of pain when you not only lose someone but also don't have the freedom to talk about them. Anytime a memory pops up and you have to beat it back down, it feels like another part of them dies all over again.

"I'm truly sorry for what happened."

"I want to have her faith. To share that with her, but I'm so angry all the time. So mad at Him for everything that has happened. And I don't know how to let it go."

"'I'm worn out waiting for Your rescue, but I have put my hope in Your word. My eyes are straining to see Your promises come true. When will You comfort me?'"

"What is that?"

"Psalm 119," she replies. "It's one I clung to after I lost my fifth child during my first trimester."

Pain for the woman sitting before me tightens like a vice around my heart. "I'm so sorry."

"Thank you," she replies. "I remember lying there, furious. Why would He bring me such light only to rob me of it?"

"How did you move forward? How did you forgive Him?"

"Because His promises were greater than my grief. I know that, even though I will suffer, and have suffered, in this life, there is an eternity of peace awaiting me. It was when I fully turned to Him in those moments of pain that I felt His hand on my heart. His love surrounded me and reminded me that there were still blessings in my life. About six months later, we found Lani. Tommy found her wandering the road in nothing but a diaper." Her eyes fill. "She was badly dehydrated and exhausted from walking the two miles from where she was abandoned."

"That's horrible." Disgust churns my stomach. Who would abandon their child? What monster would do such a thing?

"It was." Ruth's eyes harden with anger I haven't ever seen from her before. "He drove her straight to the hospital, and as soon as we discovered she'd been abandoned, I filed paperwork so we would be considered for adoption. This little girl needed us. She needed a home, and God brought her to us. I could feel it."

"And the rest is history."

"The rest is history." She smiles. "It was painful to lose my child. But He brought me Lani, and I love that girl as though she's my own flesh and blood."

I reach over and touch her hand. "You remind me a lot of my mom."

"I consider that quite an honor."

The door opens, and my heart jumps, half expecting to see Bradyn. Instead, the woman we were just talking about steps into the house with a duffel bag. "I have arrived," Lani announces and shuts the door.

"Thank you for coming." Ruth gets to her feet and crosses the living room to pull Lani into her arms.

"Elliot didn't give me much choice. He also didn't explain to me why I have to be here instead of my apartment."

I can't help the wave of guilt that crushes down on me. Ruth glances back with an understanding smile.

"I'm afraid that's my fault," I tell her, unsure what else to say. How do you tell someone that you brought war to their doorstep?

"Well, you can tell me all about it after I've gotten myself nice and settled in Bradyn's second guest room. Come on, Bravo, you can escort me." She pats her hand on her leg, and the dog who's spent every moment we've been here staring at the door, waiting for his dad to walk through, follows her.

Even though the idea of having her so close to me if things go badly is a terrifying one, I'm grateful she's staying here. Having a friend close by, if we're still friends once I've told her everything, will be nice.

That, and she'll make an excellent buffer for these feelings I'm carrying for her older brother. Feelings that have only gotten stronger in the hours he's been away.

The door opens a second time, and the oxygen is sucked out of my lungs when Bradyn walks in. His hair curls out from beneath the baseball cap pulled low over his eyes. One eye is black, his lip split.

But when he sees me, he freezes too, as though he's drawn to me in the same way I am to him.

"Bradyn! What happened to your face?" Ruth steps in front of me and reaches up to touch her son's stubbled cheek.

"A slight miscommunication between me and the guy who arrested me. Then another miscommunication between me and my cellmates."

"Arrested you." Ruth's face turns beet red. "I cannot believe they put you in handcuffs."

"It's not the first time, and given my line of work, it probably won't be the last," he says as he sets his bag down.

"Look what the cat drug in," Lani calls out seconds before Bravo rushes forward, tail wagging, whining in happiness that Bradyn has returned.

He kneels and pets the dog tenderly. "Good boy. It's good to see you, too. You did good, boy."

"You look worse for the wear," Lani says as she takes a Poppi from the refrigerator. After popping the top, she takes a drink and sets it down. "Are you okay? Need medical attention?"

He chuckles. "No, thanks, Doc. Besides, I've looked worse." He straightens.

I'm afraid to ask him if he's okay. Afraid to know what they did to him in there. But I can't tear my eyes away, even though in some capacity, I can recall we're not the only ones in the room. But he's here.

Standing in front of me.

Alive.

That flicker of hope that went out long ago flares to life again. Maybe this time can be different. Maybe, just maybe, we'll all walk away from this. After all, Bradyn Hunt walked into the belly of the beast and *survived.* Doesn't that mean something?

"Lani, think you can come help me prep dinner?"

"I sure can." Lani pats Bradyn on the back. "Glad you didn't get worse."

"Thanks, sis."

"Anytime. See you in a bit, roomies." She heads out the door with Ruth, and they shut it behind them.

"I'm so sorry," I say, the tears breaking free. It feels as though I've been keeping myself together with paperclips and they're all popping off.

"For what?"

"You got arrested because of me. And your face—what did they do to you?" I ask, rushing forward to touch his cheek.

Bradyn covers my hand with his own then reaches out and cups my face with the other. "Nothing happened to me," he says. "I'm fine."

"Your face—"

"Will heal. I'm okay, Kennedy." He pulls me in and

wraps his strong arms around me. I breathe him in, enjoying the steady beat of his heart against my ear. He really is okay. Really is back.

*God, if You're up there and listening, thank You.* The thoughts echo through my mind, and I feel a bit of myself soften to them. To the idea that we're not all alone. "I wasn't sure I'd ever see you again. I thought you'd end up just like Olivia. Like the others."

"Nah. I told you, I'm a hard man to kill."

# CHAPTER 28
# BRADYN

Seeing her standing here in my living room is undoing me.

I'd decided on that plane ride that I needed to pump the brakes on everything I've been feeling because those types of emotions only complicate situations like this. You can't think clearly, strategically, when your mind is clouded.

But those best-laid plans went right out the window the moment my gaze landed on her. Barefoot and looking absolutely stunning in a pair of sweats and a T-shirt, her hair loose around her face. When she wraps her arms around me —I know that I'm done.

A goner.

This woman owns me.

"He's no longer hiding that you aren't Olivia," I tell her as I step back, putting distance between us so I can at least hope to think rationally as I recall everything that happened over the past few hours.

"He told you the truth?"

"He told me that you're wanted for murder." I nearly kept that part to myself, but keeping her in the dark will do no one any favors.

She pales. "Murder? What?"

"It's a way to draw you out." Honestly, I won't be surprised if he blasts her face all over the news along with a heartfelt plea from the senator begging for his daughter's killer to be brought to justice.

It'd be just the kind of move that would not only ensure he gets sympathy votes but also keep Kennedy from being able to run anywhere. Then again, doing so would bring unwanted attention. Especially if the wrong people find her.

She takes a step, and I notice that, while she's still having some trouble with her foot, it's not nearly as bad as it was. *Good.* That'll make running a lot easier if it comes to that.

"This is insane. How can they possibly think they'll get that to stick?"

"Deep pockets. They managed to get an entire precinct to pretend I wasn't being hauled downstairs to have my teeth kicked in."

The shade of red her face turns in her fury is both impressive and utterly adorable. Her hands clench into fists at her sides. "They did *what?*"

"Jaxson's lawyer, Beckett, got there before they could finish what they'd started, but he was hoping it would soften me up. Unfortunately for him, the soft was kicked out of me a long time ago." Moving into my kitchen, I reach into the fridge and grab a can of Poppi. "Want something to drink?"

She's staring back at me. "You're talking about it like it's no big deal."

"It's not. He knows where you are, and he can't get to you. It's infuriating him."

"He's going to find a way," she says.

"Not before we crack this code open and get that evidence turned over."

"For all we know, it's worth nothing." She groans. "And if we go to the authorities without actual proof, they're going to arrest me for murder. That would be just my luck." She takes a seat on the couch, so I walk over and drop down beside her, enjoying the comfort of my own place.

To be gone for as long as I was and then to only be back a short time before having to leave again? I missed it.

I close my eyes and let myself fully relax for the first time since the fire. It's been one chaotic moment after the next, and if I can just get one good night of sleep, I feel like I might just weep with joy.

"What is that?" The tip of Kennedy's fingers brush over my collarbone, and I open my eyes. Big mistake. Because when those twin pools of blue are staring back at me, I lose all rational thought.

I have to force myself to look away before I do something really stupid and kiss her. Glancing down, I notice the puckered scar sticking out of the top of my T-shirt. "Gunshot," I tell her. "I have a few of them."

She pales. "You've been shot?"

"A few times."

"How many?"

"Four or five. A few different circumstances. One of them was after I got out. It was our first search and rescue mission. Before we had the dogs. We were focused on some activity straight ahead, and they flanked us."

"That's why you got the dogs?"

"One of the reasons." I reach down and pet Bravo. "It's an adjustment. Going from having every moment of your day planned out and waking every morning, not knowing if today's the day you'll be knocking on heaven's door, to coming home and suddenly being in control of your own life again. Bravo helps me with that." I don't even tell her that it was the nightmares that nearly did me in. And that when those terrors hit me in the middle of the night, Bravo comforts me.

"I can imagine."

"You'll have that too, you know. Where you're still trapped in fight or flight and unsure if you'll ever get out of it."

Kennedy tucks her feet up and wraps both arms around her knees. Blue-tipped toes peek out from beneath her sweats.

"You painted your toenails."

"What?" She glances down then back up to me.

"They were pink before, right?"

"How did you—"

"I pay attention to details."

"We were on the run for our lives, and you noticed my toenails?"

"It's what I do."

She smiles, a radiant smile where all guards are momentarily dropped, and it steals my breath. "That's quite a skill set, Hunt."

"It's what makes me good at my job, Smith."

She laughs softly then rests her cheek on her knees and stares into the crackling fire. "I wonder what it will feel like."

"What?"

"To not have to run anymore. To be able to actually unpack my bag and settle in somewhere. To own more than two pairs of shoes."

"I don't own more than two pairs of shoes."

She snorts and then covers her mouth in embarrassment right before she breaks out in a laugh so melodious I want to remain wrapped in it forever. "I haven't snort-laughed in forever!"

"It was pretty adorable." I laugh, and before I know it, we're both laughing, neither of us worried about what tomorrow might bring. Just two people brought together in the midst of chaos, enjoying a moment of peace.

It feels good.

Like home.

---

KENNEDY IS fast asleep on the couch, covered in a blanket. She'd been asleep long before Lani came back with dinner for both of us, so my sister sat with me while I ate, and we put Kennedy's food in the fridge.

Lani tells me that she hasn't eaten or slept since my arrest. Elliot picked her up in Tulsa; then Jaxson and Elijah flew home to their families and to work on the drive some more since most of Elijah's equipment is back in Hope Springs.

He'd burned a copy of the data for Tucker too. Between the two of them, I have hope they'll be able to glean something so it's not what Kennedy fears it is—useless.

I glance over at the closed bedroom door where Lani is sleeping. I'm grateful that Elliot thought to bring her here to keep her safe. He'll be going with her to and from work, ensuring that she stays that way until this is all over.

Men like Klive and Alexander Brown wouldn't hesitate to take her out just to spite me.

The Bible in my lap is heavy tonight. The weight of the life I took at that motel is settling onto my shoulders. It's not the first man who's fallen at my feet, and as much as I hate to think it, I doubt it'll be the last.

Not with what I do. I save innocent people from bad men. And sometimes, you can't stop a bad man with anything but force.

But that doesn't make the loss of life any easier.

Ecclesiastes sits open to chapter three on my lap. It's one of my favorite books in the Bible and one I've spent a lot of time in over the years. It puts things into perspective for me when I'm feeling overwhelmed by everything going on in my life.

My gaze drops to the text.

*"For everything there is a season, a time for every activity under heaven. A time to be born and a time to die. A time to plant and a time to harvest. A time to kill and a time to heal. A time to tear down and time to build up. A time to cry and a time to laugh. A time to grieve and a time to dance. A time to scatter stones and a time to gather stones. A time to embrace and a time to turn away. A time to search and a time to quit searching. A time to keep and a time to throw away. A time to tear and a time to mend. A time to be quiet and a time to speak. A time to love and a time to hate. A time for war and a time for peace."*

Aside from when I was a child, I don't know that I've ever known a time of peace. Though I've never actively sought violence, I am not a man built for peaceful times. My desire to defend the innocent is too strong.

In those rare moments when I'm sitting still, all I can think about is the people I'm not helping. My thoughts remain on those suffering.

I glance over at Kennedy. I *know* that God brought us together for a reason. That He wants me to help her. I can feel it down to my very soul. And even as we don't know each other well, I know that, if anything were to happen to her, I'd be changed forever.

I'd be less.

*God, help me, please. What am I doing here? How do I help her? Guide me, Lord, I can't do this alone. Please be with me. Guide me so that I am doing Your will and not my own. I ask this in the name of Jesus Christ, amen.*

Kennedy stirs and stretches out just enough that her toes brush against my thigh. I long to take them into my lap and let her stretch out completely so that she might find better rest.

But I'm afraid that every move I make in that direction will only lead to disaster. She's spent the last two years of her life on the run, and this ranch will only serve as a reminder of that.

So what if she doesn't want to stay when this is all over?

Kennedy's eyes flutter open, and she stares at me for

just a moment before smiling, her eyes still full of sleep. "Sorry, I crashed."

"Don't apologize. It's okay."

She sits up. "At least, you got a shower."

I grin. "Did I stink that bad?"

"No, but it felt good, didn't it?"

"It did."

"Your mom made me take one when we got back. She told me it would make me feel so much better, and even though I had my doubts, given everything, I have to say she was right."

"She usually is."

Kennedy stretches her arms up, and I have to force my gaze away from her. Desire hums through my veins. Every moment I spend in her presence, I find myself falling harder. Every single second I'm near her leads me deeper down the rabbit hole. And what's even more terrifying is that I don't want to make my way back out.

"Bible study?" she asks.

"Ecclesiastes," I tell her.

"Everything is meaningless. Like chasing the wind."

I arch a brow, surprised that she can quote even a bit of the Bible with the lack of faith she's been upfront about.

"It was my mom's favorite. That and Job. She loved them because they showed just how important it is to appreciate what we have. She also loved Psalm 46."

"Your mom had good taste."

"She did." She looks over at my arm then at my face. "You're in a T-shirt."

"I am."

"I've never seen you in a T-shirt before today."

"That's because I'm usually outside where it's too cold for one," I reply with a laugh.

"Well, yeah, but I didn't know you had tattoos."

I glance down at the sleeve I had done over the course of a year. I'd just gotten back from my first deployment and wanted to feel in control, if only for something like this. So I went and got inked.

"It looks good," she says with a smile. "Did it hurt? I've always heard they hurt."

"Not as bad as you'd think," I reply.

She stands. "I'll be right back."

I remain where I am, unsure exactly where she's going, but about a minute later, she's coming back down the hall with a worn leather Bible. "This was hers." She hands it to me, and I try to ignore the small droplets of dried blood on the cover. "She had it with her when she was killed."

I run my hand over the leather, noting just how broken in it is. Well-loved.

"I don't remember a night when she wasn't reading this. Or a morning when I came out of my room and she wasn't sitting at the table. Cup of coffee and this open in front of her."

Because I sense she needs to just let it out, I remain silent, holding the Bible in my hands.

"I hated it for a long time. It's silly, I know, to hate paper and ink. But I was so angry that she died. That she and my dad didn't get a chance to retire and spend their life the way they wanted to. I'm still in so much pain knowing that I'll never get to see them again. But I think I'm—" She closes her eyes and takes a deep breath. "Being able to talk to you about them has made the pain more bearable because it feels like a part of them is still here with me."

I reach over and take her hand in mine. "A part of them will always be with you."

"I want to let go of the anger. I want to have the same understanding that you do. The same faith. I just don't know where to start."

*God, please give me the right words here.*

I hand her the Bible. "It starts right here, Kennedy. In the word. Reading His promises. Asking for Him to open your heart."

She clutches the Bible to her chest, holding on to it like a lifeline.

"Why don't we start together?" I offer. "We can read together. Would that help?"

"Really?" Relief floods her expression. "You'd do that? Help me get started?"

*There isn't a single thing I wouldn't do for you,* I want

to say. Instead, I shove that declaration back down and simply say, "Absolutely."

# CHAPTER 29
# KENNEDY

I close the Bible in my lap and set it aside to stretch. It's nearly ten in the morning, and I've already been up for what feels like half the day. I wish I could say it's getting easier to be trapped inside all the time, but that would be a lie.

Truthfully, it's triggering a whole bucketload of fear, given the last time I was in this similar situation, I didn't see the attack coming. I try to tell myself it's different this time. That this time around, it's not U.S. Marshals guarding the house but soldiers. People who came to my aid when they didn't have to. They chose to help me. They weren't ordered to do it.

After grabbing a glass of water from the kitchen, I head into the bathroom where the only window I'm allowed to look out of resides. It's blocks of frosted glass, so while I can see the natural light outside, no one can actually see me.

This is miserable.

Not that being in this house with Lani and Bradyn has been awful. In fact, they're the best parts of it. We've spent almost every night this past week playing board games or watching old movies.

While Tucker and Elijah haven't gotten any closer to cracking the code without a key to go off of, Bradyn remains hopeful that they'll figure it out and promises me that he's working on a Plan B if that one fails.

Something that will free me from these chains.

With nothing else to do, I head back into the kitchen and check the cookies I put in the oven. It's my mom's recipe, one I memorized since I'd helped her in the kitchen for as long as I could remember.

*Mom.* My eyes get a bit misty, and I take a deep breath. She would've loved it here on the ranch. Every year, we'd binge-watch cheesy Christmas movies where the big city girl fell for the flannel-wearing cowboy and gave up every-thing to move to his ranch. Dad used to joke that it was the only real fear he had.

I smile to myself and set the hot pan on top of the stove to sit for just a few minutes before I move the cookies to the cooling rack.

The front door opens, and Bradyn stalks in. I start to

greet him with a smile then notice the twisted rage on his face. "What is it?" All happiness drains out of me.

"You need to see this." He grabs the remote from the end table and turns on the TV. After flipping a few channels, he stops at the news.

Senator Alexander Brown is not a man I'll ever forget.

I only met him once, when he'd shown up at our dorm to talk to Olivia our freshman year. But the darkness in his eyes still haunts me even to this day. In some of my most recent nightmares, it's him holding the gun when that door opens—not Vincent.

"I stand before you, a father terrified for his daughter." A picture of Olivia smiling pops up on the screen, and a stabbing pain shoots through my chest at the sight of her. "She's been troubled since the sudden death of her mother and even dropped out of college to spend all her time at home these last two years." He sucks in a breath and wipes the tears from his eyes. "She went out to meet her friend two nights ago and never returned." He closes his eyes and pauses a moment while I continue staring at the screen, sure that I must be imagining all of this.

The image of Olivia disappears and is replaced with one of me. My student ID image from UC Davis. "This is Kennedy Smith. She's the friend my little Olive Bug went out to meet, and she's missing too. Kennedy has always been a troubled girl. It's how they bonded, but where Olivia tended to withdraw from the world, Kennedy had a violent streak. I am asking for your help in locating both of these girls so I can make sure my Olive is safe and Kennedy gets the help she needs." His gaze shifts to the cameras, and it feels as though he's looking directly into my soul. "Kennedy, if you're watching this, please reach out. Let me know that Olivia is safe so I can have my daughter back. Whatever you need, I'm here to help you."

The blood drains from my face, and I stumble back into the counter behind me. Breathing ragged, I'm trying desperately to separate the anger from the fear. *How dare he.* How dare he stand there and taint Olivia's memory like that! A troubled girl? She was only troubled because of what he'd done to her!

"Breathe, Kennedy." Bradyn places both hands on my shoulders. Where did he come from? Wasn't he across the room?

"I took that picture of her," I say, my voice shaky. "Me. We went to the park after finals were finished, and I took it. He used a picture *I* took to condemn me to the world." I'm rambling, and I know that, but I can't seem to find stable ground. "And she's dead! He knows she's dead! He killed her, and he's acting like—" I suck in a breath and close my eyes.

"Breathe," Bradyn says again then pulls me against his chest and wraps both arms around me. Focusing on the steady beat of his heart against my cheek, I manage to catch my breath. But only barely.

"My parents are dead. Olivia is dead. And he's just standing up there, asking an entire country to track me down and hang me for it."

"That won't happen, Kennedy."

I pull back and start to pace, desperately needing fresh air but knowing I definitely can't have any tonight. "Bradyn, I'm dying here. The entire town has seen my face. They *all* know I work here. They're going to come looking. They're going to—"

"Even if they do show up, they're not getting through the gate," he assures me. "No one is coming for you, Kennedy. He knows where you are, but he knows he can't touch you. Not yet. It's why he's trying to get someone to turn you in."

"He just put out a massive wanted poster with my picture on it, Bradyn. All they have to do is say I might be here, and the police will be beating down your door." My chest aches, panic squeezing my heart like a vice, so I press the heel of my palm against it and rub. "I'm never going to get away from this."

"Yes, you will. We'll get it figured out."

"You've been saying that for a week. At what point does running make more sense?" I ask, tilting my face up to look into his gorgeous hazel eyes. "At what point am I going to have to disappear again?"

A muscle in his jaw ticks, and his gaze hardens. "You won't have to run."

"There might not be a choice. There's already not a choice." I throw up my hands. "I can't even go outside. I'm trapped, waiting for someone to kick in the door all over again."

"That's not going to happen," he insists.

"Bradyn."

"No." He crosses toward me and stops a few inches in front of me. He raises his hands and grips my biceps, gently stroking in his attempt to offer me some form of comfort. I've gone cold, though. Cold and afraid. "You're not going to have to run. I promise we're going to find a way."

"I don't see how."

"Don't you trust me?" he asks.

I tilt my face up. "With my life. Haven't I proven that?"

His gaze flicks to my mouth for a second, and my heart jumps. Then it travels back up to my eyes, and I momentarily forget all the reasons us getting closer is such a bad idea. "I won't let them get to you. I just need you to hold on a bit longer. I will find a way to finish this and get Olivia, your parents, and all the others who died at his hands the justice they deserve."

I swallow hard. "I'm just tired, Bradyn."

"I know." He reaches up and runs his knuckles over my cheek. I close my eyes and lean into the touch as it soothes some of the brokenness in me. Then he's gone. Moving away and making me long for his touch again. "Are you okay if I go finish up? I'll be back soon."

"I'm okay. Honestly, I'll probably go catch a nap."

"I'll be done soon. I just have something I need to take care of first."

"Okay. I'll be here." I turn away then remember the cookies. "Want a cookie for the road?"

"Absolutely."

I cross into the kitchen and pluck one from the pan then hand it to him. He'd eaten nearly a dozen of them between yesterday and the day before, but he takes a bite and savors it like it's the first time he's tasting it. "You have a gift, Kennedy."

"I don't know about that, but I'm glad you like them." I turn the oven off and put the unused dough in the fridge. "Thanks for letting me know."

He nods. "I'm sorry we don't have answers yet."

"It's okay." But as he walks out the door and I head down the hall toward the guest room I'm using, I realize that it might be time to permanently remove myself from this place. That way, the monsters don't drag Bradyn down with me.

---

"KENNEDY?"

I come awake quickly, shooting up out of bed, my heart racing. "What is it? Are they here?"

"No. Easy. I'm sorry." Bradyn gently runs a hand over

my back. "No one is here. It's just late, and I thought you might be hungry."

I take a deep, steadying breath, letting my panic subside. "I haven't eaten anything but cookie dough all day."

"I figured." I can hear the smile in his voice. "Come on, let's eat. I have something to show you. Get dressed and meet me in the living room. Dress warm."

"Oh, okay."

Bradyn retreats and shuts my door softly behind him. Leaving my leggings on, I pull a sweater over my head, slip into some boots, and head out into the living room. He's standing in the kitchen, wearing dark jeans, a sweatshirt with the ranch's brand on it, and a baseball cap.

He stares at me for a moment, gaze traveling over me as though he wants to memorize me. My stomach flutters.

"Are you ready?"

"For what?"

"A surprise." He grins. "Come on." He turns and heads down the opposite hall to the laundry room and entrance to the garage. A Hunt Family Ranch work truck is backed inside with the door down, which is unusual since he normally parks out front. He opens the back door and gestures. "Hop in and lie down."

"We're leaving?"

"For a bit. I'm smuggling you out." He grins. "If you're up for it."

I don't even respond, my heart leaping at the thought of being free from four walls for even a short period of time. Even if I must view the sky lying in the backseat while he drives, I'll take it because it means I can see the stars.

The truck smells delicious. A combination of his pine- and leather-scented cologne and something that smells a whole lot like food. My stomach growls.

He climbs into the driver's seat and hits a button. I hear the garage door rumble as it opens; then he turns his truck on and pulls out of the garage before closing it behind him. The road is bumpy, but the moment I get my first look at the bright stars, I feel a bit of the tension I've been carrying slip away.

I can breathe again.

"You doing okay back there?"

"Great," I reply. "Where's Bravo tonight?"

"Hanging with Echo," he replies. "Elliot agreed to keep him for a few hours."

"That's great."

"He doesn't do well without a job, so the playdate helps him relieve some of that anxiety."

"Is that why you're taking me out? Is this a playdate for me?"

Bradyn snorts. "I guess you could look at it that way."

Silence surrounds us as Bradyn drives. Given that I can only see the stars through the windows, I have no idea where we're headed. I'm just grateful to be outside—sort of.

The minutes tick by in silence with just the hum of his heater and the steady but muted road noise filling the cab of the truck. Then, he comes to a stop and turns it off. "We're here. You can sit up now."

"Really? You're sure?"

"As sure as I can be," he says as he turns back to smile at me. "Come on. Let's get some air." Bradyn exits the truck, and I climb out when he opens the door. We're standing beside a pond, the moon glittering over its sleek surface.

Large oak trees surround us, aside from the break in the road and the pond in front of us. I take a deep breath, enjoying the crisp, clean air. It feels so good to be outside, to be standing beneath the bright moon and not huddled inside, trying to soak up whatever I can through those frosted blocks in the bathroom.

I hear something behind me and turn as Bradyn lowers the tailgate of his truck. He spreads a blanket onto the cold metal then retrieves a wicker basket from the passenger seat and sets it onto the blanket.

"Dinner is served," he says, gesturing casually as though the man didn't just put together an entire picnic for me.

Just for me.

Outside in the cold January air, all because I was

feeling cooped up. The last hold I'd had on my feelings snaps. Since the moment I met Bradyn Hunt, I've been falling a bit more for him each day. It's been hardly any time at all, but I feel as though I've known him for a lifetime. I'm tired of questioning how it's possible. I want desperately to lean into it. Into him.

"You did this for me?"

"You were hungry and needed to get out. We've also secured the ranch, so the only way they're watching us is from the entrance. We'll be safe out here."

"Bradyn—" My eyes fill.

"You deserved a break," he says then takes a seat on his tailgate. "Come on. Have a seat, and let's eat while it's warm."

# CHAPTER 30
# BRADYN

Kennedy crosses over and hops up to sit on the tailgate of my truck. As soon as she's settled, I reach behind me and grab another thick blanket then tuck it around her shoulders so she doesn't get cold. At least, it's a bit warmer than the last time we were outside together.

And this time there's no sleeting rain.

Ideally, we'd remain inside until this is all over, but I don't want her to feel trapped. I feel like an idiot as it is, that I didn't put two and two together and realize she was going to feel just like she did back then.

That's the last thing I want.

"Warm?" I ask.

"I am." She smiles at me. "What are we eating? It smells delicious."

"Pot roast and potatoes," I reply.

Her face lights up. "That was the first meal your mom made when I started working for the ranch. It was the first home-cooked meal I'd had since—" She trails off. "Since Cillian took me in."

"Cillian is the veterinarian?"

"Yeah. He's great. A good man."

I take the lid off of a glass food container and offer it to her along with a fork. "Tell me about him."

She sighs. "He'd lost his wife a few months before I showed up. They'd never had any children, so he was all alone. His apartment was over the top of his clinic. He helped me up the stairs and took care of me."

"What made you leave?"

"I caught sight of two of Klive's guys on the street about three months after Cillian first found me. I was worried they were getting close, so I took off in the middle of the night. I left him a note, told him that I was sorry but I couldn't risk his life." She shifts her gaze to the pond. "I still send him postcards every so often. I don't know if he's alive or if he even gets them, but I send them."

"He's alive," I tell her.

Her head whips toward me. "What? How do you know that?"

"We looked him up. After you first told us about him. He's alive and well, still running his clinic."

Her eyes fill with tears, and I wish I'd told her this news sooner. "He's alive?"

I nod.

Kennedy smiles and closes her eyes. "Thank you, God," she whispers.

She speaks it with such confidence that my heart soars. This woman, who a week ago was closed off from her faith, has been working to reconnect with it so much so that she's seeking Him in everything.

And that, in and of itself, is a beautiful miracle.

"I'm so glad he's okay."

"When this is all over, I can take you to see him if you'd like. I can even wait outside, but if you don't want to go alone—"

"I would love for you to come with me," she says. "You can meet. Two men who saved my life."

I swallow hard. "I haven't yet."

"You have," she says. "In more ways than one."

We eat in silence for a few minutes with only the sound of the light breeze surrounding us. Does she know how much she means to me? How absolutely head over heels I've fallen in such a short period of time?

Would it scare her to know how I feel?

"Tell me something about you," she finally says. "Something I don't already know."

I laugh and set my now empty plate to the side. "I'm not entirely sure what you don't know."

"Given that all I know is that you were in the service,

still operate as a soldier, run a ranch, and have a dog named Bravo, I'd say not much."

Chuckling, I raise my bottle of water to my lips and take a drink. "I played football in high school, for a league that was mainly made up of other homeschoolers, was in both 4-H and FFA, the latter until I graduated high school, and spent every spare moment I had helping out at the church."

"4-H? FFA?"

"Future Farmers of America," I tell her. "And 4-H is close to the same thing, just for younger kids. I showed sheep when I was in 4-H then steer when I was in FFA."

"You showed them? Like a horse show?"

"Did that too," I tell her. "I enjoyed it all, but I'm not one for the spotlight to be on me, so I was glad when it was all over too."

"That why you didn't want to keep playing football after high school?"

I laugh. "Something like that. I also took a nasty hit and ended up with a pretty gnarly concussion. After that, I just didn't see the point in playing since I didn't have a desire to continue after school."

"I played chess."

I turn toward her. "Really?"

She nods. "Was pretty great too. I played competitively all the way into college." When she catches me staring at her, she blushes. "What?"

"You just keep surprising me," I tell her. "Amazing with animals, strong, beautiful, intelligent, and great at chess."

The color of her cheeks deepens, and she smiles softly. "I'm feeling more like myself than I have in a long time, Bradyn. Thanks for that."

"That's not me. It's all you."

"Not all of it." She sets her food aside and stares out at the pond. "It's beautiful out here. I don't think I've ever been to this part of the ranch."

"We don't use it until the spring," I tell her. "In early April, we'll rotate the cattle out here so they can enjoy it. But it stays vacant all winter since it's so far from the main house."

"Makes sense."

I'm not entirely sure how she's going to take it, but I'm desperate to hold her, so I push off the tailgate and hold out my hand. "Want to dance?"

"Dance? There's no music."

"I can fix that." Reaching into my pocket, I withdraw my cell phone and hit shuffle on my worship playlist. Then, after setting it on my tailgate, I hold out my hand again. "How's that?"

She answers by shoving the blanket from her shoulders and taking my hand. I pull her into my arms, and she snakes one hand over my neck while I place one on her waist. The music is steady, and I move slowly, carefully pulling her in closer.

Kennedy leans in and rests her head against my chest.

And in this moment, all is right in my world.

There is no danger looming overhead. No mysteries.

Just Kennedy and me.

"I haven't danced in years," she says. "Not since the prom our church put on for the homeschooled high schoolers."

"It's been a while for me, too," I admit.

"This is nice."

"I couldn't agree more."

We keep moving slowly, and I lose myself in the feel of her pressed against my chest. This beautiful woman who's suffered more than her fair share of trauma but still manages to keep her head up.

What strength one must have to do that. To face down the darkness and refuse to bow to it.

The music shifts from one song to another, and Kennedy pulls back to look up into my eyes. "Thank you for tonight, Bradyn. I can't tell you how much it means to me."

Because I can't help myself, I raise the hand that was on her waist and brush some hair out of her face. My gaze drops to lips I've wanted to taste from the moment I first ran into her on the street. And even though I have no idea what the future holds for us, I lower my head and capture them with mine.

The world tilts, pieces fitting together like they were made for each other. Like *we* were made for each other. Desire hums through my veins, and I lose more of myself to her in this moment.

"I've wanted to do that since we first met." My voice is breathless as I speak, my mind already on kissing her again.

"I've wanted it too," she replies. "I've wondered what it would feel like since we bumped into each other. Even though I also knew it was a mistake since I had no idea how long I was staying." Reaching up, she touches my lips with her gentle fingertips.

"Life is uncertain," I tell her. "But does that mean we shouldn't live?"

"No," she replies. "It doesn't." Kennedy pulls me back down, and I capture her lips again. She opens beneath me, and I lose myself in the kiss, burying my hand in her thick hair.

She grips my shoulders, pulling me in and stretching up on her tiptoes to get closer.

I'm surrounded by Kennedy Smith.

Utterly and completely captivated.

And I never want to let go.

Even if it kills me.

# CHAPTER 31
# KENNEDY

My mind is still on that kiss.

I was up nearly all night, staring at the ceiling, grinning like an idiot because all I could focus on was the way his lips felt on mine. I've been kissed before, once upon a time, but it never felt like that.

As though my entire life was waiting to begin until the very moment my lips met his.

The alarm on the bedside table beeps, so I reach over and turn it off then throw the covers off of me, pull on some leggings and a sweater, and head out into the living room. Bradyn should be getting up any minute now, and I want to have his coffee ready to go.

After the care he took in providing me with just what I needed last night by getting me out of the house, I want to show him the same type of attention. And not just by baking cookies he gets to enjoy.

I'm stepping out into the hall when Bradyn opens his door and comes out. We nearly smack into each other, and I jump back. "Sorry!"

"Sorry!" he says at the same time then laughs and runs a hand over the back of his neck. "You're up early."

"Early riser," I remind him.

"Yeah." He tilts his head to the side. "This is weird. Why is this weird?"

*Because you made me see stars with that kiss last night.* "It doesn't have to be." I head into the kitchen and start the coffee I prepped last night.

"Did you sleep okay?"

"Not even a little," I reply honestly. "But it was all self-inflicted."

He laughs. "Same."

Lani comes into the room and yawns. "Good morning," she greets.

"Morning," Bradyn and I both reply at the same time.

She arches a brow. "You two are in sync today. How was dinner?"

"It was great," I tell her as I get another cup down from the cupboard.

"Good. I'm glad. I bet it felt good to get out."

"It—" A loud explosion rocks the windows of the house. Bradyn immediately yanks Lani and me down to the floor, and Bravo starts barking at the front door.

"What was that?" Lani yells.

"Stay down," Bradyn orders me as he reaches into his pocket and withdraws his ringing cell phone. "What was that?" he demands. His gaze locks on mine, and I know—I *know*—that whatever it is, it's happening because of me. "I'm coming. Stay put until I get there." He shoves the phone into his pocket. "Your old cabin exploded," he tells me. "It took out the rest of them."

My stomach plummets. "Injuries?"

"We don't know yet." Bradyn gets to his feet.

"I'm coming with you," Lani says as she gets up.

"Me, too," I say, prepared to run down there straight into the flames if need be.

"Kennedy, I need you to stay here."

"Bradyn—"

"They can't see you. If they see you, they could turn you in. No one can know you're still here."

"But—"

"No. I'm sorry. I promise to tell you everything, but please just stay here where it's safe."

Lani comes rushing back down the hall with her medical bag and heads straight for the front door.

Bradyn tugs me close and captures my lips, stealing my breath with a kiss before pulling away and rushing outside to join her, Bravo on his heels.

I remain where I am, frozen in place, staring at the door, and knowing I can't even look out the window to see how bad things are. Though even as the employee cabins are a good distance from here, I can see orange flickering in the small window at the top of the door.

A phone rings.

I turn and scan the room for it, but I can't figure out where it's coming from. Rushing down the hall, I check all the bedrooms then come to a stop outside the back door. It sounds louder here.

It stops.

Seconds later, the ringing begins again. Even knowing I shouldn't, I unlock the back door and peer outside. A small phone has been dropped on the mat just outside. Reaching down, I pick it up and bring it inside.

The pit in my stomach tells me I should leave it, but when it starts ringing for a third time, I give in and answer it. "Hello?"

"Kennedy, I have to say, it's good to hear your voice."

My blood goes cold, my body rigid. I'm frozen in place, trapped in fear.

"Nothing to say? That's okay, I have enough to say for the both of us," Alexander Brown says into the phone. "There will be deaths that came from that. At least one, maybe more."

The explosion.

It was him.

"Tell me, Kennedy, how many people are going to have to die before you give me back what belongs to me?"

"I don't know what you're talking about."

He chuckles into the phone. "You know, I never particularly thought much of you before, Kennedy. But you've impressed me these past couple of years."

"Glad to hear it." I rush into my bedroom and retrieve my gun then take a seat in the corner of the room where I have a vantage point of the door. "What do you want?"

"You're not even a little curious as to how I managed to get a phone on the back door of your boyfriend's house without any of his cameras picking it up?"

"I imagine you're going to tell me."

"A drone. Rather clever contraptions, really. They can even deliver—say—bombs, without so much as a single boot on the ground."

My stomach lurches as I think of the innocent men staying in those cabins. How many died because of me?

"Now, I have a really great view of your boyfriend at the moment. Big guy. But they fall too, you know. And all it would take is the press of a butto—"

"No! Please no. What do you want? Just tell me what you want."

"Don't play stupid with me. I want what was stolen from me."

"If it's Olivia back, I can't give you that. You know, since you had her killed."

He's quiet for a moment. "I want the thumb drive, and I want you to bring it to me."

"Oh, is that all?"

"You don't want a war, do you, Kennedy?" When I don't immediately answer, Alexander clicks his tongue. "What a shame it would be to see that ranch leveled to nothing but ash. To die knowing that this family who took you in would be buried just as your parents were. With no funeral. Just their once-warm bodies lowered in the cold, hard ground."

I swallow thickly, trying desperately to keep the panic out of my voice.

"What a sad outcome that would be for everyone," he adds.

I don't want to die, but I will not sacrifice a single inch of this ranch to save my own life. Not when my death could save them all.

"I want you to bring me the thumb drive. So I can deal with it and you appropriately and end this thing once and for all."

"I'll give you the thumb drive for the ranch. I can mail it to you. Overnight it. Meet in a coffee shop and hand it over, whatever you want. You can have it if you'll leave them alone."

"You have cost me two years of resources. Two years of trouble. So the thumb drive isn't enough."

"You want to kill me."

"I don't like loose ends. If I thought you'd managed to get information off of that thing, there'd be no choice. I'd be leveling that ranch and killing every single person who might know anything about it. Make your choice, but stop testing my patience. Either do what I'm asking, or they all die."

"I—"

"I'm not a patient man. There will be a car waiting to pick you up once you've gotten off the property. The second I see you leave that house, I'll have them bring the drones in, and your cowboy will be safe. But deny me any longer and—"

"I'll do it." Tears stream down my cheeks as I speak the words. Bile rises, burning my throat.

There's no other choice, though.

He has us.

"Good girl," he says. "I promise it will be quick. You have five minutes to walk out that back door." He ends the call, and I drop the phone, choking on a sob. My entire body is shaking.

Five minutes.

I have five minutes.

Folding my hands, I drop my head. "God, please help me," I sob. "I'm so scared. I'm so scared something will happen to them. Please keep them safe. No matter what happens to me, please, Lord, let them stay safe."

# CHAPTER 32
# BRADYN

The damage is substantial, but no lives were lost.

The blast from Kennedy's place took out a wall into the next cabin as well as all the windows, but we were able to keep the fire at bay long enough for the fire department to get here and put it out before the flames damaged the others any further.

A gift from God above, for sure.

But, man, two fires in as many weeks on the ranch? Not a great start to the year.

"Any idea what caused this?" Elliot asks as he comes to stand beside me. It's still relatively dark with the sun just starting to creep over the horizon, so there's not much we can see except what's illuminated by the work lights.

"Not sure yet. We'll have a better idea tomorrow when they've been able to see it in the daylight."

"Gas line, maybe?" Tucker offers.

"Possibly." But my gut is telling me something is off. These homes have buried propane tanks, and both cabins were empty since one was Kennedy's and the other Arthur's. Which means the theory of someone forgetting to turn off a stove is not a likely one.

"No one needs anything more than some minor stitches," Lani says as she comes to stand beside me. "They were all really lucky."

"God had His hand on them tonight, that's for sure." Elliot sighs.

"Amen to that," Tucker adds. "Dylan and Riley headed up to the house to let Mom know. She's pretty shaken up about the whole thing. And Dad is struggling, too."

"Understandable." I pull my hands out of my pockets. "I need to check back in with Kennedy. Let her know that everything is okay."

"Is it, though?" Tucker asks. When I turn toward him, he continues. "It seems strange, doesn't it? The first fire, sure, storm-related. But the cut fence and tire tracks? This explosion?"

I can see the lines he's drawing because they're ones I already have. "I'm wondering if it's all connected, too."

"The cut fence could've been someone scoping out the tree lines. Seeing how close they can get before the cameras catch them," Elliot offers.

"My thoughts exactly." Tucker shakes his head. "It just all seems—"

Bravo lets out a warning bark, and both Tango and Echo join in.

The dogs are staring off in the distance, their hackles standing on end.

"What is it, boy?" I ask, turning to face the same area they are. I half expect to see Kennedy strolling toward us, tired of being cooped up, but there's no one coming.

Something shifts in the shadows above us a heartbeat before the soft whirring of a motor fills my ears.

"Get to cover!" I yell seconds before the gunshots begin.

Grabbing Lani, I throw her behind my truck and cover her with my body as I withdraw the pistol that stays holstered at my waist. In the pause between the firing, I peek up over the bed of my truck, take aim, and fire.

One hit.

Two.

The bullets tear through the metal, and a drone crashes down onto the ground in front of us. I'm momentarily stunned. What in the world is a drone doing—

"What on earth was that thing doing—"

Elliot doesn't even have time to finish vocalizing my question before I'm jumping into the UTV he drove here and racing up toward my house. The adrenaline in my system is nothing compared to the fear.

*Please, God. Please let her be okay.* How did I not plan for this? Why did I think she was safer alone?

But I know the answer.

I got emotionally involved and lost sight of the fight ahead of us. I was too afraid one of the ranch hands would collect on that reward money and turn her over. To me, that was the bigger risk. I was wrong. So, so wrong.

Throwing the UTV into neutral and shutting off the engine, I jump out and race up to the front door. "Kennedy!" I bellow.

She doesn't answer.

"Kennedy! Please answer me!" I sprint down the hall, checking every bedroom and closet then heading back down the hall and into the kitchen. Panic claws at my chest, tightening around my heart and bringing the walls crashing down on top of me.

I turn in a slow circle, trying to find anything that might clue me in, and then I see it—a note on the counter along with a cell phone—and her Bible.

Rushing over, I read the note.

*Bradyn,*

*I'm sorry. He told me that he was going to kill you all, and I can't risk him following through with it. No one else can die because of me. I hope you understand and that, someday, you'll find it in your heart to forgive me for leaving. If I can get the key and escape, I'll contact you.*

*He caused the explosion and is using drones to bypass your security. He also used one to deliver this phone. I thought you might be able to use it to put him away even after I'm gone.*

*But don't come looking for me, Bradyn. Not this time.*

*Just turn him in. Let the authorities do it. Please don't risk your life.*

*Always,*

*Kennedy*

I crush the paper in my fist, my entire world crashing down around me. I left her here...alone. Vulnerable. Because I was too absorbed in what was growing between us and lost sight of the fact that she was a job.

And now she's gone.

Breathing ragged, I stare straight ahead, though I see nothing but red.

My door opens, and Elliot races in, Tucker at his side.

"What happened? Where is she?"

I hold out the crumpled note, too shaken to read it aloud or even speak the words.

"Did she take the thumb drive?" Tucker asks. "Did you find it anywhere?"

I shake my head. "She would've taken it with her."

Tucker pales slightly, his eyes going wide. "Then we have another problem."

"What is it?"

He hesitates a moment. "I switched the drives."

"You did *what?*" I growl, taking a step toward him. I love my brother, but right now, I want to level him where he stands. "If she doesn't come with the right drive, he's going to kill her!"

"He's going to kill her anyway," Elliot tells me, stepping up toward Tucker. "You have to breathe, Bradyn. This isn't the first time a plan has gone awry."

"Kennedy is gone. *Gone.* And we may not even have time to find her."

"Think about it," Elliot says. "He's going to want to know where the drive is, right?"

I consider, hating what that would mean for Kennedy. If he's trying to get information out of her—I shiver. I can't think about that now. All I can do is focus on the task at hand—which is tracking her down, wherever he may have taken her.

I turn to Tucker. "Find out where those drones came from."

"On it." He turns and sprints out of the house.

Elliot remains where he is. "You're in love with her."

I can't even deny it, not that I would. "I am. And I'm not even entirely sure how it happened so fast." I can barely breathe as my mind is flooded with horrific imagery of things that could be happening to her right now.

Of things that could happen soon.

What if I'm too late?

Elliot puts his hand on my shoulder. "God, we ask that You watch over Kennedy. Please guide us so that we can get to her and bring her back safely. I ask this in the name of Your Son, Jesus Christ. Amen."

"Amen." I can barely get the word out, but after a few moments of silence, I'm breathing easier. "As soon as Tucker has an address for those drones, we're rolling out. Call Jesper and have him on deck, ready to go."

"You think they left the state?" he asks at the mention of the private pilot we hire for jobs where discretion is of the essence.

"I think it's more than likely they're headed back to where this all started."

"California," he says.

"Exactly."

———

"DRONES ARE A DEAD END."

Frustration ebbs at my frayed nerves. "You couldn't find an address?"

"Nope. They're unregistered. The only thing I can tell you is that they were scoping us out for a while. Flying just above our radar and only ever at night." Tucker turns his tablet to show us shaky footage of the drone flying over the ranch.

"Spying on us. Learning our routines." Dylan shakes his head furiously.

"The explosion was a distraction," I say. "He knew that

he had to get low enough to drop the phone off safely, and we'd catch him on the security footage if he did."

"Unless no one was watching the cameras," Lani interjects. When we all look at her, she shrugs. "I don't know why you're staring at me like that. We all grew up playing army."

"He used the explosion to mask the drop because he knew you wouldn't let Kennedy out of that house—for fear either one of our employees or a firefighter would recognize and turn her in."

"Well, joke's on him because I too can pull surveillance photos." Tucker sets one on the counter before us.

I lean in to study it. "What's this?" A massive house sits on the top of a hill. It's surrounded by brick walls and iron gates as well as a scattering of security guards crawling the grounds. The gate blocks off entering from the road, and from what I can see, there are no visible weak points.

He crosses his arms. "A surveillance image of the senator's home in Southern California."

"How did you get this?" I ask.

"Nowhere legal. It's better you don't know," Tucker replies.

Dylan leans in and studies it. "This is his home? It's a compound."

"It's well protected," Tucker agrees.

"But?" I ask, knowing that Tucker has the innate ability to see what others miss.

"I found a hole." He grins at me.

"Where?"

"Here." He points to the back wall and, more specifically, a grate just outside of it.

"What is that?"

"Dude has a pond on his property. There's a gap between the bottom of the brick wall and the top of the water. It's not huge but large enough that we should be able to get in undetected. It's getting back out that will be the problem since I doubt we'll be able to use the same entrance."

"What if she's not there?" Riley questions. When we all glance back at him, he pushes off the counter. "We could go in there, guns blazing, and she's not even there."

"She is," I say, studying the photograph.

"How do you know that?"

"I feel it," I reply. "Before he kills her, he's going to want to check that the information on that thumb drive isn't corrupted. With how well protected that is, my guess is the key is there, too. It wouldn't make sense to keep them in two separate places when he thinks he has everything he's wanted."

"Everything we need, right there, in one place," Dylan says, studying the photograph. "We've taken on bigger enemies. Larger compounds. The place we pulled Silas out of in South Africa comes to mind."

That was a dangerous mission, but somehow, this feels

worse. Likely because it's not a Navy SEAL on the inside to offer assistance but someone who is unarmed and untrained.

"Not stateside," Riley says. "And not without the authorities backing us."

"This will be a totally rogue mission. We have no proof without that key." I look around at my brothers. "So if any of you want to sit this out on the off chance we get caught, I don't blame you."

They all look at each other then turn to me.

"You're kidding, right?" Elliot shakes his head.

"Aren't you supposed to be the wisest given that you're the oldest?" Dylan clicks his tongue. "You know we won't let you walk in there alone."

"We'd storm the very gates of hell with you, brother," Riley adds.

I take a deep breath, feeling overwhelmed and completely supported all at the same time. "Then let's gear up. We've got a plane to catch."

*God, please let me be right. Please let her be there. And please keep her safe until we arrive.*

# CHAPTER 33
# KENNEDY

Not a word has been spoken to me since that phone call.

When I'd arrived at the car that was waiting for me, someone got out, patted me down, took the thumb drive, then shoved me into the back seat. All without a single word.

Hands tied behind my back, I'm in another car now after riding in a private plane for four hours on our way to California—something I only know because of the billboards I saw when we drove from the airport into Alexander Brown's massive house.

Even with as good of friends as we were, Olivia never brought me here. I wonder now if she was always trying to protect me because she knew what kind of sinister life was led behind these stone walls.

My body aches from being tied to a chair in what appears to be a study. Leather-bound books line the walls around me, and a massive mahogany desk takes up most of the room. The décor is impersonal, just empty photographs and random items, including an old globe and what appears to be a few rusted chain links. The fireplace has no fire in it, and curtains have been drawn over the windows.

I'm completely shut off from the outside world.

My thoughts drift to Bradyn. Has he found the note? Was anyone hurt in that explosion? So many questions that I'm going to die without having answers to. Fear tries to claw its way to the surface, but I beat it back down. I made my peace with dying a long time ago. I always knew this was how it was going to end.

At least, I tried.

The door opens behind me, but I remain staring straight ahead.

Alexander Brown comes into view and leans back against the desk. "Well, well, well, Kennedy, we meet face-to-face. Again."

I don't speak.

"You know, I thought we had a deal. You come here. Bring the thumb drive. And I won't kill your boyfriend and his whole family."

"And I followed through," I snap. "I'm here, aren't I? You have your precious thumb drive."

"But do I?" he asks, moving to sit behind the desk. As he does, he sets the thumb drive down on top of the desk.

"It's literally right there."

"We both know that's not the right drive."

I gape at him, that fear coming through again, though this time, it sneaks past my quiet resolve. If that's not the drive, and he thinks I have it, then this was all for nothing.

He's going to go after the ranch anyway because he'll think it's there.

"That's the one Olivia gave me."

He lifts the drive. "This is not the drive she stole from me." His cheeks redden. He reaches into his pocket and withdraws a drive that looks exactly like mine. "This is the key that unlocks it. One is completely useless without the other, yet this one"—he points to the one I brought—"is useless regardless."

The key.

It's right there.

Renewed purpose fills me. If I can get the key and somehow get out, then I can finish this once and for all. But how?

"I despise having my time wasted, Kennedy, and right now, you're proving to be one massive waste."

"I'm telling you, Olivia handed me that drive. It's been around my neck ever since she gave it to me—" Until we got back to the ranch and Tucker took it to download a copy of the data.

He'd had it for a few hours.

What if—

"You seem to be elsewhere now. Remembering something?"

"Just thinking back through my steps over the last two years. Things are a bit hazy, given the whole running for my life."

"You'd better think hard. My associate is counting on this being what he's looking for. And if you don't have the information I need by the time he gets here, he'll make everything I've done look like a walk in the park." Alexander pushes back from his seat.

"Why did you kill her? She was your daughter."

"She was *not* my daughter," he replies. "And she proved to be just as much trouble as her mother—if not more."

Olivia had told me that her mother committed suicide. That it was sudden and she still harbored anger over it. In fact, she struggled to even tell me that much. But the way he's speaking—"Did you kill Olivia's mother?"

"Not personally," he replies. "I have people for that." He walks around the desk then stops in front of me and leans back against it. "People you're going to meet a lot sooner than planned if you don't get me the information I need."

"I don't have the information you need," I insist. "Why would I knowingly walk in here with a useless piece of metal? Why trade my life if it wasn't going to do any good?"

He studies me. "I'm honestly not sure. Stupidity, perhaps? Olivia wasn't the sharpest tool in the shed. It seems fitting she'd run with someone just as dense."

"Olivia was the smartest person I knew," I growl. "She was ambitious, friendly, and you ruined her!" I scream it, so furious that I don't even see the hand before it cracks across my cheek.

Pain sears the side of my face, and copper fills my mouth.

"You'll do good to remember who you're speaking to."

"I won't," I reply, hoping it comes across as a threat rather than compliance. "So, tell me, *Senator,* what is it you're wrapped up in? What about this lifestyle wasn't enough for you that you had to go and get into something so illegal it's worth killing over?" I consider mentioning that I know they're shipping logs, but if I do that, he'll know that I had the real thumb drive at some point. So I keep my mouth shut and hope he believes Olivia gave me the wrong one.

"I only have this lifestyle because of the generosity of my associate. He gives me support and status, and I make sure he can do his business unbothered."

"Dirty politician. How original." I spit on the floor, blood splattering onto the white rug. "Oops," I say. If he's going to kill me, which he's made clear he is, I won't go out without a fight. Even if it's just bravado.

*God, if You can hear me now, I'm ready. Please help me find my way to You. I need You. I won't survive this alone. Please, God.*

"What, you've got nothing else to say?" he asks.

"Nothing that matters."

He shakes his head. "You act as though the cards are in your pocket. I could have that entire ranch wiped out before breakfast, and there's not a single thing you can do about it." He considers. "There's a thought. If you don't give up the information I need, then perhaps that's the route we'll go. You can watch them all die in HD." Alexander gestures to the TV on the wall. "It's where I watched your old cabin go boom." He grins. "Think about it. I'll be back."

---

At some point, I must have drifted off because, as I open my eyes, the sunlight that had crept through the closed curtains is gone. *What time is it?* My entire body aches, my neck stiff from being in the same position for who knows how long.

Fear creeps up my spine. How long *has* it been? Have I been out only a few hours? Or an entire day?

The door opens behind me, and I jolt in my seat. "So this is the troublemaker, then?" a deep voice booms as a man I've never seen steps into view. "She doesn't look all that intimidating. Pretty too." Reaching forward, he runs his finger along my cheek. I try to pull away, but he grips my face, holding it hard enough that I know my cheeks will bruise.

If I'm alive long enough for that to happen.

Wearing black jeans and a leather jacket, he looks every bit like someone willing to tear me apart for the information he wants.

"Hi, darling, it seems we need to have a talk." He releases my face, slams both hands down onto my strapped-down forearms, and squeezes.

I wince, tears burning in my eyes as pain shoots up both arms. "I already told him, that's the drive Olivia gave me."

He flings me backward, chair and all, and my head hits the ground with a hard *crack*. Pain explodes behind my eyes. He comes into view above me. "I don't play the same games Alexander does, something he should have warned you about." Walking around, he grabs a fistful of my hair and jerks, setting my chair back up.

Some hair rips free, and I scream.

"There we go. Now we're getting somewhere. So I'll say it again. We need to have a talk. And I'm not leaving here until you've given me every answer I need." He slips out of his jacket, revealing a large gun sheathed in a shoulder holster.

Crossing his arms, he leans back against the desk across from me.

My blood goes cold, and that fear turns to panic.

But even as it tries to overtake me, a sense of peace settles in its place. A thick blanket telling me to just hold on a little longer.

Just a little longer.

# CHAPTER 34
# BRADYN

I t only took us fifteen minutes to get through the grate leading into the compound, but it felt like lifetimes. Especially once we'd gotten confirmation that the senator's plane landed at a private airstrip and Kennedy was among the passengers.

Something we only know because Tucker hacked into the hangar's security cameras and pulled the footage for us. She's close. I can feel her.

*God, please let me get to her in time. I need You to guide my steps. Guide us.*

Still dressed in the black wet suit I wore through the water, I keep my assault rifle at the ready as I creep forward through the grounds. I'm moving soundlessly and sticking to cover as I can, all of my brothers moving in formation behind me. Bravo walks at my side, silent but at the ready.

Echo with Elliot.

Romeo with Riley.

Tango with Tucker.

And Delta with Dylan.

We're a team—the ten of us. And with God on our side, we'll finish this mission and free Kennedy. "Two up ahead on the right," Tucker whispers into the earpiece.

I see the guards up ahead, their backs toward us. Elliot takes the one on the right, and I go left. We move as one, both of us snaking our arms around the necks of the guards and squeezing, holding until their bodies go limp.

Quickly, we zip-tie their hands together, remove their weapons, and tuck them out of sight. They'll be out for a while, hopefully waking just in time to have those zip ties swapped for cuffs. That is as long as the voicemail I left for Frank Loyotta earlier gets heard in time. Otherwise, we're truly on our own.

Lifting my weapon again, I fall back into formation, and we sneak around the side of the building. We're so close. Right near an entrance.

"Incoming!" I hear someone yell and plaster myself against the wall. Bravo moves with me, my entire team pressing our bodies against the wall, just out of view as the large iron gate opens and a black SUV speeds in.

The car slams to a stop, and two men get out, one of them looking absolutely furious.

"No one can do anything right, George. You know that. No one. You want a job done, you have to do it yourself."

"Yes, boss," he replies.

He says something else, but it's muffled as they slip inside the house. Yet he didn't need to say anything more for me to understand just why he's here. *Kennedy.* My heart begins to pound.

"We have to move," I whisper into the earpiece.

It's a delicate balance, moving fast enough to get there in time but not so fast we risk bringing attention to ourselves. A full-on midday assault is enough of a risk.

We creep toward a side door, and I step back as Tucker moves to the front, placing a lock break onto the keypad. Within seconds, the light turns green, and he removes it then falls back into place behind us.

I glance back, gesturing toward the door to let them know I'm going in. Weapon at the ready, I shove against the door.

The hall is empty, so we flood it in formation, clearing every room we pass. So far, we see no guards patrolling the interior, nor house staff. Not unusual for places like this—most of the security is outside.

We've only made it through part of the downstairs, and there are two other floors to get through. She could be anywhere, and I get the feeling we're running out of time.

*Come on, Kennedy, where are you?*

A scream tears through the house, and my heart slams against my ribs. *Kennedy*! I pick up speed, no longer caring if we get spotted. All that matters is getting to her.

I have to get to her.

We reach a door right before a set of stairs, and I press my ear against it.

"Please, I'm telling you that I don't know anything!" Kennedy screams again.

"I will not be lied to! Come on, sweetheart, we're just getting started. Be honest with Ralphie, and I promise to make this quick."

She screams again, a heart-stopping cry of pain.

I slam my boot into the door, and it flies open. The man reaches for a gun holstered beneath his arm, but I'm faster. *"Fass,* Bravo!" I order. Bravo lunges forward, his jaws clenching around the man's forearm. The man screams in pain, and I disarm him, ripping the firearm from his grasp while Bravo takes him to the ground.

The other dogs all stand at the ready, growling low and deep as the man stares at them in fear, his eyes wide. "Get this mutt off of me!" he yells.

"Keep squirming; it only makes him bite harder," Elliot replies as he withdraws zip ties from a pocket on his vest.

*"Aus*, Bravo," I order. *Let go.* Bravo releases him, and Elliot's quick with the zip ties, securing his hands behind his back.

With him no longer a threat, I turn toward Kennedy. Her face is bruised, her lip split open, eyes bloodshot. Blood slicks against the skin of her arms where her sleeves were cut off—long cuts from the blade discarded at her side.

There's a bit of blood matted to her hair and dripping down her forehead.

Fury ignites in my veins. A thirst for vengeance that will not be quenched until this man is dead. I start to turn toward him.

"You came for me." Kennedy's soft voice grounds me, and I remain where I am. She's top priority, and vengeance is not mine to have. Not when God can deliver far worse than I can if He so chooses.

I rip the knife from my boot and cut the ropes binding her. "Of course I came for you."

She tries to smile, but she winces and reaches up to touch the cut on her lip. "I told you not to." Her wrists are covered in bruises from the ropes as well as burn marks where she tried to get free.

I swallow down my anger and do my best to only focus on her. "I've always struggled with following directions."

"We need to get out, brother," Tucker says. "Otherwise, we're about to be sitting ducks."

"You're already sitting ducks, you fools. You won't make it out of this alive, and now I'll really make her suffer."

A heavy thud masked with a soft grunt has me turning my head. Dylan slowly lowers his boot back to the ground, and the man lies unconscious on the floor. "Don't act like none of you wanted to do that and so much worse."

No one says a word, and I know that, in this moment, we all appreciate Dylan's temper. Honestly, he probably saved the man's life by knocking him out.

Kennedy rests her head against my chest. "Alexander has the key in his pocket. We find him, we have the proof."

"That's good," I tell her. "Because I've already made a call."

---

"THIS IS GOOD, HUNT," Frank Loyotta says appreciatively as the senator is loaded into the back of a police cruiser. While it's not necessarily his wheelhouse, Frank has connections that I don't. Connections that led to the Department of Homeland Security showing up on Senator Brown's door, along with multiple media outlets and a slew of local police.

I smile. "Thanks for showing up."

"Anytime. Turns out the guy you found in there with your girl is Rice Berns. He's wanted in four Countries and has been on the FBI's most-wanted list for a decade. The good senator there tried to save his own hide by telling us Rice was behind everything and he was only being blackmailed. We got both him and his son, Klive, trying to escape out the back. And wouldn't you know, the senator had a thumb drive in his pocket. Think we'll find anything on that?"

"I would think so. It's likely the key. Tucker has the main one. He can get it to you before you head out. You'll need one to read the other."

He nods. "Seriously, you did great work. Again."

"It's a team effort," I reply.

"You and your brothers ever want to come work for me, all you have to do is say the word. I'll make it happen."

I shake his offered hand. "Appreciate that, Frank, but I'm really looking forward to some quiet time after this." My gaze lands on Kennedy. She's sitting in the back of an ambulance, a blanket over her shoulders.

She turns toward me, and our gazes hold. For a moment, everyone else just fades away, and it's just her and me.

*Thank You, Lord.*

"Ahh, I get it now." Frank clasps me on the shoulder. "You know where to find me if you change your mind."

"That I do."

"You should know, though, after we got off the phone, I did some digging. I have a friend in the marshals, and he looked into what happened that night."

"The night Oliva Brown and Kennedy's parents were killed?"

He nods. "It was all buried pretty good, and Olivia's

identity was hidden, but he pressed in the right places and got his hands on the real file."

"They'll get justice then; that's good."

"That's the thing, though. Aside from the three marshals, only one other body was recovered that night."

"What do you mean?" I turn away from Kennedy and focus fully on him.

"The murders were called in by a man who was also living at the residence."

"What are you telling me?" I don't dare read into what he's saying because, if I read between the lines and I'm wrong—well—I don't want to be wrong.

"I'm telling you that not everyone died that night," he says. "There were two other survivors."

"I really am okay," I insist as Bradyn carries me up to the porch of his parents' house. He's insisted on waiting on me, hand and foot, from the time we left the hospital this morning to our arrival back here tonight.

Staying by my side the entire time the hospital kept me for observation. His brothers went home, taking Bravo with them, but he stayed there. Right at my side.

Bradyn Hunt has been my rock while the world cascaded around me, a rushing river that might sweep me away.

"I know you are," he says with a smile. "Maybe I like feeling you in my arms."

"Maybe I like being in your arms."

His smile spreads, and he leans down, capturing my lips

with his. Then he pulls back and rests his forehead against mine. "You have my heart, Kennedy Smith."

*Lord, how will I ever thank You enough for bringing this man to me?*

"That's good, because you have mine, too."

He smiles and pulls away then reaches for the handle, but his mom pulls it open first. She beams at me.

"Kennedy!" Rushing out, she wraps her arms around me and pulls me in for a hug. "Let me look at you. You look good. Are you good?"

"I am," I reply, appreciating her lie. I know I don't look good. I'm bruised head to toe, and I look like I've been hit by a truck which then had the courtesy to back over me.

But I'm alive. And that's all that matters. Everything else will heal.

"Thank God for that, darling. Come in, come in." She ushers me inside. "We have some guests, too. And I think you're going to want to see them."

"Who's here?" I ask, noting that all of the brothers, Lani, and Mr. Hunt are lingering at the edge of the living room, smiling softly at me. "Bradyn? What is it?"

He lifts my hand and presses a kiss to it then releases me and steps away, joining his family.

I eye him nervously, trying to figure out just who would be here, but then a man comes into view. I stare, unsure if what I'm seeing is real. Surely it's not. It can't be real. Can it?

And then a second person comes around the corner, a worn Bible in her hands, and my chest feels ready to explode. "Mom?" I choke out, my eyes filling with tears. "Dad?"

"Dee." My mom rushes forward and wraps her arms around me. My dad joins the hug while I stand there, completely stunned and so absolutely overwhelmed with love that I'm not entirely sure what to do with it.

How is this possible?

"I don't understand." I choke on the words, tears streaming down my face. "I don't understand. You were dead. I—"

"We thought we were, too," my dad says as they release me. He cups my face, thumbs stroking my cheeks. "But thanks to God, we somehow survived. Even the doctors didn't know how we were still breathing." Tears slip from his eyes. "My baby girl. We've been so worried about you, but they wouldn't tell us where you were. They said it was for the best, that if we were separate, you had a chance at surviving."

"Who?" I ask.

"The marshals. We were taken in again, and they wouldn't let us have contact with anyone outside of this tiny house in Florida we've been living in for the last two years. We prayed for you. Every night. Prayed you would find someone to help you."

"Oh, baby," my mom coos. "Your face. Are you okay? They hurt you."

"I'm okay, Mom. I'll be okay. You're alive. You're really here? This is really happening?" I look back at Bradyn.

"Frank Loyotta," he replies. "He made a call to find out what happened that night and discovered that you weren't the only one who walked out of there. Elliot and Riley flew out to Florida and picked them up once the marshals released them. They got here about an hour before we did."

I'm speechless.

My heart's so full that I feel like it might burst. "God," I choke out. "He did this. He brought you back to me."

"He brought *you* back to us," my mother says then pulls me back into her embrace. My dad wraps his arms around both of us, and I breathe in the scent of his familiar after-shave, letting it absorb into my memory because I have him back.

I have them both back.

*Thank You, God.*

"I love you both so much," I manage even as my throat burns while I try to keep myself at least partially together.

"We love you too, Dee."

THE CHILL in the air can't cool the warmth radiating through me.

I sit on the porch in the early hours of the morning, swinging softly as I wait for the sun to rise over the ranch.

Bradyn had left for his house two hours before my parents called it a night around three in the morning. They're currently sleeping in a guest room in the house behind me. Sleeping. I'll get to see them in the morning. I'll get to laugh with my mom and tell jokes with my dad.

They're alive.

A tear slips from my eye. I still can't believe it.

We'd talked about everything. About how my dad taught the marshals guarding them how to play chess and how my mom started knitting blankets for the local children's hospital there, and the marshals delivered them for her.

I told them about Cillian, and they've asked to meet him one day. Something I'm incredibly excited about. I haven't even had the chance to call him yet, but I'll be doing just that tomorrow.

This huge weight has been lifted off of my shoulders, the demons clinging to me over the past two years defeated.

I feel free.

Unburdened.

"God," I say aloud, closing my eyes and tilting my face to the sky. "I don't have the words to describe to You how grateful I am. How I know that I didn't deserve any of this.

Especially after not placing my trust in You when I should have. But You blessed me anyway. You brought me to Bradyn. You brought my parents back and delivered me from hell on this earth. Thank You, God. Thank You for everything." I keep my eyes closed, my face tilted up, as I imagine what it will feel like one day to meet the One who created everything.

Who delivered me.

"So are you an early riser too?"

I open my eyes to see Bradyn leaning against one of the cedar posts, looking far too handsome for his own good. The familiar phrase brings that memory to life in my mind, and I grin. "I like to get the day started early. Helps the day go by smoother."

He smiles and steps closer. "Leave anything for anyone else?"

"I like to be busy."

He closes the distance between us, so I stand. His hands go to my hips. "Something I relate to all too well. It's Kennedy, right?"

"That's right," I reply, wrapping my arms around his neck and stretching up to press my lips to his. It feels like lifetimes ago I was desperate to hear him say my real name.

I know that I've only known Bradyn Hunt for the span of a few weeks, but it feels like we were made for each other. Like there's been something missing from my life until the moment he walked into it. "Why are you up this early?"

"I don't mind the dark," he whispers against my lips then kisses me again before pulling back. "I like to catch the sunrise."

"Sounds peaceful."

"It is," he replies. "Feel like joining me this morning?"

I smile against his lips. "It doesn't sound like a two-person job."

"No, but the company would be nice. And the view is just breathtaking." He kisses me again, passionately stealing my breath here on his mother's porch. I lose the ability to think, to breathe, when his mouth is on mine.

Desire hums in my veins. This man undoes me. And now that we have forever ahead of us, I can't wait to see where God leads us.

"See, breathtaking," he says, tone low and husky.

I pull back and stare up into his gorgeous hazel eyes. "I couldn't agree more."

# EPILOGUE: BRADYN

I've faced down enemies on the battlefield that would terrify even the most conditioned soldiers.

I've fought, bled, and nearly died. And I did it all without so much as a single anxiety-ridden moment.

But this evening, as I make my way up toward the large barn decorated for the town's summer kick-off potluck and dance, my stomach is a pit of nerves. Dressed in my nicest jeans and button-down shirt, a cowboy hat on top of my head, I stop right in front of the door.

The music is loud enough that I can hear it clearly, and I know she's in there. Like a moth drawn to the flame, I can feel her. My love. My Kennedy.

Reaching down, I pat the box tucked away in my pocket.

"You look positively terrified, big brother."

I turn as Lani steps up beside me, already dressed for

the dance in a light blue dress and cowgirl boots. "What are you doing out here?"

"Needed some air for a minute. I tried to wave you over to the picnic tables, but you weren't paying attention to anything but the barn." She laughs, gesturing to where she was sitting off to the right.

"Sorry."

"Don't apologize." She bumps me with her shoulder. "She looks beautiful tonight. Radiant."

"She always looks beautiful."

"True, but I thought my repeating it would help you get through the door."

I laugh. "That obvious?"

"You're standing here staring at it as though you expect it to open by itself."

"I'm nervous."

"You don't need to be. You know she's going to say yes."

"Do I?"

"You do." Lani loops her arm through mine. "But I'm here to help you get through the door."

"I love her."

"She loves you."

I take a deep breath. *God, please grant me courage.* Reaching forward, I pull the door open and walk inside with Lani. A band plays up on a makeshift stage while people dance on the floor in front of them.

The potluck is set up on tables across the event space while more tables line the walls.

Riley is dancing with Betty Phillips, a woman of about sixty, the two of them laughing happily, while Dylan, Elliot, and Tucker are all seated at a table, eating with Mom.

I spot Patrick and Melissa, Kennedy's parents, on the dance floor as well, smiling and holding each other as they spin around and around. Cillian, the veterinarian who helped Kennedy, is even dancing with Patricia Gorden, a woman who owns the local dance studio.

I'm scanning the room for Kennedy when she comes into view. Wearing a beautiful white dress that falls to her knees, cowgirl boots, and a jean jacket, she looks stunning. Absolutely perfect. Her hair has been curled softly, her lips painted in soft pink, and she throws her head back and laughs at something my dad says. He's currently leading her around the dance floor.

The song ends, and after giving her a hug, he heads back toward the table. She turns, and her gaze lands on me. A wide smile spreads across her face.

"Go get her," Lani urges, pulling her arm free and giving me a little shove.

I take a deep breath. I can do this. Right?

"Hey, stranger," Kennedy greets, lifting onto her tiptoes and kissing me softly.

"You look beautiful."

"Why thank you. You clean up nice too." She cocks her head to the side. "You okay?"

"Yeah. I was wondering if I could talk to you for a minute? Please?"

"Sure thing." She links her fingers with mine, offers Cillian and her parents a quick wave then leads me toward the door. As soon as her back is turned, her dad gives me a thumbs up and a big grin while mouthing the words, "You've got this."

Oh, I hope I do.

We head up the stairs and out onto the terrace. Fairy lights are draped over us like stars glittering in the night.

The music has started back up and is drifting upstairs, a slow song that makes for a wonderful backdrop.

"Want to dance?"

"We could have danced down there." She laughs but loops her arm over my neck anyway. I place my hand on her hip, keeping my other hand in hers, and we start to move.

"But down there, we weren't alone."

"True." She rests her head against my chest, and I hold onto her, moving slowly and enjoying every moment.

"I love you," I tell her.

She pulls back. "I love you too."

"I can't tell you how many nights I prayed for this. For what we have." I spin her gently then stop moving and take her other hand in mine. "You are everything to me, Kennedy."

"You're everything to me too," she says softly.

I release her hands then reach into my pocket for the box before dropping to one knee.

Kennedy's eyes go wide and fill with tears. She covers her mouth and stares down at me.

"I want to spend every moment of my life loving you, Kennedy. Will you marry me?"

"Yes. Absolutely yes." She throws her arms around me, and I nearly fall backward. She kisses me, gripping both sides of my face.

"Yes?"

"Did you really doubt it, Hunt?" She stares down at me, bathed in the light from the twinkling fairy strands above. I take the ring out of the box and slide it onto her finger, sealing the promise.

Then I stand, pulling her up with me. "I love you, Kennedy Smith. And I can't wait to spend the rest of my life with you."

"Did she say yes?" someone calls through the door.

"Of course she said yes," Lani whispers loudly.

"I said yes!" Kennedy yells.

The door opens, and my entire family, the Smiths, and Cillian rush out onto the balcony. Lani immediately heads for Kennedy and hugs her while Patrick comes over and offers me his hand.

"I'm beyond happy that you and Kennedy found each other," he says.

"Same. I don't know what I'd do without her."

Patrick wraps his arm around his wife, who beams up at him. "I know that feeling."

My gaze shifts back to Kennedy as she turns and smiles at me, her entire face radiant in her joy. I've spent years bringing the lost back to their families. But I never expected to find a piece of myself in the process. Yet, there she stands, right in front of me.

A part of my soul that I didn't realize was missing.

Silently, I promise myself that I will do everything in my power to give her the happily ever after she deserves. I know that, no matter what life throws our way, we have God, and we have each other.

And that's all we need.

---

Thank you so much for reading! Keep turning the pages for the first three chapters of Elliot's book, ECHO! Coming soon!

# ECHO: JANE DOE

He's going to kill me.

There's not a single doubt in my mind that I won't live to see another sunrise. Unless, of course, I'm granted a miracle. I pump my arms faster even though every single muscle in my body aches from being hit by that car.

How I walked away from that, I have no idea. I do know, though, that if I'm caught, I won't be walking away. Not this time.

A gunshot rings out, and I stumble, slamming my knee into a rock. I choke on a scream. I can't let him know where I am. It's dark now, and the shield of trees is keeping me relatively hidden. Out of sight, out of aim.

Another shot. Wood splinters off the tree beside me, and I fall once more, shredding the hem of the t-shirt I'm wearing. It tears as I push up from the ground. Every move is agony, but I keep going. Keep running.

I have to keep running.

Ahead, headlights illuminate the highway as cars pass by. Hope fills me with renewed strength. If I can get up there, I can get into a car before he reaches me. Then I'll be able to survive. Then, I can get help.

I push harder. Faster.

Until—I slide to a stop at the edge of a river.

Water roars, blocking me from the highway. Thanks to the heavy rains we've had over the past couple of days, there's no hope of me getting across without being swept away. Still, maybe—

"I told you I'd find you. I will *always* find you."

Dread coils in my belly as I turn to face my attacker. His smile is sinister, his eyes dark. "Please, let me go. I won't say anything."

He raises the gun and levels it on me. "It's too late for that, darling. You know that."

A gunshot echoes through the trees, and the bullet tears through the flesh of my abdomen. I fall backward. Until icy cold envelopes me, dragging me down to the depth of darkness.

# ECHO: ELLIOT

"That ought to do it." I finish turning the wrench one final time then slide out from beneath the old truck. As soon as I'm standing, I tap on the hood so my brother, Riley, can turn the motor over.

It purrs to life, sounding better than it has in over a decade.

Riley grins at me. "Good work, brother."

"All in a day," I reply then head into the shop to retrieve a bottle of sweet tea from the refrigerator. It's not nearly as good as the stuff my mom makes, but it'll do in a pinch. "Want one?"

"I'll take one, thanks."

I offer Riley a bottle of tea, and we both take seats on the old couch kept in the shop. It's worse for the wear with grease stains and the smell of motor oil clinging to it, but it's comfortable and reliable. And after a day of working underneath a truck older than me, it feels darn good to sit on.

My service dog, a German Shepherd named Echo, lies on an old blanket in the corner alongside Riley's dog, Romeo. Both pups enjoying a relaxing afternoon. You wouldn't know by looking at them that they could be lethal, or that they spend a good portion of their lives chasing bad guys and bringing people home to their families.

Hunt Brothers Search & Rescue is a job that leads us down some dark roads, but it's one I wouldn't trade for anything. We bring lost people home, and that's a calling that I'll answer until I draw the very last breath from my lungs.

"It's so hot already. How is this April?" Riley asks, rubbing an old handkerchief over his forehead.

"That's Texas for ya," I joke. "One day it's freezing, the next it's summertime."

"Isn't that the truth." Riley downs the rest of his tea then gets up. "You coming in yet? I'm guessing mom will have supper ready to go here in the next hour or so."

"I'll be in soon," I tell him. "I want to check a few more things before calling it a night."

"Sounds good." He turns and offers me a wave over his shoulder. "*Heel*, Romeo."

His dog hops up and joins him, and the two of them head out of the shop together.

Even though we each have our own houses on the

ranch, my mom still insists on cooking dinner at least once a week. More if she can get us there. She loves it, and frankly, so do we.

I'm helpless in the kitchen, despite her best efforts, so during the winter when grilling is unpleasant, it's frozen dinners for me. Except on the nights she cooks. Given that I'm thirty-five now, I probably should have figured out how to cook at least a basic meal without a grill, yet here I sit, still hopeless.

It's something I can live with.

After taking a deep breath, I toss my bottle into the recycling bin then head out into the early evening. It's not quite six yet, so it's still bright enough that I can get one final ride in before the end of the day.

That in mind, I head toward the barn. Echo falls into step beside me, the dog never straying far from my side. He's my best friend and the greatest partner I could ask for. Truth be told, he's saved my life in more ways than one.

When I'd gotten back from my final deployment, I'd been a mess. The things I saw—I shake my head, not even wanting to relive them for a moment. I'd struggled with the transition into civilian life. But getting and training Echo had been the best decision I made.

Each of my four brothers has his own service dog. Bradyn has Bravo, Riley—Romeo, Dylan has Delta, and his twin brother, Tucker, has Tango. Each of us with our own lifeline.

Or, at least, that's what I consider them. Attachments that tethered us into the real world when we'd been so lost.

The barn is empty right now, with our three ranch hands likely finishing the new section of fencing dividing a pasture into two. Most of the horses are gone, including Bradyn's horse, Rev, and his fiancé's horse Midnight.

"Hey there, boy." I reach over and run my hand over the forelock of Bobby, my quarter horse. I saddle broke and trained him, and he's like an extension of me. He nuzzles me in response, so I retrieve his halter, slip it over his head, then open the gate and guide him over to the tethering post.

After brushing him out, getting a saddle onto him, and slipping the bridle over his large head, I guide him out of the barn.

"Hey, just heading out?"

Bradyn's fiancé, Kennedy, asks as she dismounts from Midnight. Her blonde hair is braided down her back, and when she smiles, there's no longer darkness hidden behind her bright blue eyes.

Bradyn has been good for her. Just as she's been good for him.

"Yeah, I want to take a quick ride over the ridge. Spent all day working on that old Chevy, so I'm wanting to stretch Bobby's legs a bit."

"Totally get it." She beams at me. "The new fencing looks great. Bradyn's finishing up out there then heading in himself."

"Date night tonight?" I ask, knowing that they're in the final preparations for their wedding and likely spending the evening going over the last-minute details before their walk down the aisle next month.

"Yes." She grins. "We're so close to having everything ready. I can't wait."

She currently lives in one of the ranch hand cabins on the property, though she spends quite a bit of time with her parents in town. They just bought a house a few weeks ago, and she's been helping them get everything unpacked and in its rightful place.

"It's going to be great to have you in the family." I smile then climb onto Bobby's back.

"Hey, I thought I already was a part of the family?"

I laugh. "You know what I mean."

"That I do. See you later!" she calls out.

"See ya!" I urge Bobby into a trot while Echo runs silently beside us. The ridge is a nickname my brothers and I gave the tallest hill on the ranch. It leads into some thick oak trees, and we used to use them for 'cover' when we'd play Army as kids.

A game that turned into a desire to serve our Country for the better part of a decade. Until we all felt pulled back home.

I reach the bottom of the ridge then ride up, stopping only once we've reached the top. From here, I can see the entire ranch. Two hundred acres of beautiful bliss with our houses scattered just far enough apart that we get privacy but close enough that family is never too far away.

Clicking my tongue, I urge Bobby to head down the other side. With it being spring, we've had a lot of rain recently, more so than usual even this time of year. Not that I'm complaining. The creeks are all full, and the pastures are green, which will make for happy, healthy cattle.

Ahead, the largest creek on our property is overflowing with glistening water. It's fed by the Red River that runs along the border of Oklahoma then splinters through our property and even on into the next ranch.

My brothers and I spent many summers swimming in this creek as it's a good fifteen feet across and typically has at least a foot of water in it at all times.

Today it's nearly spilling over, though, and I won't even pretend that, if it wasn't warm enough, I wouldn't be jumping in to cool right off.

I keep riding, continuing up the creek a bit, enjoying the solitude. Birds chirp overhead, and somewhere, a bullfrog calls out. Man, I love spring. It's my favorite time of the year. I love how everything just comes back to life.

Favorite time of—Echo lets out a warning bark. Instinctively, I reach behind me, my hand closing over the grip of my pistol. It's more than likely a coyote or other wild predator, but just in case, I withdraw my firearm and climb down off of Bobby.

He's not the least bit spooked, which wouldn't be typical if there was an animal nearby. So what's going on?

"What is it, boy?" I ask, walking to Echo's side.

He lets out another warning bark then heads toward the creek. I follow on foot, leading Bobby behind me.

We make it five steps, and I see exactly what caught his eye. *Oh no.*

I drop the reins and rush forward, holstering my weapon as I jump into the creek. The water is cold against my legs and hits up to my waist, but I push forward through the current to get to the slender body draped over a tree limb, partially hidden, thanks to the canopy of trees draping over this side of the creek.

Shoving the branches aside, I get my first full view, and the blood drains from my face. *No. It can't be.* Water sloshes around my waist as I move closer, shoving the impossibilities aside and focusing on the now.

A cascade of soaking wet, red hair is matted and tangled in the bark of the fallen tree, but I manage to brush it aside and check for a pulse.

The body is cold, but there's a weak pulse.

I do my best to untangle the hair so I can retrieve the body and get whoever this is to safety. I roll the body into my arms and find myself staring down at a woman so pale, so cold, it's a miracle she's even alive.

With her in my arms, I see the differences, but they're

not enough for me to ease the emotion searing me from the inside.

And then I note blood on the front of a white, man's shirt. Saturated enough that even the creek didn't wash it away. There's so much. How is she still breathing?

"Hang in there," I mutter to her as I carefully make my way across the creek. As soon as we're on the embankment, I lay her down and strip out of my jacket.

Echo rushes over and starts licking her face, whining as he moves around the body. He's trying to wake her up. I brush the hair from her face, noting a silver cross dangling from her neck. It's the only jewelry she's wearing.

Quickly, I cover her with my jacket then carefully raise it and the shirt to check her injury. The black dress beneath the shirt has a hole in the abdomen.

A gunshot wound.

She's been shot.

How did she get here?

I reach into my pocket, only to discover my cell phone completely dead, thanks to the water. Knowing I don't have much time, I lift her into my arms, draping her over one shoulder carefully, until I get situated on Bobby and can lay her over my lap.

"*Heel*, Echo." I push Bobby into a run, and we race over the ranch. I just hope we get there in time.

# ECHO: JANE DOE

I'm moving.

My body is cold, unbelievably cold, and I begin to shiver as I come awake. I'm lying on something, and the first face I see is that of an incredibly handsome man wearing a baseball cap. His jaw is stubbled, his face serious.

Who is he?

Whatever we're on jolts, and I hiss as pain shoots through my body. The first real thing I've felt in the moments since I first opened my eyes.

He looks down at me, and our gazes hold. Beautiful hazel eyes that somehow seem so kind and harsh all at the same time. "Hang in there, okay?" he says to me, his voice deep.

"Okay." I'm not sure what else to say. Hang in there for what? My body aches, my stomach feeling like it's full of heavy stones. I manage to tilt my head enough to see blood staining the front of my shirt. Panic thrums through my veins. "What happened to me?" I try to sit up, but the stranger holds me tighter.

His arms feel strong. Good. But the panic mutes whatever comfort he's trying to offer.

"Stay still," he orders. "We don't know how extensive the damage is yet. I'm getting you help, okay?"

I close my eyes and nod, obeying him because lying still is easier than moving.

"Bradyn!" he roars.

"What is it?" a second man calls back.

"Call an ambulance! I found her in the creek. She's been shot."

Creek? Shot?

I've been shot?

We come to an abrupt stop, which jolts me, and I hiss in pain once more as it radiates up through my body.

"Bradyn called," a woman says, though I can't see her face.

"Hold her steady so I can get down," he says.

Slender hands hold me up while he climbs down then reaches up for me. His strong arms surround me once more, pulling me down off of what I now see is a horse. The man shifts me so carefully I might as well be made of delicate porcelain. He carries me into the house and sets me down on a couch.

People move around me in a blur of movement, but he's all I can see. The hazel-eyed stranger. He kneels beside me, and his face contorts in anger as he reaches up and brushes wet hair from my face. "Who did this to you?" he growls.

"I don't—I don't know," I stammer. I try to remember, but everything is blank. Everything, except for this man's beautiful face as I woke.

"What is your name, honey?" An older woman pushes through and presses a clean towel to my abdomen.

I groan, pain shooting through me.

"I'm Ruth Hunt," she says. "What is your name?"

"I—" I trail off. What is my name? Panic pushes through the pain. Why can't I remember? Why don't I know? "I don't know my name." My heart begins to pound. "Why can't I remember? Who am I?"

"Easy," the stranger says, reaching up to rest his hand on my forehead. I stare up at him. How can he calm the storm so easily? Who is he?

"Hey! Is dinner—what happened?" Another woman pushes through the crowd, and the man pulls away.

I want to call him back. My heart begins to hammer again, and I try to steady my breathing, but the panic is too much. It's all too much.

The woman kneels at my side, her nearly black hair braided back. "My bag is in my car. Grab it, please."

"On it," an older man replies as he leaves the room.

The woman's face is serious as she lifts my shirt and checks the wound. "Is there an exit wound?" she asks.

"I didn't check," the man who'd brought me here says from somewhere out of view. "Bradyn called an ambulance."

"Good." The woman reaches into her pocket and withdraws a light then holds open my eyelids and shines it in. The brightness has me seeing spots. "What is your name?"

"She said she doesn't know it," Ruth answers.

The other woman nods. "She's likely in shock. My name is Lani. We called an ambulance, but I'm a doctor, okay?"

"O-okay." I want to ask where the beautiful man went. I want him back here at my side.

"Do you have any idea what happened to you?" Lani questions.

"No." I suck in a breath as a fresh wave of pain shoots through me.

"I found her in the creek. She was draped over a fallen branch."

*There he is. Come back.* His face swims into view, and my heart stops racing so fast. Do I know him? Is that why I feel so calm in his presence? But I immediately brush that thought aside. If I knew him, he would know me. Which means he'd know my name.

Unless—did he do this to me?

But I disregard that thought the moment our gazes hold.

*"Who did this to you?"* Would he really ask that if it were him? Would he have tried to save me if he'd been the one to put me in that creek?

My vision blurs, and I close my eyes. I'm so tired.

"I need you to stay with me, okay?" Lani says.

I try to open my eyes, but they're heavy. Everything hurts. I just want it to stop hurting.

The voices begin to fade, and a numbness settles over me. If I can just linger here long enough, I feel like I'll be okay. Like everything will be back to normal. If only I can remain in this place of peace.

---

I come awake slowly. My brain is foggy, my vision a bit blurry. I rapidly blink to clear it and find myself lying in a hospital room full of beeping machines.

How did I get here?

I try to sit up. "Easy, you need rest, honey." A woman comes into view and gently presses me back onto the bed.

"Ruth?" I choke out. That was her name, right?

She smiles softly. "Yes, honey. That's right. Do you happen to remember your name?"

I shake my head and lie back down. A tube of oxygen blows cold air up my nose, and whatever drugs they have me on have taken the pain. I glance down at my belly. I'm covered by a blanket, so I slowly push it down and gently touch the outside of the gown. "I was shot."

"Yes. Doctors had to go in and get the bullet out. You were just moved here from recovery about half an hour ago."

"Who shot me?"

Her mouth flattens in a tight line. "We don't know, honey, but we'll get it figured out, okay? You don't worry about such things right now. You worry about getting rest."

"Where is the guy?"

"What guy, honey?" she asks, her eyes full of concern.

"The guy. The one who saved me."

"Oh, Elliot. He and his brothers are combing the ranch, looking for any sign of what happened to you."

*Elliot.* "His name is Elliot?"

She nods, a soft smile replacing the worry. "He's my son."

The door opens, so I turn my head as the dark-haired woman I'd seen before—Lani? Was that her name—walks in carrying a clipboard. She's wearing a white coat and blue scrubs.

She looks up and smiles. "I see you're awake."

"Am I going to live?"

"Yes, you'll be fine." Lani smiles. "We were able to get the bullet out. We're not sure how long you were in that water, but I do know that the only reason you survived is because of it. The cold slowed the bleeding. Otherwise, you probably would have bled out before Elliot found you."

"I would have died?"

She nods. "Do you have any idea what happened to you?"

I try to think back, to come up with anything that answers her questions, but I come up completely blank. "No. I have no idea."

She smiles. "Mom, can you give us a minute?"

"Of course. I'll be right outside." She gently squeezes my foot then leaves. As soon as the door has closed behind her, Lani sets the clipboard aside.

"What is it?"

Lani takes a deep breath. "I want your permission to check for signs of assault."

"What?"

"You were found in a party dress with a man's shirt wrapped around you."

"I was?"

She nods. "I want to make sure nothing happened to you. And if it did, we might be able to pull some DNA. That's if the water didn't wash it all away."

Tears blur my vision. Surely this nightmare won't get worse, will it? "I don't feel different." My stomach rolls at the mere idea. Would I feel different? Surely, I would, right?

"It's totally up to you," she says softly. "No pressure

from me at all. I cannot even begin to imagine how confused you are, and the last thing I want to do is be pushy. I can even perform a quick physical examination that will tell me if there's any cause for concern. I can look for bruises or any other signs of trauma. But I won't do it without your consent."

I swallow hard then nod.

"Okay." She reaches down and squeezes my hand gently. "I will come back in and do it in just a few. Right now, there's a deputy from the Sheriff's department here, and he wants to speak with you."

"Okay."

"We'll get you taken care of, okay?"

Unable to stomach saying the word 'okay' even one more time when I feel anything but, I simply nod.

"Come on in, Gibson," she calls out.

The door opens, and a man wearing a brown and black Sheriff's uniform strolls in, notepad in hand. He looks friendly and offers me a soft smile. "Ma'am," he says. "I just wanted to ask you a few questions."

"I don't know how helpful I'll be. I don't even remember my own name."

"We can get all of that figured out." He reaches into his pocket and withdraws a device that looks like an oversized cell phone. "With your permission, I'll scan your finger-prints, and we'll run them through our database, see what pops."

"Yes, please." Eager to find out who I am, I offer him my right hand. He quickly scans my fingerprints by pressing them onto the glass screen then shoves it back into his pocket.

"I'll let you know if we find anything." He makes a note on his pad. "Now, can you tell me the last thing you remember?"

"I remember waking up and seeing Elliot. Right after he found me."

"Not anything prior to that?"

I shake my head.

"That's okay," Lani insists. "Sometimes a traumatic event can cause memory loss."

"Will it come back?" I ask Lani.

Her expression is one of hope. "Only time will tell."

The officer makes a few notes on his notepad then puts it back into his pocket. "Until then, we'll do everything we can to find out who you are and who did this to you."

---

Get your copy of ECHO and continue the Hunt Brothers series!

# ABOUT THE AUTHOR

A USA Today bestselling author of over sixty novels, Jessica recently felt her faith pulling her in a new direction. Now, her focus is inspirational romantic suspense with characters who fight to find their faith in even the darkest of moments, because, as she has learned, it's then we should lean on God the most.

She lives in Texas with her husband and homeschools her three kids. She is an Army veteran and has written multiple bestsellers since debuting in 2016. Find out more on her website, www.jessicaashleybooks.com or by joining her Facebook group, Coastal Hope Book Corner.

# ALSO BY JESSICA ASHLEY

**<u>Coastal Hope Series</u>**

Pages of Promise: Lance Knight

Searching for Peace: Elijah Pierce

Second Chance Serenity: Michael Anderson

Tactical Revival: Jaxson Payne

Perilous Healing: Silas Williamson

———

**<u>The Hunt Brothers Search & Rescue</u>**

Bravo: Bradyn Hunt

Echo: Elliot Hunt

Romeo: Riley Hunt

Tango: Tucker Hunt

Delta: Dylan Hunt